BRANDED VENGEANCE

DARK RANGE
BOOK THREE

RANDI SAMUELSON-BROWN

WOLFPACK
PUBLISHING
— EST 2013 —

Wolfpack Publishing
9850 S. Maryland Parkway, Suite A-5 #323
Las Vegas, Nevada 89183

wolfpackpublishing.com

Paperback ISBN 978-1-63977-602-3
eBook ISBN 978-1-63977-794-5
LCCN 2023942246

BRANDED VENGEANCE

PROLOGUE

THE SHEDDING HORSE MOON SHONE FULL AND BRIGHT, ICY cold of a strange breathtaking whiteness that cast down onto the Colorado landscape below. A radiance which failed to penetrate the outcroppings and gullies that obscured the secrets and misdeeds hinted at by the wind. Perhaps a lunar reflection of the human heart, the vagaries of the terrain lurked in those shadows carved out by treacherous hues of gray and something yet darker and ill-defined. The mountains kept their impassive watch, silhouetted against the anthracite velvet of the spangling midnight sky. A soul penetrating sky punctuated by boundless flakes of mica-glinting stars that spoke of nothing more than cold remoteness.

Of planets that spoke of nothing more than lies.

A rutted, threadbare road cut into a slope of no certain character, no different than countless other trails and traces veering off deeper into the wild, deeper off into isolation. The crooked spine backbone of the region, those mountain ranges waited poker-faced, dangerous, a flashing knife blade seeking an opportunity to wound. Like gamblers in a crooked game, the mountains held their cards and bided their time, outwaiting their opponents—hard men that they themselves had spawned and bred.

During those dark hours of the frigid clear and glinting night, trouble careened along that rutted road. Trouble accompanied by the song of the coyotes and of wind rattling the scrub, smelling of faint mineral dirt and sage.

Huddled inside the battered pickup's cab, if anything, the two men smelled the sweat coming off from each other and of their unwashed clothes plenty far gone and turning ripe. They smelled of rotting teeth and foul breath, of death and decay brought about by dirty money.

Dirty money they hadn't yet managed to lay their hands on.

No, each of the men in the pickup remained oblivious to the dangerous beauties of that night and engaged in no banter. Each turtled down into his collar, sweat prickling beneath his clothes, oblivious to the night that fell clear and cold. And the men carried a primal sense of threat unspoken, laying like lead in the pits of their stomachs that neither would ever confess if given the chance. Both strained to listen past the engine and past the wind rushing down from the higher peaks, scouring the ground and making the scrub rattle.

The two men hunched down and progressed without headlights as a precaution—the moonlight creating shadows and treachery where none previously existed. Eyes wide open and peering into that which could only be gambled, the driver fought a losing battle against the dips, ruts and holes whittled out over time, use, and weather. Even without the moon's incandescence, odds prevailed that they would have reached the ranch gate in complete darkness in one fashion or another, perhaps a bit more bruised, perhaps courage a bit more dented. Gravity always maintained its pull, and they pointed downhill toward a predictable conclusion.

What remained unpredictable remained the given task at hand.

Driving by memory and feel with neither man a stranger to that place, neither proved the most observant of subjects but the land didn't care. The old wagon ruts marked the way, although at times the route proved a crapshoot marking where the road ended, and the boulders and scree held sway.

Wham! Thud!

"Shit!" one of the men in the cab exclaimed, or maybe both simultaneously. Not that it mattered.

The jarring impact found every loose bolt and metal clatter as the two in the cab lifted up, airborne for a couple of disorienting seconds—the passenger, having nothing to hold onto, hit the roof hard, head smacking against the ancient, depleted padding that did little to soften the blow.

One of the thuds belonged to the corpse slung into the bed of the pickup truck. He didn't have anything to hold onto, either, but such considerations no longer mattered or concerned him. Not, at least, since some undisclosed time back.

"Ouch! What the hell—you're going to break the axel driving like that."

The driver slammed on the brakes—skidding to a stop. Dust and rocks rolled and skipped out and away from beneath the worn and balding tires that failed the penny test.

For a brief, tense moment, the driver's eyes searched

the passenger's, incredulous that they hadn't collided with a hidden boulder. Shocked by the sudden, brutal violence of the impact, the driver remained clinging white-knuckled to the steering wheel as the other rubbed his now pained head.

"Son of a bitch," he complained.

Each appeared wide-eyed and fearful, like a hard-eyed horse ready to spook.

"Shit," the driver said again, still hanging on to the steering wheel from a curious sense of self preservation, buried deep. Then he remembered his cargo. "Is he still back there?"

The passenger, none too bright, peered through the back window. "Shit, if he ain't, I ain't gonna pick him up to load him in there again. He can just stay where he damn well landed."

"Moron!" The driver peered through the window himself. "Like hell you will, and son-of-a-bitch, he's not back there now!"

The driver slammed the gearshift into Park, threw open his door and hopped out, stumbling slightly in a shadowed rut, his boots crunching on the ground.

He peered over the side of the truck bed.

"Damn it all to hell…oh wait. He didn't go anywhere —just slid around a bit."

Indeed, the corpse had changed positions. Only to be expected, really, on account of all the bouncing and the slamming of brakes. The body landed bunched up against the back of the cab, as if, although lifeless, hanging on for dear life.

Originally wrapped in nothing more than an old, worn sheet, all of the jostling and bouncing rolled the body clear from cover. The rope, tied in a hangman's noose, remained in the bed of the truck, waiting off to the side.

Neither of them had thought to tie the sheet, just like they hadn't thought to put on their seatbelts.

The dipshit got out of the cab, and taking his own sweet time, glanced over the side of the truck and into the bed half fearful.

"Aw man, now we can see him and his face! Now what?"

The driver glared at his companion, features clear enough in the moonlight to get his point across. "Who the hell cares? We were going to have to see him sooner or later. Shit. Now let's go."

"Cover his face," the passenger pleaded.

"With what?" the driver asked.

The dipshit passenger delved into the cab and came back with three grocery bags and held them out for the driver.

"Put these on him so we don't have to see him."

The driver muttered, glared at the other man, but stuck the bags over his head, tying them under his chin. "Now are you happy?"

The other man didn't respond to that question, mind on other topics. "Guess you might be willing now to put on the headlights. *The moon is bright enough*, my ass. I mean, who in the hell is going to see them?"

The driver's eyes raked over the dipshit. "No, we can't turn on them lights. They could be seen from the road."

"I don't know how we got talked into this in the first place."

The driver wagged his head, halfway toward mournful. He stood by the truck's open door, hands tense and splayed wide. "We got talked into this for two hundred dollars each. Now, come on. Let's just get 'er done. Then I'll buy you a beer once it's finished."

"There's a bit more to it than that, and you damn well know it. And I'll want a shot," the passenger accomplice whined from the ingrained habit of trying to sweeten a deal.

"Fine. And a shot. Just as long as it's not one of them girly ones."

"From your part of the proceeds. And drive more slowly, would you?"

The driver only grunted, climbing back in and slapped the transmission into Drive. The whiner climbed into the passenger side, slamming the door shut as the moon beamed down and the shadows obscured, magnified, and flattened the ruts of the road.

Another jolting mile—more cautious in their approach—brought them to the crossbar. The conversation between the two completely dried up and died out as the passenger shifted in his seat, and the driver swallowed down his bile and a case of the jitters.

Pulling up beneath the crossbar, the driver killed the engine. Eyes glued to the top of it, he estimated the height, snatched the rope from the back and lobbed it over the beam, grabbing at the loose end as it swung by. Rope controlled for the moment, he hefted it upwards to lob it around again.

"Hell, I've never done any shit like this before," the driver muttered under his breath, considering the hangman's noose, and taking in the dimensions of the dead body in the back of the truck.

"I guess use the winch," the dipshit said.

That observation gained a modicum of respect, for the driver hadn't thought that far ahead. "Yeah, that should work. Then we'll tie the rope off to one of the sides and get the hell away from here. That ought to keep 'im in place until morning, if not longer."

They both appraised the body, reluctant. "Let's flip him over and get the noose down around his neck and string him up."

"Just like that?"

"Just like that."

The driver went back into the cab, pulled out a piece of white carboard. With a thick marker, he wrote out the words *HORSE THIEF* on it. Taking a roll of grey duct tape from the cab along with the crude sign, he then walked behind the truck, knelt down beside the corpse, and flipped it over. He tore strips of duct tape from the roll using his teeth to secure the sign on the front of the dead man's shirt.

The dipshit wagged his head. "That seems like overkill to me," he lamented.

"And you ain't paid to think," came the reply.

1

STANDING AT THE GATES
OF HELL

MODERN-DAY SHOOTOUTS WEREN'T SUPPOSED TO HAPPEN, but they still did. And Hugo provided dead-and-buried proof, literally. He died from gunshot wounds taken during a battle that never could be considered his own. He never should have taken part in any of it. As a result, Emory buried Hugo Werner's lifeless body in their family cemetery to show their deepest mark of respect. None of the events that led up to the violence were his fault—*other than for his fundamental mistake of falling in love with her.*

Brushing away the nuisance of tangled hair as she drove, the memory of that gunfight still seared like an invisible brand.

So did the guilt. Guilt stemming from different reasons.

Had it been love that caused her to run out to his life-less body, despite the bullets flying? Or had it been guilt. Deep down, she knew the answer to that question, and it made her feel unworthy.

If she had died on account of someone already bled out,

although her father never held that out to her, *then where would they all be?*

The Lost Daughter Ranch came first. She only got part of that equation right during the gunfight. For the time being she was the last of the line—and the Cross line needed to carry the ranch and the family over into the next decades.

Emory Cross' right hand clenched the steering wheel, knuckles white and pronounced. And so she ate up miles on the highway, uncertain, unhappy, and ashamed.

She drove deeper into northwestern Colorado to take up a temporary assignment she neither asked for, nor wanted.

"No need for a death-grip," she muttered after a time. "It's still just Colorado and I can manage."

Still Colorado and 'just down the road' in the fickle month of April still offered challenges. The snowiest month in the mountains provided plenty of obstacles. Travelling to her new post hadn't turned out straightforward, either. Forced into taking the long way around on account of a semi that jackknifed at dawn or in the early morning hours before first light, she had to turn around, change directions, and take the long backroad to Vermillion. Whenever the accident happened, it closed down the mountain pass that offered the only direct route from Stampede.

Perhaps the semi drove too fast, or the driver fell asleep at the wheel. Maybe he swerved to avoid a deer or hit the creature head on and then panicked. Then again, black ice remained a danger, and one not easily interpreted until it proved too late. Any way a body chose to read it, the semi jackknifed, and the state patrol turned frustrated drivers around.

The pass would remain closed indefinitely. Buying

time for the proper authorities to analyze the cause, and the workers to clear the result.

Buying time for some, cost money for others.

It came as no great revelation that mountain passes and semis often didn't make the best of friends, and those flatland drivers learned about gradients the hard way. The locals and tourists both suffered as a result. Jackknifed semis and closed down passes pissed everyone off without question.

She set out with the intention of getting an early start, but any hopes of being in Vermillion by ten that morning faded. The only upside that she could find meant fewer cars were on the roads at that early hour, and the detour gave her new land to consider and admire.

One thing held for certain—driving always left plenty of time for thinking, and that might not have been such a good thing. Not in her case.

If she stared too long and too hard into the darkness, a rockslide of jagged emptiness tumbled in and hurt.

And so, turning around she backtracked to pick up I-70, and upon taking a further exit she threaded along another backcountry road with only a number and not a name. Kai was loaded into his trailer and coming along for company or sanity—she could take her pick. Coming along to keep her honest. Horses had a way of doing that, every single time.

She rolled down her window a crack, to let the fresh air blow in.

Heading off into the farthest remote corner of north-western Colorado, *literally*, she couldn't help but feel relegated to a distant outpost. True, so far it struck as an outpost that remained impressive despite the gas pipe-lines marring the view. Ignoring those impediments, the region boasted plenty of rugged views to go around. One of the brand inspectors in that region retired, leaving a hard-to-fill post vacant. Her boss, Senior Brand Inspector Terry Overholzer, conferred with the powers in charge, and they all decided she needed a change of scenery.

She disagreed.

The senior brand inspectors, no doubt prompted and bolstered by her father, prevailed. And so, she drove. Twenty-four years old and feeling closer to forty.

They said she would get over that part. She differed on that score, as well.

More than a few four-lettered words came to mind at the time the decision arrived by decree, but she held her tongue as a form of penance. Hoping that somehow, her silent acquiescence would lead to absolution.

In the end, she accepted defeat and what amounted to banishment. The most that she had a right to hope for was the pain of Hugo's untimely death to ease.

When those guilts and regrets passed, so might the sepia tint that colored everything around her. Time healed all wounds, or so the songs sang, but misgivings lingered and weighed heavy.

"Change the tune, sister," she sighed aloud, realizing with a jolt she had taken up the habit of talking to herself. Another caution right there.

She didn't want people to feel sorry for her, or to become bitter and crazy. Not yet. Not so young.

Focusing on the scenery beyond didn't help matters all that much because that part of the drive boasted a whole lot of dried scrub and the ever-present mountains in the distance, some better than others. Tapping the steering wheel as she tried to dredge up a reasonable distraction, she searched her memory. The name of

Brown's Park came to mind and beckoned. All but forgotten, Brown's Park owned a tarnished history of outlaws and rustling. It still cast a long shadow among those who *did* know. If her family's history proved anything to judge by, she ought to fit right on in there. But she wouldn't be working in Brown's Park, but the nearby town of Vermillion instead, nearby posing a relative term. Probably eighty miles one way, if she counted. The Lost Daughter Ranch was located one hundred or so miles going the other direction from the town.

The remote region remained largely undisturbed and bisected by few roads—one of which was the back road to the infamous Baggs, Wyoming. Many a chasing posse and outlaw travelled that worn path in yesteryear. Then she wondered why in the hell she debated the merits of Baggs. She ought to worry about Vermillion, where she'd be setting up for her temporary job.

Fresh scenery and all.

Switching on the radio and twisting the dial, in that early morning hour she found nothing but religious sermons and static. Emory flicked it back off with a sigh and settled further into her seat.

———

OUT INTO THE oil shale basins she travelled, seeing firsthand where the extraction industries set down roots and the resulting pipelines blossomed, jutting out of the ground in proliferation. The Utes once called the shale, *rocks that burned*. She could always try to set one on fire for the sheer hell of it.

Those pipelines carried and pumped liquid money.

Money the likes of which the region had never seen, and coming from shale, of all things. The ranchers who owned land along the deposits certainly cashed in where they could, and she didn't exactly blame them. But the river meadows remained serene and beautiful beneath the faceted, crenellated cliffs that towered and observed the passing of the seasons as they had throughout the ages—forever, in fact.

Intrusions aside, the terrain looked like country worth fighting for, even well before the vast shale deposits were discovered and exploited. In the 1870's, the Utes rode their horses over the land unfettered before the ranchers moved in and settlement began. In truth, it all amounted to a land grab, and the outlaws followed close on their heels sensing blood and easy money.

The terrain of sage and scrub carried the same feel as renegade country, perhaps even more so than did Stampede. Hell, there her family provided the outlaw contingent, and not much had changed on that score.

An underlying flash of sharp, red pain at the admission of the truth seared.

Outlaws suffered pain and deprivations the same as anyone else. True, they tended to alleviate their shortages by theft. Injuries and maimings—well, the outlaws bled the same as their victims, the same as anyone else. Honest people never worried much on that score—they believed outlaws reaped their rewards. Especially swinging at the end of a rope.

She leaned forward, peering through the windshield of her grandfather's old Ford F-150 pickup, sizing up the rugged landscape beyond. Gas pipelines marred the view of the basin, but the scrub land ranchers pocketed cold, hard cash when that deal arrived new and in the offing. *Land.* That's what people in their part of the state had. A whole lot of acreage, and not much else going by the way of hard cash, other than for cattle, sheep, and horse sales. Until recently, livestock provided the main source of their cash crop in that part of Colorado. That, and plenty of high-altitude land.

Emory Cross glanced first into her rearview mirror and then over to the side mirror with a practiced eye, checking on the horse trailer and by extension Kai within. Everything travelled along as it ought.

And she returned her attention to the infinite soaring blue promise above.

She glanced at her phone displaying the time as 7:36 on a Saturday morning.

Practically alone on the empty road, she encountered few trucks or cars as she wove her way through long intervals of high-altitude prairie offset by mountain nothingness between.

The weight she'd carried upon her chest lightened, lightened ever so slightly.

Maybe a slight hope burrowed in, just beneath the surface.

THE ROAD THREADED north as the miles fell away, the hum of the pickup's tires on the pavement mixed with the whistling wind through the window gap. Together, they lost her in a song of the region's own making. Hardscrabble ranches, old, weathered structures, and tumbling fences scattered along, shored up by the ever-present strung barbed wire that meant business. The discarded, forgotten, and washed-out heritage buildings faded against the promise of spring around the corner, easing down, leaning into their surroundings, and succumbing to age. Relics that held every intention of transforming into the ghosts of an era.

Time marched on and would not stop.

An old single-track road, no different than any of a dozen others, snagged her attention for no particular reason. She eyeballed the dusty dirt ribbon, noting the crossbar which predated the county road, standing at least an eighth of a mile away.

She slowed. There was a reason.

A large mass hung from that old crossbar, out of place, and an ominous whisper from the past rose up her spine.

Emory glanced in the rearview mirror to verify no one followed besides trusty Kai, safe and secure within his trailer. Braking harder than intended, the turn pulled sudden and heavy.

"Hang on, Kai," she muttered, knowing her voice wouldn't carry as she angled the sharp left onto the dirt road, her eyes glued to the crossbar ahead.

She blinked. That shape sure struck like a body dangling. But such a notion struck as plumb crazy—in the year 2023. Whatever the object turned out to be in actuality, it had to be some sort of an effigy warning away potential trespassers. All of a sudden, the Lost Daughter's skulls paled in comparison, coming across as mere child's play.

That couldn't be right.

Frowning, she killed her speed upon approach. The truck crept forward, tires barely turning.

Details coming into focus with each yard advanced.

No, in front of her hanged a dead body all right.

The corpse's hands stayed out of view, presumably tied behind his back. Head jutting forward as if the neck broke when the rope snapped, his face was covered by grocery bags, pulled down to cover his features. Tied beneath his chin, those bags hid the exact gruesomeness from view. The heavy rope, knotted in a hangman's noose, secured both the body and the bags into place.

Whoever he was, the killer likely did his shopping at the City Market.

"Shit. Shit shit shit!" She braked to a dead stop about twenty yards away.

On the man's shirt, a rectangular white duct-taped sign stood out, bold.

Again, she rolled the Ford forward about five more meager yards, squinting to make out the words.

Horse thief, it claimed. Written in stark block capital letters.

2

CENTURY BE DAMNED—THEY HANGED A MAN

Emory stared at the apparition straight out of the nineteenth century where it belonged. What in the hell had she stumbled across?

NO ONE hanged horse thieves anymore.

Correction—make that *almost* no one.

Her phone, discarded on the seat alongside her, finally registered. Checking the reception bars she found it as suspected—out of range and out of coverage. She had a choice. She could turn around and leave, or she could try to make sense of the hanging and help. But help how?

Emory knew what an ordinary, sensible person would do. *Leave. And leave immediately.*

Instead, she cracked open the truck door, and stood upright half way out. One elbow laid across the roof for support, and the other balancing on top of the door frame. Half in and half out, she felt a strange reluctance to leave her truck. Considering the dry ground below, she'd leave footprints if she stepped down and wasn't certain that she wanted to do that. Not in those circumstances.

The hanged man wasn't going anywhere, that much was for damn sure.

Plenty wary, she sniffed. The wind blew in from behind, carrying in the wrong direction for her to catch any hint of rotting or decaying flesh.

Logic dictated, both by the lack of scent and the lack of law enforcement, that the hanging had to be recent and fresh. And say what anyone would, even in the Colorado hinterland, modern day hangings would summon a whole lot of law enforcement attention—and probably from five counties over. Had this been reported, the surrounding landscape would have crawled with badges and uniforms.

She had a badge, too.

Just not the kind that most expected.

The silent body dangled unmoving as three ravens flew overhead. Of course, she watched them, and took them as a sign.

Bad energy abounded.

"No shit, ravens," she said into the wind.

Her attention fell to the ground beneath the crossbar, and the tire tracks that imprinted into the dry dirt.

Why to any and all of it. Who was that man and who had done such a thing to him?

Someone plenty pissed off, came the obvious answer.

Those damn tire tracks provided a clue, but getting any closer would disturb the evidence. Knowing the direction the tires travelled would prove useful, but her tracking up the road would amount to crime scene contamination—and she'd been taught far better than that.

Peering at the corpse's blue jeans and crotch, they appeared dry—but with dark blue, dirty denim it remained hard to tell. She'd heard that men pissed themselves from fear, or simply from their body shutting down and evacuating once life drained and fled.

She spared Hugo that indignity.

To hell with the guy's crotch. If this body followed that same biological course, he'd have had enough time to blow dry.

Again she traced the line of the ranch road, the best lead so far. It branched out in different directions once it separated along the slope and travelled further in.

Whoever used those roads would likely know of grudges, fights, or hard feelings that fueled the hanging, whereas she didn't know a damned thing about the area —beginning with something as fundamental as to how many spokes that dirt road split into, and the owners of the land in question.

Giving up, she dismounted, adding her boot prints to the scene. Hell, implicating evidence of her presence already abounded. While she could erase tire and boot tracks with a bit of effort, that didn't mean that someone else wouldn't drive by as she did, sparking up a whole lot of suspicions.

In any case, such actions would just throw everyone off and probably lead to more trouble in one form or another, and for no real reason. No real reason other than she had stumbled on to a modern-day hanging. Any deception on her part, if detected, would cast a whole lot of questions her way.

Damn.

Once on the ground, Emory turned in a slow circle. Whoever hanged the man could have as easily travelled from the county road as from the ranch roads in the distance.

In every single direction, she raked the landscape

noting strategic spots falling within easy rifle range. She'd always been that way—but had turned doubly so since the gunfight. Clean-shot vantage points abounded, both where she stood and at the crossbar behind her.

But this hangman, for obvious reasons, didn't act the part of the shooting kind.

She tried to pick up on the sense if she were being watched and decided not. If she made a mistake on that count, it could prove fatal.

But no. The landscape felt empty and deserted.

And obviously, the hangman wanted his handiwork found.

Senses remained on high alert, but for the moment it all boiled down to just her, Kai, and the corpse. Standing in the breeze and wondering about a practice that crossed century lines and common sense.

The Old West lived and rode on.

She really ought to ride on, too.

3

A PARTY OF THREE, AND
ABOUT TO GET BIGGER

BUT SHE DIDN'T.

Her rifle, stowed and locked in the truck's steel box close by, remained far enough away. No one, including her, moved as fast as a bullet.

Still, a small reedy voice ran through her brain and down her spinal cord with timeworn advice.

Don't pull out a weapon, unless you damn well plan on using it.

If the hangman waited and watched, and if his aim proved halfway decent, she could be dropped in an instant. The sight of a drawn rifle, in old West standards, provided reason enough to open fire.

On that count she couldn't blame them, but she'd come out dead.

Wrong place, wrong time, and planning on phoning the sheriff to boot.

Frowning, she withdrew inside of her Ford, made a wide U-turn, and pulled Kai and his horse trailer back out of whatever the hell she had stumbled into. They headed uphill to the comparative safety of the county road. A road that offered the chance of testifying witnesses if events took an even further southward turn.

Coming to a stop, she checked her cell atop the road's rise. Two bars popped up. The nearest mile marker read twenty-nine.

Still within sight of the body, she mulled what to disclose—and how not to sound like a crackpot while doing so.

Emory hopped down from the cab and circled around to the back of the trailer to check on Kai, all the while scrolling to find the contact email outlining her reporting directions. Standing alongside the back of the trailer and Kai's brown rump, she found the number she wanted and clicked on it.

Two rings.

"Josh Tucker," the voice answered.

"This is Emory Cross, your new brand inspector for the Bassett County district?"

"Is that a question?" the man teased with a touch of underlying concern.

"No, not exactly. I'm on the road from Agency to Vermillion, and I saw something hanging from an old crossbar near mile marker twenty-nine. It looks to be the body of a man who's either been hanged or committed some weird form of suicide, but he wouldn't have been able to pull it off alone. Anyhow, he's got a note duct-taped to his shirt that says, 'horse thief'. Do you have the number of the local law enforcement out here?"

A ripple of well-earned distrust. "Is this some sort of a joke?"

"No, sir," Emory replied. "My badge number is Colorado 10549. Emory Idella Cross."

"What in the hell," he swore. "Stay right where you

are, Emory. Sorry about that. I'd come out to help you myself, but I'm about one hundred miles away. I'll call the Sheriff for you right now, however. His name is Joe Hammond."

"Will do," she replied, clicking off and still uneasy.

Old traditions died hard if they even died at all. In her heart, she knew and understood the desire to adhere to the old ways as much as possible—just bolster them with better technology and equipment. In short, to modernize.

However, anyway she considered it, hanging people from ranch crossbars in this day and age went a step or three too far.

Not to mention that the explanatory note might be a ruse. Or it might be the truth. If it were true, the outcome might be considered just another form of rough justice by some.

Surprisingly, she remained uncertain whether she fell into that camp or not.

Stealing horses, however, provoked and demanded a strong response.

"I brought us out into horse-thief country, Kai." Then again, she wondered if that was the truth, despite appearances.

Either way, there seemed no sense just standing out in the open acting as a target to practice on, so she climbed back inside of the truck and waited for the real law to materialize.

THE SHERIFF MADE good time driving at what appeared, to the untrained eye, a speed of about ninety miles an hour. He pulled up a short twelve minutes after she wrapped up the incident call, sirens off but lights flashing the standard red and blue strobe.

Emory climbed back out of her pick-up at his arrival, staying out of the way as his vehicle skidded to a stop, churning up dirt and spitting out rocks low. The dust cloud hadn't yet entirely settled upon her approach.

And he certainly wasn't paying attention to her.

She noticed how the sheriff's eyes bugged out as he surveyed the hanging body through his windshield. Lips pressed in a tight, thin line he stepped out of his truck, fixated on the apparition.

"Shit," he said by way of a greeting.

"Yeah. That about sums it up. I didn't get any closer than about halfway down," she offered. "No reason to mess up the scene."

"Of all damned things," he groaned. "He sure wasn't here last night when I passed by." The sheriff stuck out his sinewed right hand. "I'm Joe Hammond. Josh said you were the new brand inspector."

"*Temporary* brand inspector," she countered.

A quick sideways dart. "This got you spooked?"

"I'm not exactly happy about it, if that's what you're asking."

Mindlessly, she grabbed her left wrist with her right and gave it a twist. *She shot left-handed.* They both heard the snap.

He grunted, noting the odd reflex but bigger problems mocked, right in their faces. "Can't exactly blame you there. Let's go take a gander at what we've got."

Their footsteps crunched on the rocky dirt. Good land for grazing livestock, and not a whole lot else.

Standing shoulder to shoulder they stopped, both now staring up at the hanging body. Although tall, the sheriff topped her by about three inches.

"You have a lot of horse thieves around here?" She tossed the question out nice and light, as if embarking upon an easy conversation.

"That's your department," he replied in the same neutral tone.

Emory gave him a long-eyed stare, which he caught. "The coroner will be along any time now." He obviously felt the need to explain. "Since the sign says he's a horse thief, I guess that part falls in your jurisdiction."

Emory stiffened. "Yes, as you've already said. But I guess the murder part falls into yours."

There. Take that.

"Sure does." He stink-eyed the sign. "So does tampering with a corpse."

He stepped closer to tracks, analyzing the ground with professional rigor—tire and boot prints. "No sign of struggle."

Emory scanned the clay castellated formations yet again. Nothing stirred other than the long, dried grasses swaying in the wind. The white and brown cliffs contributed to the pretty spot for a hanging—offsetting the ranch gate and the mountains beyond. She then returned to the hanged man, following the sheriff's gaze.

"It'd be a lot of work—to hoist a body up like that. Dead or alive."

The sheriff shifted, eying her with interest. "Have a lot of experience in hangings, do you?"

She read his expression, square and head-on. "No. Don't suppose you have any theories on all of this, do you?"

The sheriff dropped his head for a brief second, lowering his glance before lifting back up, eyes narrowed. "Stringing up someone as a horse thief? Hell, no. We've got a few candidates for Pueblo, but nothing like this."

The sound of an approaching motor carried through the clear blue quiet morning. He tore his eyes away from the corpse, away from her, and over to the approaching utility van with lettering along the side. CORONER. "Here comes Greg now. I've already alerted two of the county deputies, and they're waiting on standby. Don't need them underfoot right now."

The sheriff spat into the dust, and a vein in his jaw throbbed. If anything, Emory would say he was mad.

4

BADGES AND BODY BAGS

Words used up, the sheriff placed his hands on his hips, feet apart in a wide stance. They watched in silence as the coroner's van came to an unhurried stop.

Guess there's no hurry when someone's already dead. Not for someone used to dealing with death all the time.

Windowless except for the windshield, the coroner emerged, frowning at the hanging body. He glanced at the sheriff before his attention landed full stop on Emory as a stranger.

"Meet the new brand inspector," the sheriff explained.

"Temporary," Emory insisted.

"Yeah, she keeps pushing on that. She's the one that found him. This is Greg Foster, our coroner."

"Rough start," he remarked, walking away, and clicking pictures of the immediate vicinity and the so-accused horse thief—scrutinizing the tire tracks on the ground underneath the crossbar.

"You see these?" he asked the sheriff.

"Yeah. Not a matched set, and a bald one to boot. The

tires are probably in the same condition as fifty percent of the county. Those are my tracks on the edges there."

The coroner grunted at the truth held within those few words. Pocketing his phone, he placed his hands on his hips and stared at the hanged man, trying to figure out how on earth the corpse possibly could have gotten himself into such a fix.

Holding his face upwards at an angle allowed Emory the chance to study him. The balding man styled his hair in a combover that didn't do so well in the blowing wind. He dressed for a casual Saturday in a gray misshapen sweatshirt and jeans sagging down in the ass and appeared about sixty years old, the same approximate age as the sheriff. Both men's faces bore the marks of life lived in the outdoors at altitude—crow's feet at the corners of their eyes, and the planes of their faces lined and wrinkled from the wind and the sun. Their bodies leaned toward spare from either physical activity or good genetics, but the sheriff wore his weight a bit better —the more muscular of the two.

Or maybe the uniform just helped.

Judging by their footwear, neither were ranchers by background or inclination.

The coroner's eyes narrowed at the corpse.

"If this don't beat all," he mused to himself, then his mind settled on something beyond her reach. Then in a stronger voice: "Call in your troops."

Receiving the instruction, Joe Hammond strode over to his truck, picked up his radio's handset and issued his own set of directions.

In the meantime, the coroner turned toward her, curious. "What did you say your name was, Ms. *Temporary* brand inspector?"

"Emory Cross," she offered, nodding toward the

swinging man. "Do you know him?"

"Oh…not through the grocery bags," he chuckled, shooting a glance over at the sheriff, still speaking into his radio. "Sorry. Coroner's humor and all. Let's wait until we cut him down to make that determination."

He eyed her more closely. "I've got to say that you're handling this all remarkably well."

"Am I?" She felt a dreaded blush spread. *He guessed that something was wrong with her.* "Maybe it's just because I don't know any of you yet. Best behavior and all."

"You're tough," he said with obvious respect.

"I grew up on a ranch."

"Must be one hell of a ranch."

"Sure is," she replied.

The coroner did a doubletake, tilting his head as if catching the whiff of something not quite right.

She tamped being a smartass down. It would get her nowhere at this point.

Emory occupied herself by taking out her phone and snapping a few pictures of the corpse and the tire tracks for herself. "For brand inspector records," she explained, although no one asked. "Just in case he really is a horse thief."

"What a pile of guano," the coroner said to no one in particular, waiting off to the side.

Emory wrinkled her nose. "What's guano?"

"Bat shit," the man explained.

For one, she didn't know anything about bat shit, but she did know about sirens. The plaintive wail approached, threading around the curves of the mountain road.

"Here they come now," the sheriff announced in a foregone conclusion, leaning against the roof of his car. "I suspect they were waiting just around that bend."

Sure enough, two more pickups came tearing down the one-laned county road, slamming on the brakes hard. They skidded, too.

A day late, and a dollar short to Emory's way of thinking.

Both deputies emerged from their respective vehicles, acting all official. One—a man with weasel-like features, dark hair slicked back and a thin mustache—gawped. "Would you look at that!"

The other deputy, a taller, more circumspect man with sandy hair stuck his hands in his back pockets and frowned.

"Did one of you remember to bring a ladder?" the sheriff barked.

"Yes, sir," they replied in unison.

Again, drawn to the ranch roads, Emory took their measure, wondering where they led. "I suppose you all know who lives along this stretch, right?"

The sheriff nodded. "Yep. This crossbar belongs to the Flying X, but there are some offshoot roads that go to other ranches further back. I'll talk to them all, never you fear." He turned his attention back to the deputies. "Cut the body down. Let's take a look at who we have."

The quieter of the two deputies pulled a ladder out of his truck bed, which he carried with ease over beneath the crossbar. The aluminum rasped and echoed as he extended it out to its full length. Everyone eyeballed the ladder, estimated the height of the crossbar, and theorized about the hanged man.

"Just cut him down?" the darker one asked, eyes darting over to Emory where they lingered a split second too long, before returning back to the sheriff. "The body'll land on the ground."

"You got a better idea?" the sheriff asked.

"No, sir," the dark deputy responded, unhappy but professional.

"Put on your gloves and just cut him down," the sheriff replied. "Dustin, do you want to do the honors? We'll take the rope in as evidence. It's the only way to get 'im down that I can think of."

The two deputies glanced at each other, uncertain. The dark one held out a sheathed bowie knife for the climbing deputy. The sandy-haired climber stuck the knife into his back pocket, exchanged a pained expression with the earthbound deputy, and climbed. The darker one kept his foot on the bottom rung, holding onto the sides of the ladder as a precaution.

In silence, the elevated deputy consulted with the sheriff when he reached eye level with the corpse. With careful movements he pulled out the sheath from his back pocket and removed the knife within.

The sheriff nodded.

He sized up the task, placed the blade against the hemp and sawed. The taut rope held firm, and he sawed harder. The rope frayed slowly as he applied more pressure, cutting through one ply after another.

He kept on sawing as the rope kept on fraying.

Everyone exchanged nervous glances, shifting their weight and waiting for the body to fall.

The body remained suspended as the rope remarkably continued to hold—the deputy kept hacking his way through.

Finally, with about two plies remaining whole and intact, the weight of the body proportionally increased to snap the rope. The corpse plummeted to the ground, landing with a sickening, crunching thud.

The deputy wiped his forehead with his sleeve, disquieted although trying not to show it.

Everyone contemplated the body heaped sideways upon the ground. The only sound came from cautious footsteps ringing down the aluminum ladder rungs.

All of them that remained on the ground didn't move, but stayed exactly where they stood when the whole process began.

The deputy sniffed when he reached the ground, dabbing his nose with his shirtsleeve.

"Sorry," he apologized to Emory.

She tilted her head in a way to say that it didn't matter.

The coroner and the dark-haired deputy took pictures of the corpse where it landed in the dirt, presumably for The Record. Next, the coroner pulled on his gloves and stooped over to remove the grocery bags knotted around the person's neck. With the utmost care, he peeled back the bags, one by one. Holding them out for the deputies again, one by one, to bag as evidence.

"Now we can smell him," the coroner half sang, bending over and going about his business, unhurried and unbothered.

Half of Emory really didn't want to look, the other half did. Probably each one of them struggled in the same way, but to differing degrees.

Of course, with them being The Law and all, they encountered more of this type of thing than she ever would.

Staring death in the face amounted to a deep and ingrained primal instinct. Somewhere beyond the level of will-I or won't-I stare at a mangled car accident along the side of a highway.

In this case, the conclusion came as a given and viewing the corpse won out.

Bags pulled away; the man's grayish skin cast

displayed an unhealthy hue. Expected really, with him dead and all. And his lank brown hair certainly needed a wash.

Hell. He probably still got carded for buying 3.2 beer.

Face sprouting a ragged, wispy beard growing in uneven patches, his lips drew back to show teeth that weren't any too pearly white from what Emory could tell. Eyes at half-mast, she noted that at least his tongue didn't stick out and felt grateful for that small mercy.

She had no desire to go any nearer, feeling strangely hollow and detached toward the stranger.

Judging from everyone else's reactions, none of them recognized him, either.

Intent, the coroner snapped yet more pictures, scribbled a few notes into a well-worn leather-bound booklet, and turned the man's head a bit to the side.

"Deep furrows, however, none as expected where the noose meets the vertical stretch of rope. As it is, I'd suspect he's been dead for two or three days but will have to get to the lab to make the determination." The coroner sat back on his heels. "I don't believe I've ever seen him before. Joe?"

The sheriff also squatted down on his haunches to peer into the man's face. "No," he said clearly surprised. "Can't say that I have."

Again, the coroner eyed Emory with more curiosity than concern. "Are you OK?"

"Relatively speaking," she replied, bothered. *Hugo had been killed at twenty-seven, four months short of his twenty-eighth birthday.* "Does he look hanged to you?"

"Meaning was that the cause of death?" The coroner glanced at her, then back at the young man. "No, I don't think so. Not based upon the contusions. But that's not final."

"He's younger than I expected," Emory murmured, "and it doesn't look like he put up much of a fight. I don't know about him, but if someone was about to string me up, I'd fight like hell to make sure that didn't happen."

The two men exchanged pointed glances, which she intercepted.

"I'll remove those hand ties once I get him back to the lab, but you're right. There are no bruises on his face. Then we'll search for needle tracks, signs of foul play, or pure medical causes. In short, establish the cause of death."

Still sitting back on his heels, he stared into the face a moment longer.

With a groan, he got up from that low position, his knees creaking and popping as he straightened. "Old age," he said.

"Happens to the best of us," the sheriff replied.

"Well, I don't hear your knees creaking. I'll go get the body bag and the trolley." The coroner's voice remained weighted down, sad and resigned. He limped a bit as he returned to the van, opened the back doors, and pulled out a gurney.

Maneuvering the jangling trolley over to the corpse, the small wheels struggled on the uneven surface. The two deputies arranged the body flat on his back before hefting him into the body bag, the metal zipper sounding both terrible and final. They placed him onto the trolley with another dull thud. Arranged and ready for transport, Emory and the sheriff stood silent as the coroner led the procession near the body's head. The two deputies struggled behind, pushing the trolley uphill from the rear and grasping the side to help steer toward the waiting van.

The metal folding legs collapsed with a ring, sliding the body into the waiting vehicle.

The rear doors slammed shut.

The coroner and the two deputies rejoined them, everyone standing around, uncertain.

Emory broke the silence. "If you don't need me here any longer, I'd like to go on into Vermillion to get the horse settled. I've matters to attend to before I start work on Monday. Can't say I feel good about leaving Kai in a boarding stable if there are horse thieves roaming around."

The coroner frowned. "Just because he's wearing a sign doesn't mean that he is one—a horse thief, I mean. Joe, do you know anything this *temporary* brand inspector ought to know?"

"I'd have said. Nothing's come across my desk. Either of you hear anything?" He glanced at his deputies, but his expression didn't hold out much hope.

The deputies, judging by their body language, had no idea. "Nah," said the one who didn't climb the ladder. "You'd best keep your eyes open, however. It seems like a lawless element has rode into town."

The other deputy stared at him like he had lost his mind.

"Jackass," he spat, turning to Emory. "Where are you boarding your horse?"

"Just outside of Vermillion," she replied. "Their name is Weaver."

"Hey, they're my cousins," he replied with a relieved smile. "Your horse will be just fine out there, I promise. My name is Dustin Weaver. Tell them I said hello."

He held out his hand for her to shake.

"Emory Cross," she replied, clasping his hand in return.

"And this jackass is Frank Deacon, but we often don't pay any mind to what he says. For obvious reasons."

Frank twittered, as if the words spoken meant nothing more than a joke. None of the others joined in his laughter.

"Hey, Emory," the sheriff interjected, breaking off the banter. "Don't mention anything about the hanging to anyone. And I do mean *anyone*. I'd like to keep it quiet as long as possible, knowing it'll all get out soon enough. Then I won't be able to do a damned thing other than answer calls and questions."

She nodded. "I know how to keep my mouth shut."

The jackass deputy snickered.

Emory stopped, turned to him, and stared him down. "Problem?"

He turned a bit red, and a vein in his neck throbbed. "No," he replied, defensive and arrogant.

Emory never let her gaze waver, as she locked eyes with him, feeling more than just a little inclined toward smacking the hell out of him and his smirks and snickers.

"My new boss called you for me, so he knows about this—to a degree."

She could swear that all the men exchanged veiled glances.

The sheriff cleared his throat. "Just tell him, should he ask, that it's an ongoing investigation, and you're not at liberty to discuss."

"That should work," the jackass snarked.

"It had better," the sheriff snapped, in a comment aimed at them all.

5

SCRATCH THE SURFACE AND SEE WHAT COMES OUT

Stampede's version of the wild west had nothing on this part of the state, for damn sure. The area surrounding Vermillion acted like the Wild West on steroids.

While the men of the local law enforcement found her odd, she knew she hadn't acted as most women would do in the same circumstance. Dealing with such matters as hangings was hardcoded into her DNA, but they wouldn't know that. The ability to stare death down remained a family badge of honor. Crosses could, and would, deal with such matters without flinching.

That contributed to a fair-sized portion of the shame hanging over her since Hugo's death. While she hadn't fallen apart exactly, she hadn't followed the rules. Crosses knew about gun fights. She had undoubtedly let their side down.

The budding emphasis on Kai's safety held far more weight than it had only a few slim hours earlier.

The bond forged between a rancher and his horse, or her and Kai, held strong. They were a team. And one half of the team didn't allow the other half to be stolen without one hell of a fight.

Half-way tempted to turn right around and drive Kai back to the Lost Daughter even if it meant a late night, she fixed her eyes firmly on the road ahead of her and pressed the gas pedal down. *Stick with the original plan* unless something proved so plainly amiss that it defied common sense.

Men with nooses around their necks and hanging from ranch crossbars in 2023 likely qualified as iron-clad insanity in most people's books.

Maybe. She wasn't entirely sold one way or the other.

Not if he proved to be a true horse thief.

Not if he earned what he had coming to him.

Doubts, worries, and second guesses aside, Emory found the boarding stables without problem, settled on the outskirts of town.

Pulling up in front of the stables, the owner's house located right across the yard presented itself all nice and tidy. At the sound of her pickup, a muscular woman emerged through the front door smile bright and, no doubt, owning a spine made of twisted steel.

"Emory Cross?"

"Yes, ma'am. Are you Mrs. Deacon?"

"Call me Patty, but yes I am." She extended her hand. Both women returned strong, confident grasps as a ripple of understanding passed between them. Neither of them ever shirked work or backed down from a fight. Ever.

"I just met a cousin of yours, Dustin Weaver," Em offered.

A glint of perception lit the woman's pale blue eyes. "Problems, or can't you say?"

"I'd rather not say, in truth," Emory smiled. "It will all get out and make the rounds soon enough. I think I mentioned that I'm a brand inspector, right?"

"Yes, you did. Last I checked, Stampede is seventy miles as the crow flies, and about ninety-eight miles by road. How do you want to work this?"

Emory chuckled, dipping her head in respect to the woman's obvious research. "I've got transportation papers. Let me get them for you, and I appreciate you asking." Emory pulled the papers out of the glove compartment and held them out for the woman along with a pen waiting for her signature.

"Do you want to back him out of the trailer?"

"Sure thing." Emory opened the latch, freed Kai from the constraints, and backed him down the ramp nice and slow.

The woman studied the paperwork, consulted Kai's brand, and signed.

"We'll put him in that pen with the shelter next to the house while he's in quarantine," she said. "Pretty horse."

"Strong heart," Emory replied.

"Let's get that half of the team fed and watered! While we're at it, would you like some water or a cup of coffee from this morning's pot?"

Emory laughed. "No thank you, I'm fine. I need to get over to the hotel. Tomorrow's dedicated to getting the lay of the land and finding a place to live while I'm up here. Do you happen to know of a good place to start?"

The woman heard her, but her eyes followed an approaching pickup truck. "Here comes Myra," she sighed. "Poor woman. She's tough, but still, she's taken a turn—"

Another battered pickup drove into the yard, and a

woman with fly-away gray hair emerged, eying Emory with suspicion.

"This is the new brand inspector, Emory Cross. She's boarding her horse here, and we were just going to put him in the quarantine pen. How are you doing, Myra?" Although Mrs. Deacon sounded upbeat, the concern in her voice was noted by all.

And not necessarily appreciated by some.

The woman nodded, a nugget of guarded respect shining through for the brand inspector part, and more than a trace of irritation surfacing at Patty Deacon's tone.

As a result, she didn't bother with any niceties as she latched on to a detail that put Emory into perspective for her. "You're kind of young for the job. Is this your first year? People'll walk all over you unless you're tough. And what are you better at, cattle or horses?"

The woman hit a nerve. Emory took offense at the belief that she might prove too young to handle the job. "I'm older than I look."

"Uh-huh," the woman eyed her like she might a heifer going to sale. "You're obviously on the sunny side of thirty."

"Maybe," Emory said, aware the woman wanted an age out of her. An age she wasn't about to provide. "No one's ever asked me whether I'm better at cattle or horses before, but I suppose it doesn't make all that much difference. I've got more experience staring at cattle brands than horse brands, I guess." Emory shrugged.

The woman seemed to file away that piece of information. "There's probably a lot you haven't been asked yet, and plenty that you haven't seen. Give it time."

The woman turned her attention back to Patty,

borderline rude. Or perhaps she was simply direct and straight to the point. Emory had a hard time making that distinction judging by where her words fell. "I've got some extra hay for sale now. Do you want to take it off my hands?"

"Sure," Mrs. Deacon replied. "How much have you got?"

"Two tons that I plan on selling," the woman said without a flinch. "I'll offer it to you for $400. I'm keeping the rest for the time being."

"Think you might get some more horses?" Patty asked.

The woman puckered up her mouth, sour. "Not a chance. They cost too much to maintain, and these days, there ain't anyone to ride them other than myself, and I don't have the time or inclination."

Everyone knew how high veterinarian bills could run.

"I don't want you to lose money on top of everything else." Patty searched the woman's face.

But she waved the words off as she climbed back into her truck. "Anymore, losing money is just another worry on top of a heap of others. Just don't want that hay sitting around, rotting. I'll deliver tomorrow morning, if that's all the same with you."

"Tomorrow's fine. I'll have a check waiting."

Gruff, the woman nodded her gray head. "Perhaps I'll see you around, brand inspector. Better you than that damn boss of yours."

With those parting words she drove off, dust clouds billowing in her wake.

Emory wondered if that might amount to the woman's usual manner of saying goodbye.

"Myra can be a bit rough around the edges," Patty

offered. "Her husband died a few years back, and they never had any children. It's a lot of work for one person."

For a split second, she appeared on the verge of saying something that mattered, details that might help put the exchange into context, but thought better of it. Emory remained a stranger to them, and a young one at that. No important issues were aired in front of outsiders unless it couldn't be avoided. Another Code of the West, and all three of them knew as much.

"I can handle my job just fine, no matter how old I am," Emory grumbled. "She doesn't hire help?"

"She had one guy, but he's gone. Don't know what happened there. Not sure I want to, either."

The wheels in Patty Deacon's mind turned, judging from her expression, and those turning wheels had nothing to do with Emory's age. Nevertheless, she shut the door on those notions and set her attention back to the business at hand. "Let's get your partner settled in. Provided, that is, that you think everything is suitable?"

"Looks fine," Emory replied, scanning the setting and the ridges beyond. "Nice and clean. What's the worst trouble you've had happen in your business out here?"

Surprised, the woman's eyes widened, followed by a slight frown. "An aortic rupture a couple of years back. Awful."

Emory nodded. "Not much you can do for that."

"No. Unfortunately there isn't."

"It's just that I'm fairly protective of Kai. You haven't had any trouble like horse theft or anything like that, have you?"

The woman frowned, latching on to the shadows lurking in Emory's words but surprised, nevertheless. "Horse theft? No, *we* haven't, and we intend on keeping it that way." She filed that thought away, no doubt linking it to the message Emory passed on from Dustin.

Well, that presented one sure way to get rumors started, Emory figured, none too pleased with her performance. Again. Now she could only hope that Patty Weaver upheld police confidentiality, even when it wasn't expressly requested.

If the woman noticed something amiss, she didn't miss a beat. "Never heard of anything like that in this area. Well, other than a few horses being fought over during nasty divorces. We had one man who tried to take his ex's horse, but we called the sheriff and he got that all settled. Anyhow, we've installed yard lights and an automatic gate with a code. The gate is shut and armed each night. We're light sleepers, besides. My son Dave lives in the apartment off the back of the stable block. Right now, he works at the coal plant. The one they're closing down in a couple of years' time."

Emory pursed her lips at that point of information and welcomed the change in the course of the conversation. "I haven't heard about that, but that's nothing much that I'd follow from our direction. For what it's worth, I'm sorry for everyone involved. I'd guess that's not good for the local economy." She paused.

The woman nodded, and it was Emory's turn to change the subject.

"The plan is to come out every day to exercise Kai and to check in. That is, unless I end up using him for work. In that case, I'll take him away for the day. Where do you want me to leave his trailer?"

Patty pointed to a parking area off to the side. "Go ahead and put your trailer over by those others, probably at the end unless you find a closer space you'd fit into. Beyond this property, there are plenty of trails you can ride on. There's a nice one right out that back gate at the bottom of the pasture."

"Kai's great on the trail. I think he'd get bored and fat just standing around grazing." She laughed at the truth of it. "The same could be said of me on that count."

The woman laughed and patted her hips "Let's not go there. Now, Kai's your horse, you take him whenever you want him, but let's get the quarantine period behind us unless there is a real reason to do otherwise. We quarantine for seven days, unless a longer period is required for a specific reason."

Emory shrugged at the unlikelihood.

The older woman continued, familiar words and explanation. "We've never had an outbreak of any disease, and don't plan on starting now. Do you believe that this horse is healthy?"

"You bet, and I have the veterinary certificate. Want me to get it for you?"

The woman tilted her head, ever so slightly. "If I can't trust you on such matters, who are we supposed to trust?"

"Am I able to still ride him away from other horses during quarantine?"

"Sure. There are a whole lot of trails, and not that many people riding. It's other horses that we're avoiding. Like I said, the trail out the back gate is nice, and very few people use it.

"We feed at 7:00 in the morning, and about 5:30 at night. Other than that, the horses are out in the pasture, grazing unless you say otherwise. Kai will be in that far pasture for the time being, but at least he'll see the other horses."

"That's all fine and dandy," Emory replied. "I'll take him over to the pen, then I suppose it's time to get myself sorted out." She hesitated. "You know, I toyed with the idea of bringing my other horse to keep him company, but I guess I'll see how everything sorts itself out."

The woman nodded. "Best to get your footing before hauling more horses around. Where did you say you were staying?"

"At one of the chain hotels for now. I'm going to need to find a short-term apartment if I can in the meantime. I don't know how long I'll be assigned out here, which will make that task more difficult. I guess I'm staying until they find a permanent replacement."

"We might grow on you," the woman smiled.

"You sure might," Emory agreed, "but we've got a ranch over by Stampede that needs more help than my father and his crazy cousin can likely manage, if anyone asked me. Which, it just so happens, they didn't."

The woman laughed. "There's a shortage of good workers going around." A shadow crossed her face. "But when that plant closes, chances are good we'll be turning help away."

"If you happen across someone who wants to work in Rimrock County, have them come talk to me," Emory offered, leading Kai into the holding pen. "Come to think of it, if any are used to handling livestock and have an interest in becoming a brand inspector, we sure could use them here, too. It's an option for consideration, especially if employment becomes an issue."

Finding a local, full-time brand inspector would also facilitate her return back to Greeley that much sooner.

"Hiring your replacement already?" the woman teased.

"I don't know that I'd put it that way." Emory smiled.

The woman eyed her, manner still teasing but pointedly interested in her answer. "You must have a young man waiting for you."

That remark retained the power to wound.

"Not anymore," Emory replied, and those two words sounded both pitiful and sad.

"You'll find someone else, although that may not be what you want to hear," Patty murmured.

And for a moment, Emory feared that she might break down and cry.

But she didn't.

No tears allowed.

She had to stand her ground—even if that ground was two counties over from home. If she ran scared because of the hanged man, she'd never live it down. Nor would she deserve to.

She did her best to offer Mrs. Weaver a smile. "I guess it's time to get myself settled. Thanks for boarding Kai. I'll see both of you tomorrow."

She drove away as quickly as she could.

If she called it quits, everyone, including herself, would conclude that the gunfight at the ranch had broken her spirit. Had turned her yellow. She couldn't let that happen.

She refused—flat out refused—to let the Lost Daughter down again.

6

DYING WITHOUT A FIGHT

WHAT KIND OF HORSE THIEVES ALLOWED THEMSELVES TO BE hanged without a fight? Emory wondered. She wondered because that hanged man didn't have a mark on his face.

The how and why anyone would allow himself to go down without an almighty brawl, beat the hell out of her.

That notion irritated her in all the wrong ways, and for the entire drive into the town of Vermillion, trailed behind her like a ghostly warning from the past.

Flat out, the hanging didn't make an ounce of sense.

Slayed by a heart attack sounded like a tabloid title, or maybe he took drugs. Neither of which provided any excuse for stringing him up in the first place. While the autopsy would provide answers for the cause of death, motivations posed another issue entirely.

He sure didn't come across like Dustin Pruitt with all those sores on his face. Neither did he resemble those two meth heads that ran the illegal gas pump in Stampede—*Beanie and whatever that second skeleton was called.*

Those boys amounted to nothing more than skin and bones—and sores from picking at their faces and arms.

Damn and double damn.

No, any drugs that boy took remained at the recreational stage.

Listen to you, that chiding voice taunted. What in the hell did she know about drugs anyhow? More than she used to, and the phrase 'the scourge of rural America' now meant more to her than just an idle slogan.

Maybe the hanged young man amounted to just what the note said—a horse thief, plain and simple. Which meant that vigilante justice reared its ugly, and unwanted, head. Vigilantism proved a huge problem right there, no matter how anyone viewed it. The fact that someone might be wandering around loose, acting as judge, jury, and executioner, could never be considered a good thing.

Thinking how this all amounted to one hell of a way to start out fresh in a new town, Emory surveyed the landscape of the town located in a broad, flat basin, much more so than Stampede's rugged terrain in the higher ranges. Halfway between Denver and Salt Lake City, Vermillion offered gentle hills with mountains rising in the distance beyond the rugged sage and brush. The ox-bowing river snaked through the dry chiseled hillocks of the high desert terrain, offering water's promise and relief.

Emory parked her car in the hotel's parking lot and sized up the large building for a moment.

Modern and clean. Featureless. Like nothing in the world could possibly be amiss.

Emory felt decidedly unsettled clomping through the lobby to check in, carrying her laptop under her arm and a duffle bag slung over her shoulder like a rodeo rider. She hadn't been in a hotel since the National Western Stock Show and her first date with Hugo. That memory certainly didn't strike the right note either. Yet one more stark reminder of the Texan's passing.

Emory flexed her shoulders.

"I hope you enjoy your stay with us," the girl offered, sliding the plastic keycard across the counter. "The elevator is right around the corner."

Emory nodded her thanks and found the waiting door open in a universal sign of hospitality.

She pursed her mouth, doubtful.

Pressing the button numbered five, she slouched against the back wall. The car climbed and she commanded herself to breathe. The door slid open on the fifth floor, and she launched herself forward as the search for her room began. Down the carpeted, clean hallways she walked, dusty cowboy boots muted and out of place. Room number 582 located, Emory hitched her breath as she waited to see if the electronic key did or didn't work. The green light lit up, and the door clicked open.

She exhaled, pushed through, and allowed the duffle bag to drop—relieved of one burden at least. The clean motel scent put the Lost Daughter to shame. The room's bland expanse of white walls gave off a sterile impression. Bolted-on framed pictures tried, but failed, to complement the beige and sage-green striped bedspread. But then again, she could never claim to be a decorator, giving a dismissive once-over to the caricature wild horse print—a silhouetted mustang set against a flat dark sky, mane flowing in the wind.

Modern art or cartoon art, she debated without having the answer.

Palms itching for no reason, she scratched at them absently. Itching palms meant something to do with money. Well, she could use some more of that, but it didn't drive her and never had.

Restless and off-kilter, she moved over to the window to take stock of the view. *A whole lot of scrub.* Just like where she came from.

And a hanging horse thief. Just like where she came from…well, maybe a century back.

Old West problems had followed her one range over.

Turning away from the window, the painted mustang art drew her attention despite herself. Staring at that print, she mused about the different reasons or scenarios why someone would steal a horse in the first place. Love, money, or sport. Or some combination of the three. Revenge could always enter into the calculation through any one of those motives.

"You'd better learn how things work up here," she muttered, staring at the horse print, "and you'd better learn fast."

NOTHING WOULD GET SOLVED in that hotel room by staring at the print of a stylized horse painting.

But she could check the missing and theft reports and find out a few facts while she tossed about and struggled.

Setting her laptop on the hotel desk, she figured out how to connect to the hotel's Wi-Fi system, and within two minutes the computer booted up and functioned. She entered her credentials, typed in her search, and scrolled through the information that popped up on the screen.

She blinked a few times and re-entered the search parameters.

No recorded reports were filed after 2021 under missing or stolen equines. There was a closed report of two estrayed horses back in 2021 that were recovered down the road. Report taken, filed, and closed by one Ray Thompson. More recently, in fact about five months back, a record pulled up of a transportation permit for five head of horses into Nebraska—registered under Myra Brandt. Beyond those entries, a few sale and transport records of rodeo stock came across, and nothing much else.

Whatever the case, no stolen horses were recorded within the last five years in that district.

That cast a whole new light on the accusation of "horse thief." Perhaps the man came from a few counties over. Maybe the search needed to be broadened to include all of Colorado and Wyoming.

Shoot fire.

So, the mystery wouldn't solve easily. With a distinct shortage of clues or hints, she expanded her search into the state of Wyoming. There, in the northern part of that state, she located a report filed for six geldings. That report, dated back in October of the previous year, amounted to the sum total.

Trying less-than-official channels she searched Net Posse where she located a thread concerning suspicious vehicles and an attempted horse theft down in the southern part of the state, but nothing in the Vermillion area.

Scratching the back of her neck as she stared into the computer, her stomach growled as she sat there in the sterile hotel room. Nothing dished out as expected.

ONE HOT SHOWER LATER, and feeling a bit better, she caught sight of the angry red scar on her calf, skin puckering, pulling, and only half healed. Ugly and permanent. With luck, it might fade.

Maybe people needed scars to remind them of the journeys they had taken or, perhaps more importantly, the defeats they had suffered. One thing for certain, she'd never look that great in a bathing suit again.

Not that she had many occasions to wear one in the first place.

The shaft of wood sticking through her jeans and into her leg hadn't been a pretty sight either. Worse awaited her, although she hadn't known it at that moment. Just outside those old walls.

That old twinge of guilt resurfaced. She hadn't felt as strongly about Hugo as he'd felt about her. And now he lay dead.

Again, her stomach rumbled.

First things first—she needed food. Pulling on clean underwear, she picked up her jeans laying crumpled on the floor, stuck in one foot followed by the other. Glancing at the cast aside t-shirt, she figured she'd spring for a clean one, topped off by a faded Wyoming sweatshirt. Just because the calendar proclaimed the season as spring didn't make it so. It didn't mean that the high country's night air could be considered warm by any stretch of the imagination. She raked a comb through her tangled wet hair but didn't plan on doing much more. Locking into her reflection in the hotel bathroom's mirror, she met her eyes in the reflection.

Same hazel eyes, same brown hair, same busted nose. Different town. Worse outlook.

That about summed up her prospects.

She snatched the hair dryer off the wall and switched it on to hot, not having planned on doing even that much. Being new in town, she might as well give it a half-assed attempt, but she drew the line at bothering with makeup.

Going on six on a Saturday night, Emory figured that, judging by Stampede standards, if she wanted food, she'd best get hopping before the sidewalks rolled up until the next day.

EMERGING from between the steel elevator doors on the ground floor, her dirty cowboy boots crossed the clean floor tiles through the reception area. The desk shift changed, and the girl behind the counter was different than the one who had checked her in.

"Hi," Emory smiled, walking up to her. "Don't suppose you have any recommendations for places to eat, do you?"

The girl grimaced. "To be honest, we don't have all that many choices."

Emory nodded. "Yeah, I kind of figured that much."

"There's the Mexican restaurant, the Fiesta, if you want a margarita, and their food is pretty good. There's a Wendy's and the Watering Hole serves pizza, but it fills up quick because it's small. Then there's Dusty Mike's, and rumor has it that they have sandwiches, but I haven't been in there myself. It's just a bunch of old guys hunched over their beers from what I can tell. The grocery store has food, and there's a microwave in your room…"

She searched Emory's face and tried again. "The good

news is that we serve breakfast downstairs here. It won't be too bad for a night or so…"

Emory laughed. "I'm staying longer than that, I guess. Until I find a place to live in town for a while."

The girl's eyes raked over Emory, curiosity now far sharper. "Are you working out here?"

"Temporarily. I'm a brand inspector."

Emory caught the relief that washed over the girl's face but didn't understand why.

"No offense, but I hoped you wouldn't say that you were working in the gas fields. You seem kind of nice for that type of job. Those guys can be rough. *Really* rough."

Emory cocked her head, narrowing her eyes a fraction. Likely that girl had experienced trouble along those lines. "Just checking brands and livestock. I guess it's Mexican for tonight."

The girl gave her general directions, to which Emory half listened. Nothing would be all that hard to find in that two-track town.

No, she felt more worried about the fact that she'd never eaten in a restaurant by herself before.

She climbed back into her truck and turned the key, stomach clenching. Driving along the frontage road, the temptation to chicken-out rose to the point that she almost turned around to settle for Wendy's or a frozen dinner.

No, she decided. *Try something new. Do something different.*

She would go into a restaurant by herself, order a meal, and sit there to eat it. Like she was an old hand at eating alone in restaurants.

Confident women did that, she reckoned. At least they did if they were hungry.

New in town, she didn't have anyone to eat with—simple as that.

The truth remained the truth, even if it went against how she wanted things to be.

Hugo died.

She remained very much alive.

7

WHEN HAPPY HOURS BECOME A NUISANCE

THE FIESTA DIDN'T OWN A PARKING LOT, BUT INSTEAD relied upon the open street. Plenty of trucks were pulled up outside, a sign she read as auspicious as far as restaurants went.

Emory climbed out of the truck and walked up to the carved wooden door, grasped the large brass handle, pulled it open, and stepped through into a hostess station. The Fiesta smelled of refried beans, corn tortillas, and disinfectant. Shining party streamers festooned down from the ceiling in red, blue, green, and gold with piñatas dispersed at intervals—offset by 1970's printed posters distracting from the worn linoleum floor and tables with stackable chairs. The décor might come across as a shade toward kitschy, but say what one would, the place certainly didn't show a trace of dirt or grime anywhere that could conceivably be cleaned.

The Fiesta did, however, contain a pack of grimy, dusty customers replete with reflective utility vests seated at the bar and staking it out as their own. As if by some type of internal radar, they all swiveled to take note of whoever walked in through the door that precise moment she crossed the threshold.

The 'who' happened to be her. And her resolve weakened more than just one notch. *Bullshit. She had a right to be there as much as anyone else.*

"How many?" a female voice asked her, drawing her attention away from the leering men.

"Just myself," Emory replied.

A study in neutrality, the woman surveyed the construction workers like they amounted to nothing more than restaurant fixtures under consideration. A rather critical consideration. "Perhaps it'd be best if I seat you in a quiet corner away from the bar, if that's OK."

"That would be great." Emory's voice betrayed a very real sense of relief. The hostess, who appeared to be perhaps twenty-five, smiled as she led her into a partitioned room off to the side. A two-seater table against the far wall waited.

"This is a family restaurant and always has been until the drilling, the extraction, and the man-camps moved in. If they give you any trouble at all, let me know."

Emory suppressed her own smile as she took a seat. "I'm sure I'll be fine. I just don't normally eat on my own."

The hostess, however, appeared willing and prepared to do battle with the men. "They're not supposed to bother anyone or make them feel uncomfortable. Our profits sure are up, on account of all the booze they drink. Speaking of which, can I get you anything?"

Cocking her head, Emory chuckled. "Now that you mention it, a margarita sounds good."

"A house one?"

"Perfect," Emory replied, opening up the menu.

Before the girl could even return with the drink, a

pair of dirty work boots walked up to stand beside her table. They came into her vision as she studied the menu. Pointedly, Emory refused to even glance up. The work boots cleared his throat.

Emory lifted her gaze, keeping her expression as blank as she could. "Can I help you?"

The man had brown curly hair, a beard, and a dark, work-related tan. "Excuse me, I don't mean to intrude, but are you new in town?"

She blinked twice and took her time in answering. "Why are you asking?"

That ought to put him on the back foot.

He frowned. "A couple of reasons."

The waitress came back with Emory's margarita. "Jimmy," the hostess sighed. "Are you bothering her?"

"I hope not," he replied, appalled and sincere all at the same time. "It's just that she's eating alone, and I don't have anyone to eat with, so I thought I might buy her dinner. If she'd let me, that is."

The hostess weighed that information with more consideration than Emory expected.

The men at the bar, catching wind of what transpired, started jostling each other and laughing. Laughing at the man's expense.

"You two know each other?" Emory posed the question to the pair of them.

The hostess spoke up as she set the drink down. "Jimmy here is a gentleman. He never causes any trouble. Doesn't hang out with that pack at the bar, which says a whole lot right there."

"Sure, take a seat." Emory indicated the chair across the table, before lowering her eyes back down to the menu with a studied concentration. Wondering why in hell she'd agreed to let a stranger join her in the first place. Probably on account of the fact that she didn't like those assholes seated at the bar, poking fun.

As she considered her new dinner companion again, his eyebrows arched upwards, and she realized that she'd seldom seen a more surprised expression. It took every ounce of self-control not to belt out a laugh as he slipped his large bulk into the seat across from her in nothing flat.

"No one has ever said 'yes' before," he admitted, reading her expression, halfway toward woeful.

That did it. Shocked outright at the honesty, Emory laughed—startled by the unfamiliar sound. "In that case, what does that say about me?"

Before he could formulate an answer, the hostess brought back another menu. "Your waitress will be Betty. Tonight's pretty busy. Jimmy, do you want something to drink?"

"Diet coke," he replied, then over to Emory, "I need to shed a few pounds I've decided."

Now that afforded a conversation she would never hear coming from the men around Stampede, and most certainly never at the Lost Daughter. Men didn't drink *diet* Coke. Nor did they much care about their weight— or at least not that they would admit.

He held out his hand across the expanse of the table. His brown eyes, under a smudge of dirt across his forehead, were wide open and honest. "My full name is Jimmy Hudspeth. I work for the county, in case you hadn't guessed. Here, I suppose I could take off my work vest. That might look a bit better."

"Doesn't matter to me, and I'm Emory Cross—a brand inspector." The jostling along the bar grew worse, and Emory gave them a pointed stare. "Are those your friends?"

He wagged his head, slow and drawn out. "No, ma'am. Not exactly. Those are gas field or pipeline workers. A fair amount of the population ends up in here either Friday or Saturday night, if not both. This is the warm-up. Then the progression heads over to Dusty Mike's. He's the owner and bartender over at the Rusty Spur. That's where the serious drinking takes place, but Dusty Mike's all right. As for that lot in here right now, I do my best to ignore them."

"Sounds like a reasonable plan." Emory, however, glanced past him to the general horseplay. In all honesty, she felt inclined to wade in for a fight. Deep down, she'd felt like fighting a lot as of late. Ever since...well. *Ever since.*

The waitress came up to take their orders.

"What's good here, Jimmy?" Emory redirected her train of thought away from the attraction of physical violence. But it remained lurking. Just beneath the surface. One false move and...

"I'm partial to the steak fajitas and combo number six, but I have to say, everything I've had here is good."

Jimmy's voice tethered her.

"Steak fajitas, please." She smiled, handing the waitress back the menu.

"Same here," Jimmy said.

Emory waited for the waitress to move away. "And you aren't paying for my dinner, Jimmy."

"Um, that's the price of my company," he twanged, raking his hand through his hair.

Another surprise burst of laughter. This time, he joined in. A bit late, but he joined all the same.

Emory glanced over at the dirt pack at the bar, and noted they watched. They'd also turned a bit more subdued. *Good.*

Emory backed down a notch. "We'll see, then. Are you from around here?"

"Sure am. Born and bred. You just get here?"

"This afternoon," she sighed. "I start work this Monday morning. I'm from Stampede—if you know where that is."

"Sure do. Just down the road a ways," he smiled.

"I'm boarding my horse at the Weavers. Hope he'll do OK."

He caught the note in her voice. "The Weavers are fine. Never heard anything bad about any one of them."

"So, what's the story with the pipeline workers—just a bunch of troublemakers?"

"Personally, I don't care for them much. Come whatever night is their payday, they get rowdy. Money burning a hole in their pockets and not all that many places to spend it, I guess. That's what leads to most of the trouble around here."

Emory darted her gaze over to them, then back across the table. "That sounds about right. So, what do you do for fun around here?"

"Oh, I go hunting, 4-wheeling, fishing—that type of thing. I like to be outdoors, and there's a lot of good stuff out here. Petroglyphs, wild horses, mountains. You name it, and we've probably got it. Outdoor stuff, I mean."

"I'm partial to the out of door myself. As it is, I ride horses and tend to work on our ranch in my free time. But now that I'm out this direction, maybe I will go sightseeing. Do you ride horses?"

"'Fraid not. They don't like me, and I'm not sure I like them—other than from a safe distance. There's some talk making the rounds, however. Horse talk."

That caught her attention. Just in time for their food to appear.

The waitress set the plates down, and Jimmy dug right in. Emory did the same, but unlike her companion, she had a whole lot turning over in her mind beyond what was on her plate. When a decent amount of time had passed and Jimmy made it about halfway through his meal, she broached the subject.

"Horse talk, you were saying?"

"Yes," he took his napkin and wiped his mouth and beard. "I'm sure you'll hear all about it in your line of work, but there's talk about wild horse hunting, and sending them down to Mexico to be made into dog food. Don't know if that's true, but it's upsetting all the same. It ain't right. Some of the ranchers say the mustangs are pests, but I don't get involved in all of that."

"Have you heard of any branded horse thefts?"

"Oh shoot," he replied. "I don't know anything about branded versus non-branded horses."

Emory refused to let that line of conversation go but didn't want to press too hard in case of scaring him off the topic. "Perfectly understandable. What I mean is, is there any talk about horses missing from ranches?"

"I heard of *a* missing horse, but don't know where it went missing from. The general consensus came down to him wandering off." He shrugged; the matter finished —at least in his mind.

"Hope they reported it," she said, but of course, while he wouldn't have the details about filed reports. Not to mention, nothing at all had pulled up on the computer when she checked in the hotel.

She fished in her pocket, pulled out her phone and showed him a picture of Kai—whether he liked horses or not. "This is my guy, Kai. He's a good horse."

Jimmy considered the picture for a long moment. "He

shows personality," came his studied conclusion at length.

"He's smart, too. Sometimes a bit too smart." Emory smiled, setting the phone down on the table.

The waitress reappeared with their check.

"It's mine," Jimmy said, quick on the draw.

A protest poised ready on her tongue, but he quelled that. "Like I said. That's the price you pay for my company." He pulled out his wallet and handed the waitress some bills. "Keep the change."

He then turned his attention back to Emory. "Now, I know girls like you don't go out with guys like me but let me give you my phone number."

"It's just that—" Emory started, but he cut her off.

"No need to explain. Now, my number's 970-845-1729. I can show you the countryside, answer questions or whatever. Sometimes it just helps to know people in town."

Emory punched the number in her phone and rang it. "Now, you have my number, too. And thanks, Jimmy. I enjoyed meeting and eating dinner with you. I truly mean it. Next time, however, I'm paying."

"We'll see about that," he countered, "when that time comes."

BACK AT THE HOTEL, Emory perched on the edge of the bed still troubled. Where to call when she wanted to talk about a hanged horse thief? The Lost Daughter, of course. Home sweet home.

The cell rang a few times.

"There she is!" her father's voice came through. "We

was starting to think you'd taken a wrong turn and ended up in Utah."

"Ha ha. It took longer to settle Kai in, and then to find the hotel, get cleaned up and track down some dinner. Was I supposed to call?"

"Not really. You're a grown-up now," her father crowed, leaving her to believe that he wasn't alone in the house. "Unlike Monty there. He already set fire to the bunk house by accident…"

She felt her eyebrows lift. "Now you're messing with me."

"No…" Her father's voice came across a bit morose, but playful all the same.

"Damn it, Dad. I just left there this morning…what happened?"

Monty bellyached in the background, but she couldn't quite make out what he said.

"Now, I told you he wasn't house-broke! Seems he started trying to temper a pan and forgot about it as became distracted by oiling a gun. Anyhow, it all got out of hand. It's not so bad, if you don't mind the charred wood smell."

At this rendition of events, Monty started bellowing. "If you'd just keep matters between us once in a blue moon…"

"Can he still *stay* in the bunkhouse?" Emory prompted.

"He can, but he's going to have to explain to Linda what happened…"

In other words, comparatively speaking, nothing much made cause for concern at the Lost Daughter that evening.

"Yeah, I'd like to hear how that conversation goes myself. Say…something strange is going on out here."

Lance Cross shifted on the other end of the phone.

"Someone hanged a man for stealing horses. I found him swinging from an old crossbar on the back way into town."

"Hot damn," her father replied, followed by a low whistle. Whoever 'they' were, had Lance Cross' attention...and a stiff measure of grudging respect.

"I'm not supposed to talk about it, but on his shirt, they duct-taped a note claiming, 'horse thief'. Maybe I should have left Kai at home with you two jokers, but he's getting settled at the stables, and they seem like good folks."

For the moment, her father didn't want to talk about Kai. "You found him hanging, you say?"

"Yes. First thing I've had to do is to report that damned incident. Not great."

He chuckled. "Sounds like you're starting off with a bang! No, make that a snap." He made a clicking sound. "Like a neck snapping. Get it?"

Yeah, she got it. "Very funny," she countered.

"Then how come I ain't hearing you laugh?"

8

A LONG, ROUGH HISTORY (VIGILANTES WERE THE ENEMY)

"DAMN!" EMORY CROSS SAT BOLT UPRIGHT, JOLTED AWAKE.

She had attached far too much weight and trust in that danged 'horse thief' placard.

What did the accuser want, and why?

Now fully awake, she threw back the covers, and placed her feet on the carpeted ground, square.

"A man is hanged and labeled a horse thief. It's a stereotype of the old west," she mused into the empty room with only herself to answer. "Horse thieves got hanged. So what?"

That "so what" contained plenty.

Since when did signs have to tell the truth? And as a card-carrying Cross family member with the history to back it up—*vigilantes had never been their friends.*

Crude words printed out in a rough hand provided condemnation of the *alleged* crime. Those words could lie and mislead as easily as not. The truth all depended upon the specifics. Not to mention the mechanics of the act of the hanging itself.

No, upon a balanced, careful, and rational considera-tion, it required more than one lone person to hoist or hang a man.

Especially if the man didn't go willingly. Which, apparently, this one did.

Strangeness right there—but back to the vigilantes.

Vigilantes seldom were the common man—the small-holder or the independents. No, vigilantes wielded power instead. They lied—and took what they wanted. Covering their tracks by masquerading unpalatable actions as benefitting the common good. Ridding the range of the lawless elements.

Hell.

Those realizations clanged like an iron horseshoe around a railroad spike. That certainly cast matters in a different light. She'd fallen into a trap of *their* making, believing the accusation as whoever wanted all along.

"You're turning soft," she muttered to herself.

Still, that placard on the hanged man troubled her. *Really* troubled her.

Those questions niggled and would not rest. Justice... justice sometimes landed on the wrong side of right. *Vigilantes caused more problems than they were often worth.*

Cattle Kate, a whispering voice nagged, a voice she recognized as belonging from the past.

Cattle Kate provided an example, all right. And a bad one. She fell victim to the type of things men may have considered trying against the Crosses, but the Lost Daughter outfit proved too formidable and rough.

A lone homesteading woman didn't stand a chance. Not if the local cattle barons wanted her gone.

Memory for the details had faded, so Emory got up and sat down at her computer to locate the particulars of that tragic story.

It pulled up, no problem at all.

The Wyoming lynching of Ellen Watson in 1889, by six prominent and politically powerful cattlemen rocked the nation. Ellen Liddy Watson became known as an outlaw of the Old West, although subsequent scholarship sees her as a much-maligned victim. The initial accounts of the hanging, printed in newspapers controlled by the cattle barons, dubbed Ellen Watson as Cattle Kate, the moniker by which she is known throughout history. Ellen Watson filed a homestead claim with access to water vital to the wealthiest rancher in the district, Albert Bothwell. The cattle baron accused her of rustling. Abducted from her home, the riders then went to her husband, Jim Averell's homestead where they rounded him up. Watson and Averell were lynched. Both bodies were reportedly left hanging from the same tree near the Sweetwater River in Natrona County for two days as a deterrent toward further rustling activities in the region.

The Cheyenne newspapers had crowed at the time. Another account read:

Cattle Kate, aka Ellen "Ella" Watson, survived a turbulent past and a failed marriage behind her when she arrived in Rawlins, where she worked as a waitress. There she met post-master James "Jim" Averell, and while it is unclear whether the pair actually married, Ellen and Jim joined forces and filed adjoining homestead claims. Their murders epitomized the hostilities between large cattle operations, and smaller ranching concerns. According to Averill's brother after the lynching, he claimed that Jim had carved a fine irrigation ditch through his property that the cattle barons wanted. Post-master Averill had understood the homesteading stipulations and filed his legal claim under the slim protection of the law.

Jim Averell also acted as a Justice of the Peace, and he wrote letters to the newspapers pointing out infringements, infuriating the cattle barons.

Early newspaper accounts defamed Watson as a prostitute who sold her favors for livestock. The current belief is that she purchased footsore and weary cattle from passing emigrant trains and nursed the stock back to health. It is believed that she owned twenty-eight head of cattle. At the arrival of the mounted men, it is commonly held that Watson had in her possession brand registry papers proving her legal ownership of the cattle the posse claimed she had stolen. The receipt of her purchase was locked away for safekeeping in a Rawlins bank.

The Wyoming newspapers supported murderous deed. Ridding the Range of Predators they called it.

All of which pissed her off no end. Those cattle barons must have read the homesteader's brand papers all right—but they'd hanged her and Jim Averell all the same.

Bastards. Every last one of them that rode on that day.

The entire episode of the murdered homesteaders offered yet another frontier example of the strong controlling the weak, for their own purposes and for their own benefit.

The story (or warning) of Cattle Kate provided a precedent of a very specific incident when the good guy —in this case the good woman—did not prevail.

All in the name of frontier justice.

Which brought Emory back to the here and now of 2023.

What did that hanged man have or know that drove someone else to kill?

CONSIDERING the hangings and personal Cross family history, the dark side made her father a good source to talk to. She checked her watch and did a doubletake. 8:35 made for a very late start to the morning, even on a Sunday. He'd be done haying the horses and had probably moved on to other ranch chores while she slept in the lap of luxury.

That notion alone caused her to smile, laughing at his and Monty's expense. Well, they'd given her a run for her money often enough. She'd consider it partial payment for Monty setting the bunk house on fire.

Accidentally, of course.

Padding off to the bathroom, she showered and dressed in nothing flat. Out in the hallway and hearing the elevator chime, she darted in just as the doors closed —barging in on a family with two little kids and startling them.

"Sorry."

"Are you a real cowgirl?" The little boy dressed in easter-egg colored shorts and a matching top stared up at her, all wide-blue eyes.

Emory noted her shit and dirt-stained boots.

"Austin!" his mother said.

"That's all right." Emory figured that she fell more into the outlaw camp, but she kept that part to herself. "More like a rancher. How about you?"

Shy, he edged behind his mother's leg, still staring up at Emory with those big blue eyes.

"He likes cowboys," his sister explained, taking charge. "But no, he's not one. We're from Minneapolis."

"We're going to Dinosaur National Monument, aren't we kids?" the mother prompted.

Both blond heads nodded enthusiastically.

That actually sounded pretty good, and the little girl must have read her expression right.

"Do you want to come with?" the child asked.

Emory smiled. "I'd love to, but I have work to do."

"We're not allowed to take anything from the park, like bones or rocks or anything. If everyone took something, there'd be nothing left." Her clear child's voice carried as the doors opened.

"Good for you for knowing that." Emory gestured for the family to exit first.

Don't take stuff that doesn't belong to you.

And back her mind turned to the horse thief.

AT THE BREAKFAST BAR, Emory glided through, taking note of the pre-made omelets, bacon, sausage, scrambled eggs, biscuits and gravy, cereal, yogurt, and the juice bar. The clerk from the night before hadn't lied—the hotel sure provided plenty of options, and no one would go hungry.

That marked another difference, or sticking point, between now and the 19th and early 20th centuries. Food proved a scarce commodity that required hard work back in those days, thus making it difficult and time consuming to obtain. People from those eras would be amazed at the bounty they had, right here in Vermillion Colorado in a chain hotel. Not that they would have known what a chain hotel meant, either. But back in the old settlement days, everything had to be butchered, grown, baked, or what-have-you in order to eat.

Criminals in the 19th and early 20th centuries. She'd read that jail sentences back in those days, even for murder, didn't last more than a couple of years, tops. All due to the scarcity of food. Hard-working citizens during that time didn't understand why criminals should be fed for free, when they themselves had to put forth so much effort to place food on the table, and keep their own families fed.

In any case, Emory chose a table away from the commotion of families and sat down with her thoughts. Taking a sip of strange green juice, she thought it tasted fresh, if a bit like the hay meadow. She would force herself to continue to try new things, knowing it the only way to earn different outcomes.

For her part, no matter how nice the breakfast spread, doubts remained about her own future. The nagging doubt lingered as to the advisability of accepting this temporary position in the first place. She had allowed herself to be persuaded from a sense of guilt. Had she done the right thing by letting the *men* decide the best course for her?

So many questions, and in such a short period of time.

Vermillion and surrounding area sure proved one hell of a change of scenery.

And no matter whether the year was 1873 or 2023, deep pockets landed on the winning side nine times out of ten, while the average man fought long and hard for the scraps.

It remained the way of life, but it didn't mean it came across as fair.

Restless, she cleared away her breakfast dishes, and decided to take a walk around the town.

She nodded at the man working behind the desk as she passed through the lobby toward the parking lot.

"Have a good day," he called out.

"I'll be back," she replied. "Just going out to take a look around town."

"In that case, see you in fifteen minutes," he laughed.

9

THE BOUNTY OF VERMILLION

It didn't take long to find that the desk clerk had sold the town short. Vermillion held more than fifteen minutes worth of sights to see—that much appeared patently obvious before she even parked her pickup on Yampa Street. In no rush or particular hurry, she strolled along the commercial street, window shopping and considering the storefronts. True, vacancies punctuated the business blocks as in so many of the remote, outpost towns. The sensation or feeling that Emory couldn't shake amounted to a town almost gasping, but not yet ready to throw in its hand. Few people moved about in the downtown area on that Sunday morning, but maybe it remained a church-going place. No doubt the majority of citizens who tended to their shopping chores patronized the grocery or the Walmart. Ambling down the quiet, sleepy sidewalk and drawn to a large building at the end of the next block, the massive structure appeared to be an old armory or public building of an obsolete purpose. As she neared, wonder of wonders. In front of her stood an actual museum. That beat Stampede hands down right there. Up in the second story windows, mural-type paintings of cowboys gazed out past the town and into a distant horizon. Even more uncanny, the marquis over the entrance advertised their featured exhibit: Ann Bassett's War against the Cattle Barons.

Emory cocked her head in admiration as she bit back a smile, never having been one to ignore a sign.

Pulling out her phone the time read 9:36—which made it as good a time as any. She scrolled down and clicked on her father's number.

"You gotten yourself into any more trouble?" Humor laced his voice, enjoying his joke at her expense.

"Is that how you answer the phone these days?"

"I knew it was you. And it ain't an unreasonable question, given the circumstances."

Emory glanced around the street. No one approached within earshot.

All of the five people—and she counted—strolling in that particular part of town.

"Let's talk about horse thieves. Buried horse thieves like the ones on the ranch. And vigilantes."

Dead silence. Her father didn't seem inclined to rise to the bait.

"That all came before my time," he claimed, voice slow and low and defensive.

Which earned an exasperated laugh on her part. "I *know* that. What I *don't* know is the history behind all of it. Do you?"

A grumble on the other end. "Shit, Em. Who cares?"

She sniffed, holding her breath for a moment. A long moment. "Let me try this another way. Do you believe that all people who were hanged as horse thieves actually were horse thieves?"

He chewed on that. "Maybe not the traditional definition. That hanging still got you all bothered?"

"Hell, yeah. Don't you think that's natural and rubbing me the wrong way? Anyhow, it occurred to me, however, that I might have thought about it wrong." She scanned around again, pausing. "Just because someone stuck a note on him, doesn't make it true."

Her father chuckled. "There you go again. *Thinking.*" She heard him spit, and knew he weighed his options, pondering what he wanted to disclose. Or not disclose, as the case might be. "I know of three bodies, but there might be a few more scattered throughout. That's the thing about not burying a person, they scatter. Are you out in public?"

"Yes, but no one's around."

Exasperation crept in around the edges of his voice. "Do you consider this to be a conversation to be conducted *in public?*"

"No, sir. I'll go back in my truck if you're actually going to tell me something that matters."

A resigned sigh. "Git in your truck, then."

Emory jogged the two hundred yards and jumped in the front seat and shut the door. "I'm in."

He cleared his throat, but his words still came out tight. "If you stop to think about it, a body left out in the open can provide evidence, but if you get past the point where they still resembled their former selves, the wild animals will scatter the bones far and wide. Then it's the skulls you need to watch out for, but who's to say that the skulls don't belong to some ancient Utes who went off to die alone?"

She blinked a couple of times, brain churning. Archaeologists would know for starters, but she didn't want to lure him off track. "You've found skulls?"

"Only the one, when I was a boy. And no, I don't know who that belonged to or the story behind him. But there is a grave at the bottom of the rock outcropping on the old trail back into Stampede. The one that traces along the river, crossing up into the high pasture."

She knew exactly the point where her father meant. "I never felt comfortable around there. It struck me an ambush spot, that's for sure."

"There you go," he crowed, a confident pride taking over. But whether his tone amounted to pride for her, or his ancestor's misdeeds, remained impossible to say. In the end, Emory supposed it didn't matter.

"OK." In truth, she still felt vindicated. "What happened there?"

"Like you said. An ambush."

"Whose grave is it?"

"Some range rider or hired gun from another outfit. He trespassed where he oughtn't've and paid for it. My father told me that a cavvy of riders, backed by Cooper's outfit, rode in for a fight. The Coopers contested our rights to the hay meadow..."

"*Our* hay meadow?" she asked, and he chuckled at the dawning realization he heard in her voice.

"One and the same. The bottom line came down to the fact that they wanted it for themselves. Old Hank and his boys sent them packing, and a few bodies got left behind. And no, I don't know how many."

In her mind's eye, she could well imagine a fight as it unfolded. "What else?"

"Ain't that enough?"

It ought to be, but it wasn't. "You said three bodies and one skull. What else?"

"You have a one-track mind. Did I ever tell you that?"

She didn't bother to answer.

He sighed, knowing she wouldn't speak until he came up with more information, information of the type she wanted. "Then there's bones buried out somewhere in the old yard, near to Idella's house. She shot a man and buried him where she could keep an eye on him, or so that story went. And no, I don't know what happened there. The version of the story passed around claimed that he 'got too close to the house,' but there had to be more to it than that. I don't even know his identity, or why he was there in the first place. Then there's a man who tried to rustle some of the horses back around 1905 and got what was coming to him. They buried him out in one of the pastures and let the bulls trample down the mound. The law wouldn't have been too keen to go in there to investigate." Again, that same damn amused chuckle from her father.

That's how they all were raised. Tough, rough, and ready.

"So that one was a real horse thief."

"From what I've been told. *But he trespassed on our land*. That's the main thing. You ain't thinking of turning State's evidence, are you?"

"Hell, no. What do you think? Besides, that all happened long, long ago. My question is whether that sign taped to that man yesterday told the truth. Whether he amounts to a real, dyed-in-the-wool horse thief or not. I figure vigilantes didn't always tell the truth in the past, and they might not always tell the truth now. Where'd you put that skull that you found?"

"I never said that I took it anywhere at'all."

"Come on, now. You said you were a boy. What boy wouldn't keep a human skull that he found?"

"You're just jealous that you didn't find it first. Admit it. You keep pokin' around in them old out buildings, and you just might find it for yourself. Now I gotta go unless you need me for something more than a family history lesson. A motor's busted on one of them pumps."

She had more questions, but she just didn't know what they were. Yet. "Dad?"

"Yeah?"

A scratchy subject. "You're not going to tell Linda about the bodies, are you?"

"As pillow talk? I'd have to say that'd turn her off the whole idea of me."

"Dad!" Any references to her father's sex life made her squeamish and uncomfortable. She also remembered Terry's voice chiding her about how men her father's age preferred to be thought of as sexy senior citizens. *Sexy senior citizens, her ass.*

Her father probably didn't think in such terms, but she couldn't rule it past him one hundred percent.

"Give me some credit, would ya?" And with that, the line went dead. No goodbye, or anything nearing manners.

She'd give him plenty of credit. Credit for things most people no longer knew—and things they might not have wanted to even know back in the day.

Their conversation ended. An end caused by more than just a faulty motor needing repair. Her father didn't want to dredge up any more uncomfortable facts or truths. Some old ghosts and facets of family history lingered unwanted. Accounts of violence that they didn't even like to talk about among themselves.

Those buried bodies out on the Lost Daughter provided some of those sticking points.

Emory hopped back out of the pickup, glanced at the museum in the distance, and figured it probably opened about ten. A visit there would have to wait. In the meantime, she had a background to locate for a horse thief. *An accused horse thief.* All without admitting what she had seen. No doubt that would prove the hardest part, and any questions posed would strike as bizarre if she didn't phrase them right.

The Ace-Hi always provided a reliable source for the area gossip and dealings in Stampede. Wait a minute... didn't Jimmy tell her about a local watering hole? *Dusty Mike*, she recalled as the man's name...or something along those lines. He owned or ran a place called...the Rusty Spur. She typed the name into her phone, and it pulled up right away. The best part—the establishment stood only two blocks away.

The worst part was the time: On the early side for drinking, it probably didn't open on a Sunday morning in the first place. Still, she could head over that way and check it out.

Now with a specific destination, she had an address to locate. Down a deserted street she passed, rounding the corner onto another non-descript street while pretending to take in the sights more than she did. In reality, she didn't pay attention to the properties or the storefronts at all.

Music threaded through the sleepy morning, nothing loud or brash, but it carried in the small-town Sunday quiet all the same.

Following the trail of notes and a female voice singing, she came upon a middle-aged man sweeping the sidewalk in front of a building. The broom kept time along with the beat of the music...to a degree. In the right block for the bar, she figured she had found it.

Indeed, the words *Rusty Spur* stood out bold, painted in maroon cursive and taking up most of the store front. Washed-out yellow paint covered the rest of the rough-hewn wood exterior. The door, propped open to air out last night's fun, allowed the torch n' twang lament to gently catch the breeze.

The man noted Emory's approach, pleasant and benign.

She sure didn't believe that anyone swept the sidewalk outside of the Ace High. Ever.

"Lovely morning, isn't it?" he remarked.

She approached with her best friendly smile. "Sure is. This your place?"

He stopped sweeping. "It is indeed. Mike Matthews, at your service."

"Emory Cross. I'm a temporary brand inspector for this district." She eyed the exterior.

He waited for her to say more—to offer some sort of an explanation for her stopping to chat since she was a stranger and all.

"Last night I met a guy named Jimmy Hudspeth, and he mentioned that this is a popular spot. Since I was out walking, I thought I'd take a look and here it is."

She stuck her hands in her back pockets like she had all the time in the world.

The man smiled. "Jimmy's a good kid. He's my cousin Ralph's cousin by marriage, so in a way, we're related. Do you want me to get you something?"

He motioned to the open door.

"No—no thanks." Again, she considered the exterior, and by extension, the man. "In Stampede, where I'm from, the Ace High is *the* place to get the bare bones of what goes on in the area."

His head bobbed in general agreement. *So far, so good.*

"Are you looking for something specific?" he asked. "The Rusty Spur can work that way, too. Everything happening in town is discussed, one way or another. Not that there's that much going on." He extended one arm, gesturing to the trafficless street.

Emory shrugged. "Don't suppose that you've heard anything about horse thefts in the area?"

She could have sworn his knuckles grew more pronounced as he grasped the broom handle tighter.

"Horse thefts?" He scratched his broad forehead. "Not many people keep horses around here anymore. Still, a theft would get everyone's attention, I'd assume. Right out of the old days and ways."

"Yeah," she admitted. "But rustling and thefts still happen in modern times, you know."

Dusty Mike regarded her, dead serious and eyes squinting just a bit. "Are you saying that someone's horse got stolen?"

"No, not exactly," she shrugged. *Don't come on too heavy*, she told herself. "I'm just asking if you've *heard* anything about missing horses."

He shook his head. "No, but if I do, I can, and will, let you know."

She smiled. "In that case, let me give you my card."

She pulled out her wallet, rifled through and withdrew one. "The cell number is good. If you call the number in Greeley, they'll just ask you to call my cell."

He studied the information with care, much as he would a driver's license for some suspiciously young person ordering a beer. He nodded, still pondering as he pocketed it.

"Thank you, Mike. Anything you hear about missing horses or anything else strange, I sure would appreciate a call."

"Isn't that for the sheriff?" His voice held a bit of an edge.

"Branded livestock, I mean," she hastened.

He eyed her, then relented. One degree. "Livestock. You can count on it."

With that, their conversation had reached its natural conclusion, unless she wanted a beer.

"I'll stop in sometime during regular business hours, and nice to meet you," she said as the broom rasped, and she resumed walking.

"We'll be here waitin' for you," he called out after her.

Of course, that's how reputations got started.

Maybe it was high time for her to claim hers.

10

LIES ARE THE TRUTH...WITH A
KEY PIECES REMOVED

OF COURSE, THE FASTEST WAY TO FIND OUT WHERE AND how the investigation proceeded would mean a call to the sheriff or the coroner. But should she? They seemed friendly enough on the surface, but she'd swear an undercurrent swirled about them all.

Emory knew very well that how things *seemed* and how they *actually were* often amounted to two different things entirely. And she remained a stranger to them. An outsider at best. At worst, an outsider meddling in their affairs.

Climbing back into her time-and-road-worn truck, she faced in the direction of the museum and gave the marquis a long stare before reluctantly turning the engine over. The door opened at that moment, and a woman dragged an 'open' sign onto the sidewalk.

Emory inhaled, sharp.

But no. *She needed to understand the current.*

Meanwhile, a numbered county road neatly bisected the town, and she figured the least she could do was drive it. She rumbled along in the northwestern direction. The businesses on either side of the thoroughfare gave the impression of a struggling town. A proliferation of last gasp insurance agencies snoozed from years past —Walmart now taking pride of place and pumping with the town's lifeblood. Everything else drained away. Mom-and-pop concerns declined and listed, while makeshift repair shops sprang up and proliferated like weeds.

One thing felt certain, none of that trust-fund, Hollywood, I-don't-know-where-it-came-from type of money flowed around Vermillion, for damn sure.

Plain old-fashioned services pulled double duty as residences behind the shopfronts, but even those dozed —some with junked out cars decaying alongside. Taxidermists and meat processors fared better, while fast food chains sprouted up with vibrant signs that struggled against the sense of decline.

Those bright signs didn't help all that much.

Plenty of abandoned homes and last gasp businesses faded in their slow, inevitable slide back into the dust while Wendy's signs and the like lorded over their death throes.

But the dying trees framing the old plate glass windows struck a chord within her heart and hit the hardest. Sepia-tinted snapshots in time—any fingers that had once pulled those old curtains aside were now gone and leaving nothing more than ghost memories.

For years, time drained away and the brittle, rotting fabric waited. Gap-toothed curiosity from a time long since passed, no one was likely to peer out from behind those windows ever again. Gnarled skeletons of trees that once provided shade against the relentless Colorado sun languished and choked with thirst.

So many ideals and hopes dead and gone and ground

back into the dirt which would remain longer than them all.

And one stray hanged horse thief. A strange relic from a forgotten era in a place like this. A place that boasted a Walmart with pride.

That rubbed her the wrong way, too.

It didn't take all that long before she started running out of town. On the outskirts, she pulled over to a stop.

She was missing something. Hell, everyone was.

Emory searched for the county sheriff's department in her phone and stared at the number long and hard.

What the hell.

"Vermillion County Sheriff's office," the bored male voice made it sound like the mere fact of the phone ringing disturbed him. It probably belonged to one of the deputies she met earlier—the weaselly one.

"This is Emory Cross, the temporary brand inspector. Who's this?"

"Deputy Deacon."

Bingo.

Of course he sounded cocky, but that cockiness faded as worry pressed in. "You didn't find anything else, did you?"

He sounded on edge. She would have found that funny if not for her initial impression of him. She felt nigh-on certain that he thought women shouldn't be in law enforcement and would bully if given the slightest opportunity. So, she'd serve it to him first.

"No. Did *you*? Last I checked that was your job. I check brands."

He cleared his throat, before trying to sound official. "The status of the ongoing investigation is not something we're at liberty to disclose."

Predictable, and in all likelihood, it meant 'no.'

"Can I speak to the sheriff?"

"Is it for official business?"

She wrinkled her nose, annoyed, but she tried to keep her tone light and even. Deceptively unbothered. "Are you screening his calls because he asked you to?"

That got him. "No." His chair scraped. "It's his day off. Care to leave a message?"

"No thanks." She clicked off without saying goodbye and pocketed the phone.

Failing a crime of passion, follow the money instead.

The problem behind that tried and true logic stuck out like a sore thumb. There didn't appear to be much money or passion to be found anywhere around the town that she could see.

DOWN THE ROAD a few more miles, Emory pulled into the Weaver's stable yard—the load of hay already delivered and waiting off to the side. It had to be Myra's she figured, and probably the woman arrived at the crack of dawn. An old collie came wagging its way up to her, poking its long, pointed nose into her thigh by way of a greeting.

"Bailey!" Mrs. Weaver rounded a corner. "Don't bother her!"

"It's all right, I don't mind," Emory responded, smiling and patting the dog's head. Kai, in the quarantine pen, whinnied in her direction.

"Hi Kai!" Emory called, before turning her attention back to the woman. "How are you today?" She inspected the hay from a distance. "I see your delivery arrived."

"Myra delivered first thing and stayed just about long enough to have a cup of coffee. Now I'm doing the regular chores. You know, they never end where horses are concerned."

Emory chuckled still patting the dog, who sat down and leaned into her. "That's the truth. I walked around town earlier and figured that I'd come check on Kai since I was already out in this direction. I saw there's a museum. Maybe I can make it over there a bit later. Right now, I'm just trying to get my bearings and figure out the next step."

Patty Deacon wasn't exactly interested in Emory's chit-chat, but she made an effort to play along as she bided her time.

"Oh, you found the museum, did you? I haven't been there in years. Last time there the displays had a lot about the outlaws and horse thieves in Brown's Park..." The woman's words were conversant, but her mind snagged on something of far more interest to her, as she assessed Emory.

"You know, there's a rumor going around," she offered in the end. "I think it may have something to do with what you couldn't talk about yesterday."

Here it comes. Emory nodded and waited her out.

The woman ventured a half-step forward. "You asked if we'd had any trouble, and I said that others had."

Glancing over to check on Kai, Emory nodded in an absent way before returning her gaze to Patty, a bit more pointed in her conversation this time around. "I don't suppose you could clue me in on the rumor, could you?"

Patty Weaver shook her head in disbelief. "It's outlandish. Can't be true, in fact. And before you start to wonder, none of this came by way of Dustin. You'd have to use a crowbar to get anything out of that boy."

"Aww, come on. What's not true?"

The woman waved Emory's attempt away as unworthy. "I shouldn't have said a thing," she said, stepping past her to pick up a rake.

A dry, self-deprecating chuckle escaped from the brand inspector. "Good news travels fast here, just like at home. I'm used to working alongside law enforcement, but I know I'm the new face in town. It will take a while for people to establish trust, and I understand that. Since we've hit a dead end with the other conversation, what do you think of the sheriff, if you don't mind me asking?"

"Joe Hammond? He's good. Don't like that turkey Frank Deacon he's got working for him, however. No one does, other than his mother from what I gather." Another piercing assessment. "Trust goes both ways, you know."

Emory toed the ground with the tip of her boot, thinking that provided the opening she sought. "Let me ask a flat-out blunt question. *Have* you heard of any horses being stolen?"

"No," the woman answered equally straight forward. "Not in the traditional sense. But everyone's heard whisperings of horses being acquired, purchased under false pretenses, or sold in that same way. It's hard to say for certain. The thing is, none of us know the full picture. Some of it comes down to us, meaning the ranchers, versus what we think of as the bureaucracy."

That admission caught Emory. *Follow the money.* "I don't suppose you could say more about that?"

Although thoughts and beliefs visibly turned over in the woman's mind, she shut them down as a guarded secret. Patty Weaver regarded whatever information she held as a troubling, but local, business. Nothing to banter about with outsiders.

"I don't really know anything that would hold up in a

court of law. You know, the old ranchers around here… some of them used to keep the wild horses on their properties for safekeeping. Others were mustangers in the days of old."

Emory nodded. Something bothered the woman. Something she wouldn't come straight out with.

The silence got to the stable woman, and in the end, she filled it.

"But like I said. We don't have trouble because we keep an eye out and make sure our fences stay standing and in good repair. And that's another thing. We don't associate with those types of people—the ones who bend the rules…"

That last part amounted to a slip. Emory caught it, noting that something sure as hell didn't ring true.

The woman heard her lie as well and didn't go back to correct it. "Now, I'd best get on with what needs doing instead of chewing your ear off."

Her red plaid flannel shirt-back walked away, but she called over her shoulder, "You'll be happy to know that Kai did fine last night."

And so she was. But Emory remained unhappy about the undertow. And the woman sensed that as well.

11

THERE'S A LOT OF "NOT QUITE RIGHT" RUNNING AROUND

THE NEXT TASK ON EMORY'S ROSTER WOULDN'T PROVE AS simple—finding decent local accommodation. She garnered a list of four properties to check out, surprised that Vermillion held even that many. The first two seemed fine, one appeared well-kept and presentable on the western side of town, and the other, more central, appeared likely in someone's basement. Subterranean dwelling held precious little appeal and struck her as straight out depressing. That said, she wouldn't write it off just yet, since her assumptions didn't have any facts to back them up.

Outsides were one thing, insides another. Educated guesses yet a third.

Driving toward the next property, one block back from the main drag, she passed along a nondescript residential street and located the two-story apartment building without problem. A brown, wood-sided building, it appeared kind of shabby, but displayed a *vacancy* sign in the front. A chopper, parked off to the side and on the lawn, didn't strike the best of chords.

Hard to say why exactly she hopped out of the truck, but she did. Maybe she wanted to wade into the waters to test her reactions.

Just going to take a closer look at the sign, was the lie that she told herself.

Bullshit—and the sign appeared permanent.

That part didn't strike so good either.

As she stood eyeballing at that battered and faded perma-sign, a junker roared up and parked right behind her truck. The guy who emerged looked green about the gills and hung over as hell. Hung over or not, he spotted her all right.

"Hey, don't I know you?" He shot across a grin with a missing front tooth.

Warning bells jangled. "No, I don't think so."

He came up to her, sweat and booze radiating. It must have been one hell of a night—or morning. "Yeah, I've seen you before," he countered, eyes narrowing. He puffed up and out, big and tall. "At the Fiesta. You couldn't call that clodhopper you were eating dinner with the man of the hour, exactly."

"He's nice enough." She eyed him up and down, defensive. "Does that beater even have a muffler on it?"

"Noise bother you?"

She didn't bother to answer. "Do you live here?"

"Yeah. You want to come in and have a drink?" His eyes, red and bloodshot, were both leering and glazed, all at the same time. Any more liquor would be about the last thing he needed.

"No thanks. I just wondered if the apartments were quiet and clean. I read that the studios rent by the week. Do you work out in the gas fields?"

He grabbed her arm. Not hard, but persuasive. Not to mention, unwelcome. "Sure do. It pays well. Now, come on in. You can meet some of the other guys. We'll have a party. Somebody might even have some blow if you play your cards right."

She wrenched her arm free. "I'm not going in there with you. I have work to do. And for the record, hard drugs are illegal."

"Is that so? You'll do drugs like everyone else once you've been out here a while. Pot don't exactly cut it after a while. The others help to kill the time." He grabbed at her again. "I could make some sort of deal with you."

"You touch me again, and you'll be sorry."

By damn, he grabbed her again. Emory pointedly stared at his fingers pressing into the flesh of her right arm.

He didn't remove them.

She hauled back her left, threw all her weight into it, and punched him square in the throat.

Predictably, he went down, choking and gasping.

Jumping back and out of his reach, she smirked, knowing that most women would have aimed for his balls or slapped him. She did think about giving him a good swift kick as a final parting gesture but decided to quit while ahead.

Sometimes people took that one last step too far.

Kicking a man while down presented him with one last opportunity to grab a foot and start the fight back up again in nothing flat.

She wouldn't make that sucker mistake.

Without further ado, she climbed back into her Ford and drove off. She checked in the rearview mirror before turning the corner back to the hotel. He remained lying, literally, in the dirt where she left him.

He moved a bit. He might even puke, when he got enough air back.

In the end, he'd be OK. Maybe he'd have enough sense to think twice before doing anything similar again.

She flicked on the radio, feeling better.

Good thing he wasn't the kind to call the police or the sheriff because this would be one more wrinkle she'd have to explain. The throbbing pain in her knuckles was just one more souvenir to carry along, and she shook out her hand.

She thanked Providence that she'd always been stronger on her left side. for some odd reason, people always expected a righthand throw.

Best of all, she guessed that most people didn't know about throat punches and turned up the music a couple of notches louder and rolled down the window to enjoy the breeze.

Sometimes a girl just felt like fighting.

She'd won that round.

EMORY REPORTED her new office by 7:00 a.m. that following morning as Monday rolled around. Josh Tucker, already seated and working, jumped up when she came in through the door of the office trailer. He came out from around his desk, right hand extended, the epitome of good manners and appreciation. A seemingly wide-open welcome for a sorely needed addition.

"I would tell you that nothing much ever happens around here, but I don't suppose that you'd believe me."

He held out his hand and she did her best not to flinch at her crunching bruised knuckles. He noticed the ripple of pain. "Is something wrong with your hand?"

"It's nothing," she replied. "And no, I wouldn't believe you if you said that nothing happened out here. I already had to pop a guy in the throat."

His eyebrows shot upwards, and he took a half step back. "Get in a lot of fights, do you?"

"Not as a rule," she replied, sounding a bit more on the firm straight and narrow than she'd intended. "It ran into him at one of the places for rent, and he'd been drinking."

So, she cracked a grin like that would make everything better.

Startled, he offered a half-strangled choking laugh carrying a fair amount of uncertain gallows humor. "I'd ask how you're finding everything, but now I'm not so sure that I want to know."

Now it was her turn on the back foot, because she couldn't tell if he were joking or dead serious.

"I'm here to do a job," she said at length.

"So you are," he replied. "I never said anything different."

Why would he say anything at all? Strange response, so she decided to overlook it. File it away in her mind, but it struck as decidedly odd.

If he noticed her hesitance, he didn't care. "Found a place to stay yet?"

She blinked a couple of times. "No. I've only been here two nights."

He didn't bother a glance in her direction as he turned away, picking up papers stapled together. "Some of the tourist cabins rent out by the month, in the off season," Tucker offered. "That's how I started out myself, but I wouldn't recommend the exact same one. I've graduated to a regular apartment these days."

"Are you planning on buying a house at some point?" She figured that question landed on safer ground.

"In Vermillion? No. This is just a stopping place until a better assignment comes along."

She took that under consideration, wondering what post he truly angled for. "Maybe I'll try to find one of those off-season rentals. At least I have my horse boarded at the Weavers, so that's one thing accomplished. Do you know them?"

"Not personally," he said, walking back around his desk, "but by reputation. Good people who run a good outfit from what I know. Take a seat." Half-way toward seated, he paused mid-air. "Where *are* my manners— would you like a cup of coffee?"

His tone changed entirely with that last question.

"Maybe in a bit," she answered, feeling whiplashed.

This time, the brand inspector sat all the way down. His brown eyes remained sharp and appraising. "I'll bet you wonder what you've got yourself into, don't you?"

She sure as hell did, and even more so, right about now.

Focusing on a nearby corner, she noted it stacked high with discarded boxes, books, files, and papers.

She dredged up the expected reply. "Not really. Everything is fine."

"I find that hard to believe."

"Shit happens." She eyed him. "I don't want to lie to you, Josh. I have, until two days ago, always assumed that hanging horse thieves belonged in the past. I guess I'm mistaken on that count."

"I would have said the same thing, two days ago," he admitted, still shrewd and assessing. He sat up a bit straighter. "Wait a minute. You don't think that the note is *real*, do you?"

"I have no idea."

"You can't be serious," he pressed, palms now on his desktop and leaning into his statement, coiled tight.

She leaned forward as well. "I thought the era of vigilantes was dead and buried, and maybe I got that part wrong. Why have they made a comeback?"

"They haven't! It's some psychopath or a weird suicide. What else could you be thinking?" Shock rippled, as if she had slapped him across the face. "You don't honestly believe that someone hanged a *horse thief* on a crossbar because it's *true*, do you?"

He tapped on his desk with one, solitary, squat index finger to drive his point home. "Enough with the wild west bullshit. And that's another one of the problems out here. Ignorance. That is exactly the type of thing that people out here would believe, and I would expect better from a badge-carrying member of the Brand Commission."

And while she'd hit a nerve with him, he hit a nerve within her. She might be a hick, but she wasn't ignorant and doubted the local people in the area were either.

"I'm not so certain that I would chalk any of it up to ignorance. Maybe people believe in horse thieves and take justice into their own hands." Sure, now she took the part of the vigilantes which went against her grain. She pressed ahead, regardless. "This area remained lawless for a long time. Handing down stories of hangings and frontier justice when law stayed too far away to be of much help strikes a chord within many."

He still appeared incredulous and not at all in agreement with her.

Emory held her voice even as she claimed the part of devil's advocate without intent, although that's how her words came out. "Where are you from originally?"

Because he sure as hell wasn't from Rimrock County.

He shifted in his chair, not liking that question either. "Sioux City, Iowa."

Emory quirked at that clarification.

"Nice and green there, I'd guess. Pastoral." Another one of those dang words that just slipped out. "How long have you been out here?"

Being her first day and all, she ought to at least try to back down and give him the benefit of the doubt. Maybe he simply didn't know how the game played in Colorado's wide-open empty.

"Slightly over two years. Why?"

She shrugged. "Curiosity. Just making conversation, I guess. I've always been in Colorado."

A pause.

"It's about the same as anywhere else," he claimed. "And for the record, I do expect you to apply logic to the job out here. Not spinning tall tales and yarns."

Many of those so-called tall tales carried a strong foundation in reality.

And he had just insulted the hell out of her. Tossing back her head with the hint of a smile, her eyes still narrowed. She tried to pretend that their exchange meant nothing more than a friendly introduction that wasn't going all that well. That somehow, she didn't notice the slights he served.

Her actions felt false and were false...but he seemed to buy them all the same.

Change of course. "Did either the sheriff or the coroner call you?"

"No. Why would they?"

BECAUSE A HANGED MAN WAS ACCUSED OF HORSE THEFT she wanted to scream.

"Professional courtesy," she replied.

She never experienced this many problems with

Terry and Dave, even on her worst day. Josh Tucker didn't exactly take to her. That much came across plenty clear.

"No. No, they didn't, and it's none of my business."

"Bullshit," the word flew out, and she didn't regret it.

His eyes went dead cold. Furious.

She stared back at him, unwavering. "*Have* you had any reports of missing equines?"

He glared. "No. A couple of strays a while back, but they were found. Didn't even have time to write up a report about it. A segment of fence fell down, and they wandered out along a creek bed, enjoying the scenery."

Rifling through papers at the top of his desk—still plenty pissed off—he located and pulled out a clipboard from somewhere mid-pile. Skimming the clipped paper, he held it out for her. "Here's the list of what we've got for the next couple of days. And here are the keys for truck number two."

She snatched the keys and scanned the list, willing her temper to cool. It didn't. Not all the way down to level, although she gave it a half-assed try.

"Do you want me to get started on this now by myself, or did you want to come along to see how I do?"

He didn't answer right away, and his eyes turned mean although his expression, remarkably, didn't change.

"Let me be honest with you, *Miss Temporary Brand Inspector*. I called over to the Greeley Sale Barn. Your assignment came through somewhat...different...channels than usual. Girl, they've got your past locked up tighter than any I've ever seen. Now," he said returning to seated and leaning back to eye her like a spider sizing up a fly, "why do you suppose that might be?"

Her blood ran a few degrees colder.

"No idea," she replied. "I guess they value privacy."

"Nah. That's not it. Is there some secret that you're keeping? Anyhow, those old boys must be getting toward retirement age. Maybe put a pretty face on it, and things get past them. Have they made any noise about that?"

"Pretty faces? No. And I happen to like 'those old boys' as you call them. If you're asking me in a round-about way if they are eyeing retirement, they haven't said word one about it to me. Is that what you are hoping for—Greeley as your next move?"

"Maybe. At least it's approximating a city, and some of the largest meat packing and feed lot concerns are out that way. It would be more visible than hanging out in this corner of the state. Besides, the Greeley Sale Barn has a good reputation."

"Yes, they do, and for a reason. Terry and Dave handle the big plants and feed lots for the most part. But there are also a bunch of smaller concerns."

"And you handle those." His words came out as a sneer.

"I handle whatever they tell me to handle." She eyed him back. "Anyhow, who did you ask about me?"

"I *tried* talking to Dave. Not much of a conversation-alist, I'll say that for him. Met him once. Didn't have much to say then and doesn't have much to say now. I tried a few other…sources, shall I say. Jack squat."

Emory measured him up, sensing the threat. He wouldn't quit searching for something about her or her background until he found what he sought. But the question as to what, and more importantly why, loomed and loomed large.

She gathered the distinct impression that he wanted her out of his region.

To disclose information in the face of such a threat

would be an act of plain stupidity, but so was pretending not to notice. She aimed for the center path since no one held a gun to her head. "What is it that you want to know about me? You could just ask straight out. I don't have anything to hide."

Not exactly the truth, but he didn't have to know that part.

"Ok, then. What's wrong with you? Something certainly is."

His words were a knife to the stomach.

Worse, he waited, wanting an answer.

"Nothing is wrong with me, and I have a good track record. I was asked out here."

"You must not think much of your career then, because this will certainly not do you any favors."

Meaning he would see to it that her time was spent in misery.

She waited from him to continue—to finish his piece.

"Especially not if you think hanging horse thieves are the real deal. I will say that if you can't handle your job, I won't cover for you. But it seems those old boys don't question your abilities. I suppose if they don't... Let's just say that right now, I have no reason to question their...judgment."

She didn't like the way he said *judgment*, and she didn't like his insinuations. Because she had nothing further to say, she stayed silent.

"Think you can get through that roster in one day?" he pressed.

"This has two days' worth of stops on it," she replied, "even if they are close together."

"You know what I mean. For today. Can you get through today's calls, or do I need to help you out."

"You don't need to help me out," she replied, voice trailing off as she studied him.

The roster had too many stops, but she wouldn't back down and admit as much. She'd just work longer hours if she had to. She'd call those that she couldn't reach during her shift to reschedule, or she'd work outside the normal hours.

His voice came across without expression. "I've put them into order of the furthest out, working the route back into town. I did it for you this time, but you'll be responsible for your own route going forward. As a point of safety, you will always need to carry plenty of water with you out here. And get a sandwich or something. There aren't any restaurants outside of town, other than Maybell has a general store where you can pick up something."

She nodded. "Fine. Does Google maps work out here?"

"For the most part. If you can't find something, give me a call."

That flat out wouldn't happen. She would never show Josh Tucker the slightest sign of weakness if she could help it.

List in hand, Emory headed for the door like a finish line. Hand on the burnished doorknob, she broke her stride, and tossed a glance over her shoulder at the seated brand inspector. "The sheriff and coroner asked me not to tell anyone about the hanging. Just so you know."

Josh Tucker's glance didn't waver but locked into her. "Yeah, I'm sure they wouldn't want word to get out. Stands to reason. The Old West is dead and gone," he claimed, like his words made one whit of difference in the flow of life that surrounded him. "And you know what? The sheriff is facing re-election and I'll bet this doesn't make his prospects look any too good."

In her bones she knew he was wrong on a couple of

different levels—the old west wasn't dead, and Colorado had never been the same as Iowa.

But she had brands to check and a job to do, so she closed the door behind her.

The Old West lurked right beneath the modern surface of the twenty-first century. A West, then as now, that leaned toward expediency instead of regulations. As a region or belief system, the west seldom bothered to take prisoners, preferring to kill them outright instead.

For more reasons than one.

And Josh Tucker didn't like her. Maybe she'd just have to make sure that she earned that dislike.

A smile tugged along with that new notion. All of which sat with her just fine.

12

THERE AIN'T NO EASY
WAY OUT

THAT NAGGING SENSE OF TROUBLE ON THE HORIZON OF the dry scrub hills accompanied her, the same one that she'd had since her arrival in town on Saturday. Emory travelled in the direction of Maybell, to the ranch at the farthest reach of her day's roster. Bracing herself for another day of checking brands, butts, and paperwork, she couldn't settle at all. In fact, she felt on high alert but pinpointing the danger proved out of reach, and another matter entirely. Glancing at the directions on her phone, it ought to take about a half hour to drive out to the farthest address. The unfolding landscape and the unfettered remoteness ought to allow her to breathe a bit easier, even if her nerves acted up. But that day, and in that situation, the balm didn't work.

And a whole lot of "oughts" weren't holding true.

Had Josh Tucker heard about her shooting the biker? How had the Vermillion brand inspector decided that she wasn't quite what she seemed, and why?

Dang Terry and Dave, but it just didn't sound like them.

The quickest way to solve a problem meant checking with the source.

She placed a call through to the Greeley Sale Barn. In this instance, either brand inspector would do.

"Brand inspector, this is Dave."

She warmed upon hearing his familiar voice. "Dave! It's Emory," she fairly shouted.

"Hell-o!" He sounded as pleased as she'd ever heard him. "How's everything going out there—you settling in OK?"

She halfway growled. "What do you know about Josh Tucker?"

"Oh, nothing more than he asked about you. That's what I know. Not going so well?"

"You guys didn't tell him that I go around shooting people by chance, did you?"

He guffawed. "No, I can honestly say that I did not, and I doubt Terry would either. Speaking of which, here he comes now. I'm going to put you on speaker. It's Emory."

"Hey, are you missing us already?" Terry sounded as pleased as Dave.

"Actually, I am. Say, you didn't tell Josh Tucker that I go around shooting people, did you?"

"Why in the hell would I do a thing like that?" The shock in his voice struck clear, as did the fact that he took her question as an insult.

"Technically speaking, it is true," she admitted, couching her words a bit better and making them less of an outright accusation.

She didn't have to see him to know that he wagged his head, irritated at the situation beyond her words.

"You've been exonerated, but no. That's nothing I would do. What *exactly* did he say?"

Emory scratched at her neck—another nervous tick. "He claims my assignment didn't go through the normal channels. I sure get the feeling that he doesn't like me. He flat out asked the question, even." Her voice fell. "Something is wrong with *me*. I just don't want him to know it."

She didn't have to sit in the room with them to know that the two Greeley men stared at each other.

"There's nothing wrong with you at all…" Terry began.

"I talked to him, Em…" Dave interrupted, a rare occurrence for the circumspect man. "He asked why you would be willing to go out there, and I might have said a change of scenery. Nothing more. Oh hell. Guess I shouldn't have said even that much. But I also told him that you did one hell of a good job for us."

Silence. "Terry, do you know this joker?"

"No. No, I don't. Doesn't sound like I want to, either."

A flare of pain touched too near the wound. "He said that my past came sealed tighter than a drum, or words to that effect."

"Sounds like a fishing expedition to me, and an unwelcome one at that," Dave stated. "Nothing more. Still, that's not what you want."

No, it certainly wasn't. "He and I didn't hit it off, but beyond that, I can tell you that something's wrong out here. Seriously wrong. But I'm not at liberty to say just now. This region's brand inspector may turn out to be the least of anyone's problems, including my own."

Again, a hesitant silence at the other end.

"Is there anything we can do to help?" While Terry didn't sound terribly surprised by any of that last part, his tone came across as clipped and unhappy at her situation. A situation that he bore partial responsibility for placing her in.

As such, she wasn't about to let the matter drop so easily. "Now that we're talking about it, just how did this transfer take place for starters?"

Another long silence.

"Em, I know that you think we ganged up on you and sent you out there because of the gunfight," Terry began. "And that is part of the equation. But there are also some concerns about the district. Keep that under your hat, but don't get caught up in anything that you shouldn't. Let's just say that there are questions concerning Mr. Tucker's performance and how he runs that branch."

"Can you answer my question about my posting?" She persisted.

"I'll admit it—I pulled some strings. That part's true. But it's also true that we need you out there for reasons I can't go in to right now."

"He's aiming for a post in Greeley," she offered, probably breaking a confidence. "He sure managed to get me going."

"Call if you need us. We can certainly drive out if need be."

"Will do," she replied, voice hitching. Then stronger. "I'll probably drop out of range soon. I'm headed toward a remote ranch to check out my first shipment. Talk to you guys later."

She didn't want to cut off the call but had to—offering a reluctant goodbye.

And that marked the end of it.

At least they didn't tell her that Josh Tucker enjoyed an upstanding reputation, well-liked and respected by all. Slim though that consolation might feel, she'd take it.

The truth counted for everything. Especially when nothing stood out clear.

AS SHE TURNED off the county road onto private property, the fences stood tall: well-tended and in good repair. The pickup's tires rumbled over wash-boarding of the ranch road, right before she pulled up into the yard of the Crawford property. Again, she couldn't help but be struck by the outfit's appearance. Everything from the tractor in the yard, to the house itself came across as neat and orderly—and maintained far better than the Lost Daughter could ever claim. Comparison stood one step removed from jealousy, and in this instance, she recognized the flare of unintended competition. She remained all too aware that they didn't tend to the buildings as well as they should. In comparison, the Crawford ranch lacked age and pedigree—their residence a tidy example of a routine single-level ranch house from the 1950's or 1960's, and the barn dated from the same approximate era. Neat as a pin, and bland as a pin, too.

A stab of conscience rippled through, albeit at the end of her assessment. She needed to learn not to hold the lack of history against everyone, and chuckled at her own expense for her ingrained snobbery and sense of superiority—misguided though it might be.

She killed the motor and hopped out, clipboard in hand.

A stooped old rancher hobbled out from the house— obviously he'd watched and waited for her—his weathered face lit by a pair of shining pale denim eyes.

"Are you the brand inspector now?" he asked, as if finding it all a great joke.

"That's what the truck says." She stepped forward, nice and friendly. "I'm Emory Cross."

"You're better looking than Ray, 'course it I can tell your nose got busted along the line, too …" The rancher broke into a wheezy laugh. "Let me get the grandson. He runs the place, now. Does a good job of it, too, but I don't always agree with his newfangled ideas about range management."

He sliced a whistle, loud and clear. Just like she and her father did.

"What?" he asked, catching her pained expression.

Outstanding. Now even geezers felt free to give her shit about her busted nose.

Sour responses were a dime a dozen in one form or another, but he didn't mean any harm. "That's how my father and I call to each other."

He took that under consideration. Serious consideration. "Where did you say you and your lot come from?"

She hadn't. "Near Stampede."

That caught him. "Oh?" He peered at her more closely. "Which outfit?"

"The Lost Daughter."

His eyes widened, then he belted out a laugh that came from somewhere near the region of his toes. "You're one of *them* Crosses? Hell, I knew old Chuck—a bastard if ever there was one. You've got quite a… history…behind you."

Emory quirked her head, wondering what else the old man would care to toss out for inspection. But before he could further pontificate, a tall, youngish man came out from the barn.

"This is Casey," the old man announced, appraising

his grandson. "This is the new brand inspector. She hails from the Lost Daughter Ranch. She's one of *them* Crosses."

Casey's eyes widened at the tone introduction, rather than the name. His initial surprise came quickly followed by a frown aimed at his grandfather's choice of words.

"My name's Emory, and I'm the *temporary* brand inspector, until the post gets filled—"

The old man interrupted. "Just like your boss, in that case. So, what did you screw up?"

"Gramps—" his grandson cautioned.

"What do you mean, and I didn't screw up anything." Emory stared at the old man, wondering if he were senile.

"You must have, because you're out here." The old buzzard wasn't backing down. Emory warmed, kind of admiring that about him.

"I like it out here. What do you mean about Josh being temporary? That's not the case at all..."

"To hear him tell it, it is. Don't you know that he's off to bigger and better things? He makes sure to tell us each and every time he sees up, and makes sure to express his opinion that we're all idiots. He's just biding his time with us locals until he gets a better offer. I'd sure like to help him with that part..." The old man wheezed out that last part for effect.

Interesting.

"That's not how I feel about this area at all," Emory said, and meaning it. She turned back to Casey, because the clock ticked down. "You're shipping some cattle tomorrow?"

"Yes, ma'am. Let me take you to them." He took off walking, like he couldn't get away from his grandfather fast enough. Emory, long legs notwithstanding, had to hustle to fall in alongside. She glanced back at the grandfather.

If the old man noticed anything amiss in that exchange, he certainly didn't act like it. Maybe he just didn't care, but more than likely, he felt vindicated in the telling of what he considered as the truth.

The grandson slowed once they were out of earshot and away from the old man's line of sight. "Sorry about all of that. Sometimes he gets a bit carried away."

"I'm a bit surprised that he thinks Josh is temporary." Emory tried to read the grandson's expression and make sense of the exchange.

Casey tipped back his hat. "To be fair to the old man, Josh acts like he's temporary, and we're something stuck on the bottom of his boots."

"That's not good. I don't understand why that would be."

"Simple. He thinks he's better than us. When you said you were temporary, that got grandpa going, I guess. That might get a fair number of people going along those same lines, if you catch my meaning. I hope you don't take offense at any of it."

"Of course not, and I'm glad you told me. Maybe I'll knock off that temporary part, especially if it's going to rub everyone the wrong way. Hard to get things done if everyone is pissed off. Anyhow, when I'm your grandfather's age, I plan on just saying exactly what's on my mind as well. Saves time in the long run."

Casey adjusted his hat back downward, with a spark of his blue eyes and a nod, along with a slight jut of his chin.

"Maybe so, but he could learn to temper it down a bit. He gets excited when he makes connections about people. He's the gossip of this area, although you wouldn't know it to look at him." He chuckled with a measure of exasperated pride and respect.

"I'll keep that in mind if I ever want to know the background about anything, he's a good person to have in my arsenal," she smiled.

"He'd like nothing better. He figures himself as some sort of regional historian without the book learning to go with it. Anyhow, the cattle are in this holding pen." Changing the course of the conversation back to business, he pointed to a large enclosure.

"Herefords," Emory said, glancing down at her paperwork. "That lines up."

The man's eyes sparked, amused. "Have you ever had that part NOT line up?"

"No," she replied, laughing in return. He had a way about him that pulled. "I can't say as I have. Yet. No doubt, that day will come."

She caught him eyeing her ring finger. The one that remained bare naked. Maybe for perpetuity.

"So, how long are you out here for?"

Emory stepped over one of the bottom fence rails before swinging under the top rail. Both feet on the ground and standing in the pen, the cattle churned at her entrance, eyeing her with distrust. "That's the burning question, and there's no definite date. I get the feeling that it could take a while to find a replacement for this region. Why, do you happen to be interested in the job?"

He offered a lopsided grin in response. "Shoot, no. I have enough to keep me busy around here."

Emory checked the brands and signed off on the paperwork. "Everything checks out good," she said, holding out the transportation permits.

The dusty hand that reached out had ragged nails and

dirt embedded beneath. "Gramps is obviously real impressed by your people."

Emory scratched her forehead with her thumbnail and tried to think of a suitable response that might actually get her somewhere. "It's an old ranch is all. There are some stories that go along with it. Say," she searched his eyes, "you haven't heard anything about a stolen horse or horses, have you?"

He wagged his head, considering. Finally, a shrug. "Oh, you always hear something about the wild horses, but who knows what is true?"

"But none carrying brands?"

"Nothing with brands. Why, are you having trouble?"

She shook her head. "No, not really." She offered another smile meant to emphasize her words, which amounted to a lie. She didn't like lying and felt she had done a fair amount of it for one day, and the day remained young. "Just trying to piece together snatches of conversations. Besides, in my experience it is the ranchers who really know what is going on in a district. In a way, I'm just trying to understand how everything works out here. Have you had any trouble with missing cattle, or heard of any?"

It came his turn to slowly shake his head. "No more than the occasional coyote or death for whatever reason. Supposedly there's wolves out here now, ones that have travelled down from Wyoming. But if there are, they haven't affected us. Yet."

That offered another wrinkle. The reintroduction of wolves.

"You heard of any ranchers in this area that have been?"

He shifted, uneasy. "No. We're pretty remote."

"Wolves like remote, I'd guess." She wasn't about to let that topic go so easily.

"Yeah." Something in his eyes challenged her not to go any further with that line of questioning. Curious, she dropped it...almost.

"There's a fund set up to compensate ranchers if any wolf kill happens. Do you call a state vet when one of your cattle dies?"

"Not unless it's suspicious. Those necropsies cost money, and you gotta find the carcass dang near immediately, you know. Does *your* family call on every death?"

"No. Or at least we sure didn't used to. Now, with this job, I'm trying to get my Dad into the habit, but I'll be honest with you. It's a hard sell. He's resisting unless it's something notable, strange, or a combination of both. As for me, I'm just thinking aloud, that's all." She smiled again, like the conversation she offered had no deeper, or sinister, meaning. "I thank you for your time, and I'd best get going. Nice to meet you, Casey. I gave your grandfather my card."

She held out her hand, flinching from the pressure.

He caught her wince.

"Bruised knuckles," she explained.

He didn't ask, but she could read the question in his eyes. "I'll probably be seeing you around in town."

"That'd be nice," she admitted, feeling his eyes upon her as she walked back to her truck and climbed on in.

Removed from sight she shook out her hand, realizing that she must have pulled that throat punch harder than she thought.

13

ROADKILL MEMORIES

EMORY FLICKED ON THE RADIO, A SMILE HINTING AROUND the corners of her mouth as she steered down the ranch road and away from Casey Crawford. She gazed out over the dry undulating hills, absently tapping along to the rhythm of the music.

She flexed her left hand and shook it out before regrasping the wheel. She needed to curb her ingrained habit of shaking people's hands, but it was what everyone expected. Or she could simply tell them about her knuckles. One way or the other. Damn. Those suckers still ached.

Taking a right-hand turn onto Highway 40, she drove in the general direction of town, working her way back in and down the list. Not thinking much about anything at all, she cracked open the window allowing the breeze to dance along the side of her face, twirling and tangling whisps of her long hair. The drone of a motorcycle travelled up from behind, low at first. Growing. Engine noise building and interfering, finally overpowering the music with its mechanical growl.

She turned up the volume.

The motorcycle came yet closer.

Instinctively, she glanced in her rearview mirror.

As the biker swung out to pass, she could feel her eyes narrow, picking up on something familiar about him.

He came alongside the driver's window, long hair streaming out behind like pennants. The biker looked at her the same time as she looked over at him. Their eyes locked. *Dirge.*

He gave her a two-fingered mock salute as he roared passed and cut in front of her.

She slowed, noting the large patch on the back of his leather jacket, proclaiming membership in the TERRI-TORIAL SONS.

Somethings never changed.

He pulled off to the side of the road but didn't dismount. She pulled up behind him, about ten feet away and wondered why in the hell, of all places, he'd turned up out there. Of course, she got out of her pickup, and walked straight up to him. He watched her approach in his rearview mirror and killed his motor.

"Dirge. What in the world are you doing out here?"

"I might ask you the same thing. Did Greeley get too boring for you?"

His sunglasses hid his eyes from view, she could only judge by the quirk of his mouth and the relaxed way he held his shoulders that his question amounted to a joke of sorts.

"Greeley? No, not exactly. I've kept my apartment there, in fact. A brand inspector retired out here, and they're having trouble filling the position."

"Go figure," he deadpanned.

She felt a trifle more defensive than expected and

couldn't exactly figure out why. What Dirge thought mattered very little—or at least it ought to. "I'm just working out here temporarily, until the post is filled."

He chewed that over and knocked his sunglasses back to see her better. In fact, his eyes turned sharp, as sharp as a knife blade. "Did they send you out here because you were getting into too much trouble?"

A shadow must have crossed her face which caught his attention, because he scrutinized her even more closely than he had just a moment before.

She tried to laugh off the notion. Her gut level response had been to offer a lie, saying that she hadn't shot anyone since the run-in with the bikers. "Something like that."

"Anyone get shot this time?"

She bit her lip and didn't answer for fear of tears welling up. Dirge, for his part, again read her expression. "So, they did. To hell with them. You've got good aim. Everyone'll give you that much, whether they like you or not."

"Having good aim doesn't always cut it. This time it wasn't good enough," she said, flat.

He sensed the current swirling, smart enough not to get sucked in any deeper. "I saw 'BRAND INSPECTOR' on the truck and figured the odds. Of all people in Colorado, it turned out to be you."

A dry laugh masked deeper turmoil. "Yeah, isn't that like a line in Casablanca? For what it's worth, I thought about how there really ought to be noise laws enforced about loud choppers, and it turned out to be you." She eyed the Territorial Sons logo on his tank. "And you still haven't said what brings you out here."

"Nothing much in particular," he lied. Or at least that

remained her assumption. "Just the lure of the open road."

"Bullshit."

He scanned the horizon, then his eyes travelled back to her. "Yeah. That's what I like about you, Emory. You're always straight to the point."

She cocked her head. "Saves time. But I'm guessing that you're not going to give me a straight answer. Are you?"

"What I'm doing is on a need-to-know basis. And you don't need to know. It has nothing to do with livestock."

"Or drugs." She made it a statement, not exactly wanting the answer.

"Or drugs," he echoed in what sounded almost like an innocent reply.

But, of course, they both knew better.

Deep down, her indebtedness to him remained. She knew it, and so did he. He had saved her from a rival biker gang's threat...and whether they intended to rape her or just to scare her, they scared her good. They weren't schoolboys, and they hadn't been playing around. But that was then, this was now. She had a job to do, and she wasn't naïve.

"I'm convinced that you're the one that altered that calf's brand you know."

"Ancient history," he droned, but his eyes twinkled. "Anyhow, you can't prove it."

"Still find that all funny, do you? And you're right. No, I can't prove it at all, but I'll bet your cousin is still sore about it. Anyhow, the Pruitts gave him one of their best calves to make amends all around."

"In that case, I'm free and clear."

"I don't think I'd go that far. Anyhow, I've got to get on with my rounds." She turned, took a few steps toward the truck, then reluctantly turned back to face him. "I still owe you for saving me that day, and for sticking around afterwards. I know you didn't want to."

"On that day, I had nothing to hide," he grumbled, then softened ever so slightly. "Glad I happened by at the right time."

She softened as well. A notch. In all likelihood, Dirge remained a strong one-percenter tangled up in dirty or illegal deeds. "Are you staying in town long, or are you just passing through?"

"Guess I'll make that determination once the spirit moves me. Maybe I'll be around for a couple of days, and our paths might cross again."

She nodded. "If that's the case, maybe I'll see you later, Dirge."

He turned on the engine with another mocking two-fingered salute. "It seems a definite possibility out here in the bumble-sticks."

He peeled out, roaring off down the snaking highway.

Leaving Emory to eat his dust, both figuratively and literally. A fact she noticed all right.

Suppressing a sigh, she climbed back into the brand inspector's pickup truck and checked the roster.

"Who the hell cares what Dirge is doing?" she said aloud, knowing the answer all too well.

Despite herself and by extension, she wondered about Cade Timmons, his cousin who used to work at the Lost Daughter. Of course, she knew that wondering about that handsome smartass would lead to nowhere good at all.

14

CLOSE-LIPPED LOT

THE FIRST DAY IN THE BAG, THE SECOND DAY ON THE JOB fell into pretty much the same routine. When she'd handed over her clipboard, Josh barely scanned it. He acted anxious to get out of the office and as if he felt it an inconvenience—a large inconvenience—to wait around for her return.

Emory half wondered how *exactly* he spent his day, and figured it amounted to little more than sitting around the office and staring into his computer.

Probably checking his watch to mark the passage of time and wondering how far down the list she'd managed.

In fact, the only satisfaction she received from the exchange with him on either day, came when he scanned all the checkmarks. Clearly surprised that she managed to work her way through so many appointments, especially considering the distances between, his eyes widened for a brief second.

"Time will tell if you can keep up the pace," he said at the time, the challenge clear and unfriendly.

She stared at him for a moment before rising to the bait. "I'm pretty sure I can."

On morning number three, she reported to work— and again found him already behind his desk and acting put out. Like he believed she amounted to some kind of slacker for coming in at 7:00.

"Do you need me here earlier? Because I certainly can come in at 6:00 if you prefer," she asked, feeling on the backfoot, and not liking it one whit. But her instructions directed her to report in at seven. Specifically.

"Not as long as you can handle all your rounds," he replied, with an open-ended implication left hanging.

Again, he handed her the keys to the second brand inspector truck, but that probably wasn't so odd. He might be a bit territorial that way, and she knew plenty who were the same. Scanning the roster and the addresses, she had to punch in a few coordinates for general directions and to make sure they were listed in the correct order.

Instead of using her computer in the office, she sat there in the parking lot where she had reception until she felt good and ready about the day's route and roster. No doubt he noticed her sitting out in the cold with the engine running instead of availing herself of the heated office, but he made no comment one way or the other.

He could talk to her later about idling if he wanted to get technical.

Emory reminded herself that it wasn't her job to second-guess him.

If they'd had something near to a working relation-ship between them, she would have told him about Dirge.

Then again, if he didn't care about a hanged man, he wouldn't care about a one-percenter either.

In the pit of her stomach, a strong sense of foreboding settled. Dirge's presence anywhere in the vicinity never could bode well. Not for law and order.

Reversing out of her parking space, she headed out in the direction of the back road to Agency. She'd have plenty of time to think as she drove. Just outside of the city limits, another pickup crested an oncoming hill, approaching in the opposite direction. Lights mounted on top; they weren't flashing.

Still, she slowed as the sheriff's truck neared, wondering who the driver might be.

He switched the lights on to flash, on and off—and just that quick in a time-honored signal. Of course, she stopped and rolled down her driver's window, scanning the empty road behind, and finding nothing but asphalt.

"I thought that might be you," Sheriff Hammond smiled as he pulled alongside her. "How are you settling in?"

Emory smiled, patting the outside of her car door. "Oh, we'll see. Just making the rounds today. So, what have you found out?"

"About?"

Emory did a double take, and he burst out laughing.

A regular joker, all right.

"Just kidding," he offered. "We filed a report, the coroner did his thing, and now we are waiting for the toxicology results and whatever else comes along with. Naked, that boy sure had a fondness for tattoos."

"Did he die by hanging?"

Discomfort, and a tinge of something else, flashed in the sheriff's eyes. "We don't have a definitive answer on that yet."

Bullshit.

She'd try that again. In the off chance that she'd been

a bit too direct for his taste. "Couldn't the coroner tell by the rope marks, or other indicators, whether hanging proved the actual the cause of death? He didn't seem to think that it occurred on Saturday."

The sheriff, cornered, cleared his throat, and assumed an authoritative voice. "I'm not at liberty to say. It's an ongoing investigation."

Emory nodded, as if she actually paid his response careful consideration, a consideration which it certainly didn't warrant. "You know that I'm technically law enforcement, don't you?"

"Yeah." He deflated and switched to his regular voice and demeanor. "That may very well be, but you're just assigned here temporary. According to you. Remember?"

She twitched her mouth at the reminder. "I didn't think that you would hold that against me, too. You know, one of the ranchers said that my boss acts like he's temporary as well, none of which seems to go over well out here. How well do you know him?"

"Josh Tucker? About as well as anyone, which isn't saying all that much. One cannot help but get the feeling that he wants to get the hell out of here, just as soon as he can, too."

"If you don't feel you're able to divulge the details to me, how about this then. Why don't you tell Josh what *is* going on, and he can decide whether or not to share the information with me."

He chortled at the notion. "Don't think that would be the best idea."

He made it sound final. Taking her chances, Emory pressed ahead, although along a different vein.

"I've been asking people if they have heard of any missing or stolen horses, and so far, it's come up crickets.

They probably think I'm nuts when it comes right down to it."

For some reason, that bothered the sheriff, and he struggled with what to say. "I doubt they think you're nuts. Let me know if you hear of something useful, will you?"

And with that, he rolled up his window and drove away. Leaving Emory sitting in the middle of the road.

Behind her came the travelling horn of an impatient car approaching. She put the pickup in gear and drove on, offering a half-way sarcastic wave to the impatient driver, who had every right to the road.

"If that don't beat all," she said under her breath, wincing at her grammar choice.

Something wasn't right in that district. Not right at all. As she'd noted about twenty times already.

SHE DROVE to the address on her roster, listed as belonging to people named Jackson. Nothing at all unusual there. This time the ranchers had made a purchase, and she needed to check the brands and check off on the paperwork.

She hopped out of the truck, arriving just at the same time as the transport.

"Good morning!" she called out to the group of three: the rancher and his wife and the truck driver. "I'd shake everyone's hands, but I've hurt my knuckles and you people out here have strong grips."

Laughter all around.

The rancher had a spark to him. "Old Gramps Crawford is spreading the word about you."

Emory did a doubletake with a laugh. "Is he now?

When I met him, he told me in no uncertain terms that he could tell that my nose has been busted."

"Oh, pish," Mrs. Jackson said. "He's only grown more incorrigible with time."

"Well, it's kind of hard to argue with the truth."

"He said you're from the Lost Daughter, and he accords you a great deal of respect on account of your people."

Emory inclined her head. "Stories get blown out of proportion," she said, feeling embarrassed. Like somehow, hidden in her words, she bragged.

"Mebbe so," he said, "but we like the fact that we can place you. Unlike that boss of yours."

"Not a fan, huh?"

"No, ma'am. Not a fan. In fact, when he comes out here, he's all jumpy and spooky and can't leave fast enough. Ray amounted to a hell of a lot more, and you will, too."

"At least he's fairly polite," Mrs. Jackson said, to temper her husband's account down a bit. "Even when he is hurried."

Emory bit back the part about her only being temporary. "Shall we unload these beauties?"

The trucker, paying close attention to all the exchanges, consulted with the Jacksons. "I'm planning on backing up square to the unloading area. Let's make sure that there's an easy drop off. Then, if you want to go inside the trailer and open the gate from within you can...or we can open that gate from the outside. Does that work, or do you have another way you want to do it?"

"That works. If they're quiet, I'll go in and open the gate from the inside of the trailer and let them ease themselves out. We don't want to rush them. That's how they get crippled, falling off the back of a trailer and we don't need any more hamburger right now."

The trucker jogged off, and Mr. Jackson stood by Emory. "These are actually my son's. He's riding the rodeo circuit, and he's investing his winnings in cattle. Family business, and all."

Emory glanced down at her clipboard. "It says here that you're accepting ten head today. You must be proud of him, and he must be doing pretty well."

"Yes. So, it seems."

The truck backed up, and the rancher and his wife dragged a chute over to the truck. The rancher went inside, and opened the interior gate, and the cattle ambled down the ramp nice and easy.

"No accidents here today," Emory said with a smile.

She checked off on the shipment, verified the brands and papers, and the business concluded without much of a fuss.

Emory climbed back into the truck, and reached over to check what came next on the docket.

Mr. Jackson hovered by her door. Emory glanced at him and offered a puzzled smile as she punched the address into her phone. Nothing, and no coverage. This ranch, located in a dead zone, probably relied upon cable if they wanted to do any TV watching.

Technology worked great until it didn't, and she considered the waiting rancher.

"You don't happen to know where..." she glanced back at the sheet and over at the rancher, "M. Brandt lives, do you?"

He stiffened, although the gesture remained almost imperceptible. "Sure do. That's why I'm a-standing here. I figured you'd need directions for where you'd go next."

"There's no cell coverage," Emory murmured.

"There sure ain't. Now, you go back out the way you came in and take a left back toward Vermillion. On the second left, take it and follow the road along. You'll be driving up a hill. When you come to the top, the road will drop and turn, and you'll see her house down in a hollow. That's a bad business what happened to her, but it might be expected considering who she hires," the rancher murmured almost as an afterthought, but something in his tone felt hard in the telling.

"What *exactly* did happen? You're the second person I've met who has made mention of something to that effect."

The shades in his eyes came down, guarded. "I shouldn't have said. You'd have to ask her if'n you want the details. It's not my tale to tell." He eyed her. "Let me tell you this as a caution, though. Some people around this area make loose with the rules and regulations. Now I'm not saying that is entirely a bad thing, but I am saying you want to make sure that you've got yourself covered, if you catch my drift."

"Who does she hire?"

"Men fresh out of the pen in Canon City. Now I'm not saying that can't work, and the prison administers that mustang training program and whatnot. It's good. I'm just saying there's a track record there. I guess she might pay those excons a little bit less on account of where they come in from."

He shrugged, still bothered.

Emory locked eyes with the man, whose solid gaze didn't waver. "I understand," she said slowly. "Thanks for the directions."

"See you around then," he replied. "Remember. You didn't hear anything from me."

15

LAST CHANCE TO DANCE

Myra Brandt's spread claimed a pretty setting where the house nestled down in a meadow depression. Once upon a time it must have offered a sweet vision of admirable domesticity, or foolhardy ignorance. Anyone could take their pick. Depending upon motives and perspective, the location sure wouldn't offer much defense in a gunfight. From Emory's vantage point along the crest of the hill, she noted the clean line of fire—and the ease of observation. A rifleman could pick off the inhabitants one by one as they strayed from the house or worked in the barn or outbuildings. Chances for straight, unobstructed rifle-shots abounded. Emory located three such uphill positions without even trying.

Easier to attack than defend.

She wondered how the original founders had missed, or overlooked, that very fundamental point. Perhaps they hadn't had reason to care, or never ventured into disputes.

The Crosses always knew they would have to fight—that people would come along who would try to take what they wanted. What the Cross's already owned. This group here, well, they appeared to blunder along, contented until they weren't.

Kind of sloppy, if well-intentioned.

Beyond her immediate gunfighting assessments, Emory's impression of the ranch—albeit from a distance and discounting the lack of natural defenses—amounted to that fact that it likely faced its waning years, run down at the edges. It came across in its jewel-like setting as a pretty silk dress whose fabric rotted with age and time. Who cared about domestic trappings if survival turned precarious? And Myra Brant's ranch undoubtedly appeared to face an economic fight for survival. True, the sale of hay and that conversation shaped Emory's impression, but money had to be tight, judging by the pinched look about it.

The female rancher's spread faced the same hardships that plagued many of the small hold ranches.

The way the Lost Daughter had once appeared, when her father found more interest in beer and TV than in running his ranch.

But no matter its shortcomings in a given year, the Lost Daughter remained meaner, and fierce to the core. That's what allowed it to survive from one century and pass into the next.

This one struggled.

And chances were that this woman likely needed help to run her outfit—yet Emory located only the one battered and bruised truck that Myra drove the other day, and a couple of old horse trailers that might, or might not, be serviceable.

Emory resumed down the winding road, entering into the ranch yard. The sound of her truck carried, and Myra stepped out of the barn as she pulled up.

She'd been waiting for Emory's arrival, which gave her a bit more confidence in the woman's abilities right there.

Or maybe she just didn't want to give Emory too much time to poke around, which was understandable in the situation. The Crosses operated in exactly the same way.

"So, we meet again," the woman belted out. "In an official capacity." Her words didn't sound friendly, but more like some high-desert gunslinger. The one whose aim was going bad.

"That's why I'm out here," Emory called back in return, smiling with clipboard in hand. "I'm surprised you didn't mention you were shipping the day we met."

The banter died a death, and the woman frowned at the question. "I had other things on my mind."

Emory nodded despite the ill-humor. "How many head are you shipping?"

"Don't they tell you that up front?"

Emory figured the woman tested her, so kept her tone light while she stood her ground. "You called Josh to schedule the inspection, not me. Therefor I'm getting the information secondhand. Besides, it never hurts to ask." She glanced down at her clipboard. "Today you're getting ready to sell two horses."

The rancher squinted. "It says that?"

Reading the woman's expression, Emory re-checked the roster. "More or less. Transport two horses to Utah for sale. Do I have it wrong?"

"Your boss is a piece of work, I'll tell you that, and I'll tell you that for free."

A storm brewed in that woman's words, and Myra held herself stiff, like a person preparing to throw a punch.

Emory measured the distance between them. She didn't stand within actual striking distance if the woman let one fly. Strange behavior...and irritating to boot. She'd done nothing to cause the reaction, unless sizing up her spread counted. Which, in all fairness, it might. "I'm not certain that I understand. Aren't you planning on selling horses?"

"I might be," the woman replied, cagey before offering anything near to an explanation. "I believe the sale will go through, but right now, I'm just transporting the horses. Like I *told* him."

"I understand that Josh is a bit hard to communicate with. I'm dealing with that myself, being new and all. Where are the horses going?"

"Utah. Like you just said."

Asking straight out often proved the shortest course, so Emory decided to give it a shot. "You know, Myra, I can tell that something more is going on out here in Vermillion—something that no one is telling me. People are pussyfooting around, but what I can't tell is why."

"About me?" the woman spat. "Well, don't believe all that you hear."

"Actually, I didn't mean about you specifically. But now that you brought it up, what is the problem out here? I've heard murmurings that people feel bad about something that happened where you're involved. No one provides any details..."

She left that opening plenty wide for Myra to respond. But the woman didn't.

"Anyhow, people usually believe what you tell them," Emory added as a peace offering.

"Know that for a fact, do you?" Myra stared down her nose in Emory's direction.

Emory, for her part, squinted in the harsh sunlight.

"Not in your case. Let me ask you straight out. What is the problem, because I can sure feel one."

Myra's eyes narrowed as she struggled. "I sold five horses a few months back. Had a ranch hand who introduced me to a man he knew. That little shit vouched for the man and his reputation. For the record, I won't sell my horses on to kill-buyers, no matter how old or lame they are. I simply don't believe in it. Ground up as dogfood in Mexico is something I personally take exception to."

The brand inspector halted all movement, stomach clenching. "Is that what happened?"

"I have my suspicions." The woman tossed back her head, nostrils flaring. "I called the buyer in Nebraska a couple of weeks ago to check on how they were doing. You know what? He claimed that they all died. Every last stinking one of them."

Emory pursed her lips, still not one hundred percent convinced about any of it. "Did he provide any specifics on how they died?"

"Equine flu," Myra replied, aggrieved yet defiant. "He said they got a type of equine flu virus."

Unlikely, it remained a possibility. "Like the one that killed the horses in Canon City?"

"That's how I took it."

"I read about that. It killed ninety-five of them, if I've got that right. What's his name and address? I can certainly reach out to the brand inspectors over there. In fact, I need to."

Myra just stared at her, for a long unfriendly moment. "No need. I've said my piece to him. It's too late to undo what's already been done."

"An outbreak of equine flu would need to be reported. I'll just check that they have record of it. You filed those sale and transportation papers with Josh, is that correct?"

"No, with Ray. Right before he retired."

Emory just held her clipboard and stared at the woman. "Will you at least tell me where the man lives?"

"Nebraska."

OK. The woman practically obstructed her at this point. "But *where* in Nebraska?"

The stone-faced woman balked. "I don't want to go dredging all of that up. I'm not a fan of government overreach— and this is starting to feel like it. You are meddling beyond what you've been asked to do. *Overreach.*"

Emory locked her square in the eyes, unimpressed. "Don't you worry. I'll be tracking this all down anyhow."

While the woman certainly didn't like Emory's stance, she deflated half an inch. "It would be a damn strange thing to lie about. Anyhow, why should I trust you? How do I know that you're qualified to do your job?"

There were certainly friendlier ways to phrase that same question than the route Myra Brandt chose.

Emory stifled a snarl. Somewhat. "The Colorado State Board of Stock Inspection Commissioners, known as the Brand Board, and the Department of Agriculture say that I am."

The rancher would get a whole lot further in life playing the "nice little lady" card.

"That doesn't cut anything with me."

"OK, Myra." Emory let her exasperation show. "I'm from a ranch outside of Stampede called The Lost Daughter. It's a legacy ranch that's come down through the line of Crosses. We've ranched in that valley since the late 1880's. Our sign says established in 1888, but I think we were kicking around even earlier than that. In a way, we've always been the 'last chance to dance' stop for justice in the area, but we do things our way. Is that enough of a background for you?"

The woman sized her up. "Trust is earned."

"Never said that it wasn't," Emory replied. "And that goes for you as well."

The woman cocked her head but wouldn't face her. Emory thought the glimmer of tears forming in the woman's eyes, but that might just have been a product of the wind. Besides, no rancher, male or female, wanted to be caught crying. Ever.

Emory pressed the perceived advantage. "So how did this all come about, Myra? What's the hand's name, and where is he now?"

"I canned his ass," she snarled. "That's all you gotta know."

"Name?"

"None of your business. And I hired two part-timers to replace him. Now, are we going to get on with this, or what?"

"Fine," Emory conceded, tiring of the strange fight. "Show me the horses."

16

DODGY DEALINGS

CONVERSATION DRIED UP AND ESSENTIALLY DEAD, THE TWO women walked over to a holding pen. Each angry, but for different reasons.

In the circular corral, two geldings warmed in the sunshine and picked at scattered hay on the ground.

Back to the tried and true. Emory at least held out that hope. "Are you selling horses and need that paperwork to conclude the deal, or will you be using Utah brand inspectors on the receiving end? If that is the case, all you really need are transportation papers."

"Just need the transportation papers. There's only the possibility of a sale," the rancher replied, still gruff. "As I've already told you. You don't latch on real well, do you? Anyhow, the prospective owner wants to check them over before committing."

Emory bristled from the insult.

In rapid succession, she tapped the clipboard with her pen. "I latch on just fine."

She launched into a type of Miranda rights for livestock. "Please be advised that with the transportation of horses, all we do as brand inspectors is make sure that the paperwork is correct and that the brands align. That consists of verification that you own the horses in question. As brand inspectors, we do not vouch for the medical condition or the age of any of said horses. That said, any misrepresentations will be, and are, corrected if they are caught."

It came across like she had memorized it. Probably because of the *please be advised* part. Emory smothered a smile while Myra shrugged, annoyed.

Emory eyed the horses from the distance and decided to take a closer inspection than normal.

"Do these two appear OK to you?" Myra demanded more than asked.

"Sure. Is there anything that I ought to know out of the ordinary?"

"No."

Opening the gate and entering the holding pen, the grade blood bay allowed her approach with a benign curiosity.

"Who do we have here?" Emory called out to the horses as she opened the gate, acting as if she were on a social call and the horses could answer her.

"The bay is Joe, and the one over there is Oliver," Myra supplied.

Emory cast a practiced eye over the horses.

She checked Joe's brand, checked his teeth—although not strictly protocol—and figured him about ten years old as claimed by his papers. He acted accustomed to people, and probably proved a decent riding horse. The paint, however, shied away in violent, decisive aversion. Emory waited him out, approaching on the diagonal, then changing direction and weaving her way toward him. Slowly. Ever so slowly. In time, he settled enough to let her get close. Emory noted his hot brand, but when she reached out to brush back his mane to check for the BLM freeze brand, again, he stomped and bolted away.

This horse had not been trained or worked with much, if at all.

She called over to Myra, who waited on the periphery, watching.

"Since these two horses are being transported out of state, Colorado is considered the sender state. It is my understanding that these horses are being transported into the state of Utah. If you reach an agreement to sell at that point, the transfer of ownership will take place in that state. Correct?"

"Correct," Myra agreed.

"Have you contacted Utah for their requirements for inbound transportation? You will need your ownership records, brand certificates, a current health certificate and a negative Coggins test—and that's likely the minimum. Additionally, livestock laws are different among the states regarding sales and transportation into said states. Just so you know, should the next owner decide to sell these horses on for slaughter in Mexico or Canada, they may have that legal right. In the state of Colorado, they do not, so that is a gray area in this proposed transaction as I understand it. Given the earlier conversation, I thought it best to make mention of that fact."

The woman blanched but held her ground.

In view of the earlier bitchiness, Emory made no move to comfort her but kept it all to strictly business. "Let me go get transportation papers to fill out. I'll be right back."

Emory left the pen through the gate, careful to close it behind her. She headed toward the truck.

"Have you ever sold a horse on for slaughter?" Myra's

question struck like a dagger right between her shoulder blades.

The young brand inspector paused, turning to face the woman. "I have not."

The woman jutted her chin upward in response but said nothing.

Emory resumed her task, aiming toward the passenger side of the pickup where she pulled out the folder containing transportation papers. She returned to the woman, decidedly cooler than when she first arrived. "May I see their papers, please? And for the record, I don't like signing off on potential slaughter, but it's part of the job and part of our industry."

The woman said nothing to this, but pulled out an envelope from her back pocket and held the papers out, defiant.

For the life of her, Emory couldn't figure out the exact basis of Myra's problem with her. Perhaps the rancher turned a shade toward crazy with no one else around.

It could happen.

Emory concentrated on the job at hand—reading the brand, checking the color and markings to make sure the horse and brand lined up along with verifying the owner's name and address. So far, so good. The next set of papers were old and outdated vet records, which she didn't need for shipment, but were always good to provide a full history.

"The paperwork for Joe is in order," she said, eyeing the woman, "but where's the other set?"

"Underneath," Myra replied.

"No," Emory remained as respectful as she could, shaking her head and studying the woman. "They're just vet records for Joe. There's nothing about Oliver. Is he a mustang? No brand at all. Here, take a look for yourself."

The woman's face turned to stone, the papers in her hands next to meaningless. Her eyes skimming over the words, flicking and darting. Most certainly, not reading.

She didn't answer the mustang question.

"The papers were supposed to be all together." She handed them back to Emory. "Couldn't you make an exception in this case?"

"An exception?" Emory couldn't believe her ears. "An exception to what?"

The woman wheedled. "The requirement for the transport papers. I've got to ship him to Utah, like I said."

She truly must have believed that Emory's young age meant she could be easily manipulated.

Maybe she used hostility to intimidate those who she assumed were weaker opponents.

Emory shook her head, unwilling and unable to back down. "You'll have to find his papers. Until they are located, there's nothing I can do, and you can't ship him. It's *against the law*."

The woman scoffed. "And your family are supposed to be the last of the old-time outlaws. Yeah, I already heard about you. I just wanted to see what you would say."

That amounted to an interesting, not to mention unfriendly, tactic.

Emory pulled herself up to her full height. "*Do* you legally own this horse?"

"Are you accusing me of otherwise?"

Emory stared her down, before pointedly returning into the holding pen. She approached as gently as she could. Horses sensed people's moods, and she certainly felt stressed—a stress bordering on flat out angry.

"Come here, Oliver. Nice boy." Emory stood about five feet away and waited for him to approach. She also had a couple of horse cookies in her pockets, which he detected. With a fair amount of caution, he approached lured by the scent of food.

"Can I give him one of these?" She asked.

"I don't care," Myra grumbled.

When Emory held out her palm with the cookie, the paint nibbled it up, nice and gentle. His nearness also allowed Emory the chance to check the left side of his mane, which she brushed away. No marking.

That provided a strong indicator right there.

"Why don't you give me the real story, and I'll try to help. Or if you don't want to, that's fine as well. What happens next is up to you."

Emory pulled out her phone and took a picture of the horse in question. And another of his brand. And a third for good measure on the left side of his mane. The one that held no marking.

"I'd ask you to put that phone down," the woman responded in a veiled threat.

"Now that I have what I need," Emory replied, pocketing her phone, decisive and clear. She eyed the woman, and started toward the brand inspector pickup, ready to leave.

"Wait!" the woman called out from behind.

Emory paused, again slowly turning in her direction. Giving her one more chance to come clean.

The woman took three paces in Emory's direction and stopped. "I haven't got the papers."

Emory lifted her eyebrows in response but said nothing.

"I did buy him fair and square," Myra insisted. "From

a rescue society. But they didn't give me my paperwork. Honestly."

"I'm sure that you are aware of this already, but part of my job as a brand inspector is to investigate reports of lost or stolen livestock, and that livestock includes horses. You do know that, right?"

Myra nodded.

Satisfied, Emory continued, pen poised to take notes. "Which rescue society, and when did this all happen?"

"About a year and a half ago." Before Emory could even ask, the woman added, "They've gone out of business."

Of course they had. "Do you remember the month of the transaction?"

A slow sideways, shifty glance. "No, I don't. I guess it took place in the fall."

"Of 2021. Correct? Didn't you know that you needed the papers at the time?"

"Yes, I think it happened in 2021. And of course, I knew about getting the bill of sale and the deed," she snapped, then tried to tone her response down. "I just figured, since they were shorthanded and all, that I'd let the matter slide. They used to hold their sales out at the fairgrounds. I figured we could sort it all out at a later date."

Emory held her ground. "Brand inspectors are present at those types of sales."

"Your boss is a dipshit, like I said. You'll find that out firsthand soon enough."

While No one seemed to think too highly of her boss, a decidedly shady cast hovered around Myra.

"I can ask him about your particulars and check the computer, but that's all I can do without the correct paperwork."

The woman wagged her head, slow and mournful. "I'd appreciate it," she offered, at length. "And I mean that, too."

Yeah, right. Emory nodded and got back into the truck, anything but amused.

———

EMORY'S TEMPER continued to elevate as she returned the same way she came in. On the road out, she passed a pickup truck coming in with two young men. The driver gave her the standard rural two-finger salute while keeping his other hand and his three remaining fingers on the steering wheel.

She could have sworn that they both appeared startled by her presence and worried by her official capacity. Checking in her rearview mirror, she caught them eyeballing back at her as well.

Emory thought hard about sticking to the straight and narrow. Thinking about odds and how, this time, the straight and narrow didn't hold a high probability of working out at all.

———

EMORY RETURNED to the office trailer slightly after four in the afternoon. She'd put in a full day's work but harbored more misgivings than when she'd started out. Pulling into the parking lot, her pickup truck stood lonely and forlorn—the only vehicle parked there besides the other brand inspector truck. Josh Tucker's personal vehicle had already gone, nowhere to be seen.

She tried the doorknob of the trailer. *Locked.*

"Hell's bells," she muttered. Shaking her head, she

pulled out her phone and scrolled for his number. It rang.

"Josh Tucker."

"Hi Josh, this is Emory. I'm back at the office, but the door is locked. What should I do?"

"Go home?" he suggested.

Gruff voices rose in the background—sounding for all the world like her new boss was already drinking in a bar. "Shouldn't I put my clipboard away?"

Laughter erupted. "Hang on, Bill," Josh's voice said, along with more laughter belting. "It's work."

Then back to the phone. "Just keep it with you and bring it in, in the morning."

"OK. But I want to let you know that something odd is going on with Myra Brandt."

"There's a shock. Look, Emory, I've gotta go. You can tell me about it in the morning." He yelled into the crowd. "Hell, Jake, now let me tell you…"

The phone cut off, dead.

17

SMALL TOWN SECRETS
DON'T KEEP

THE LOCAL NEWSPAPER, THE *VERMILLION SENTINEL*, CAME out twice a week. Fridays for the weekend news, and Tuesdays for the ranching reports. Emory knew nothing about it, nor did she care as her first week wound down. Friday morning, she emerged from the elevator and headed straight for the hotel breakfast, bolstering up for the day. What struck her about that particular morning, were the workers. Behind the reception desk, three fresh-faced youths huddled together, reading or studying something that held great interest, laid out flat behind the counter. *The night shift.* Intent, and heads close together, they all read at the same time—any comments whispered behind their hands or with faces averted.

Emory noticed all right, but whatever they were up to wasn't her concern. *Hotel business*, she figured.

Nothing to do with her.

Choosing eggs and bacon, she drifted over to the juices, and poured a glass of the healthy green liquid that tasted like grass, but which had grown upon her since arrival. She selected an empty table without problem and set her food down before returning for a cup of coffee. Heading back to her waiting plate, she glanced up at the hotel entrance in time to see the sheriff, Joe Hammond, entering through the sliding glass doors.

She sat down, wondering.

The staff, still oblivious on account of their reading, didn't pay much attention to the activity around them. People passed them by without acknowledgement or greeting— and that included the sheriff.

Who clearly wasn't impressed in a favorable way.

He assessed the whispering clump and scowled— pausing off to the side, seeing just how long it would take for his presence to register with any one of them.

It didn't.

Disgusted and getting on with what was, no doubt, his initial purpose, he scanned the breakfast room—eyes locking into hers. She offered a half-assed wave.

The sheriff tossed his head back in recognition, scowled again at the workers who finally noticed his existence, and strode over to Emory.

"Good morning, Sheriff. Care for a cup of coffee?" she asked with an uncertain smile.

"You seen the paper?" he growled.

"No. I just came down. Why?" The realization hit in the pit of her stomach. "You mean to tell me…"

"Yep. And I want to know what you know about it." He postured, unyielding in a lawman-type way.

Good heavens. "Nothing." Her reply came out as decisive as she intended.

"You sure about that?" Again, he offered a *hook 'em, book 'em, and cook 'em* type stare.

"I am."

He relaxed a mite. "In that case, maybe I'll take that

cup of coffee." He sat down across from her and removed his hat, which he discarded on his knee.

"How do you take it?"

Registered at the hotel, Emory rose from her chair and played the part of hostess. Surely her subservience stemmed from a sense of hospitality opposed to the simple fact of her female sex. More importantly, her display of manners did not originate from any feelings of guilt on her part.

"Black," the sheriff answered. An afterthought. "Please."

She filled a cup for him, brought it to the table and set it down three inches in front of his hand. Reclaiming her seat, she widened her eyes, indicating a readiness to listen.

He didn't latch on to the hint.

Instead, the sheriff seemed predisposed to sitting there in silence. Either that, or he ignored facial cues until he felt good and ready to respond, intentionally taking his own time.

Emory, however, didn't feel like waiting around for a particular moment that she didn't understand.

"Do *you* know what happened?" She dropped her voice right down to the level of gravel on the ground.

"That's what I came to ask you."

She shook her head. "So. You're here for me."

"That's right. Who else did you tell about this?" The question hit as direct as a rifle shot between the eyes.

Deciding against admitting to the discussion with her father and, by extension Monty, that didn't mean she came empty handed. "My boss, Josh Tucker. Remember? He called you for me."

The sheriff made a funny kind of groaning sound, patted his stomach like it pained him, stretched, and took a sip. "I remember. What else has he asked you about it?"

"Nothing much," she replied. "He just made a bit of a joke about running into trouble on my first day. Something to the effect of wanting to know whether I'd believe him if he told me that nothing much ever happened in this area. It hasn't come up since."

The sheriff chewed that over. "That's a strange and interesting lack of curiosity, I'd say."

"Maybe he's just being professional, not prying and all." Emory, scanning the breakfast room, located a newspaper discarded on a table, left her chair, and snatched it up.

"Front page," she half-sang, returning.

"Does that surprise you?"

"No," she slipped back into her chair, feeling a vague sense of guilt. "Unfortunately, it does not."

The sheriff's eyes bored into hers. "It's the most remarkable thing that's happened around these parts in years."

She forced herself not to fidget. "And maybe this is the place where I should repeat what I told you the other day. I've been asking people if they've heard of any stolen or missing horses. Just so you know."

He gave her a one-shoulder shrug. "You told me. So what? You're a brand inspector."

Emory wasn't so certain. "Let me tell you what. No one has said that they're missing a horse or have heard of any strays."

She checked around at the other tables. No one sat near enough to eavesdrop with any accuracy. The memory of Myra caused her to wince.

"Now what?"

Emory didn't exactly like ratting, but protecting

someone who didn't play straight with her seemed a tall order, and ill-advised at best. "Myra Brandt. She's trying to transport two horses for sale to Utah, but one doesn't have papers. Nor does she have a bill of sale."

"You could have told me about this before…" he complained.

On that count, she didn't bother to tamp down her skepticism one whit. "For what reason? You'd sure be one of the few law enforcement officers interested in horse shipments, especially the part about *all* the missing papers. Anyhow, those details just came to light yesterday."

"Maybe," he replied, seeming to measure up her next response before she even had the chance to formulate a sentence. The jury in his mind hadn't returned a verdict as to whether he believed her or not.

"Like your office," Emory began as if she prepared to explain the finer points of her job to a scoffer, "we wouldn't want word getting out. As brand inspectors, we work with law enforcement when, in good faith, we can't handle a situation and bring it to legal resolution on our own. Which is rare. As to any horse thefts—we're not there yet, but nothing on this matter is what it seems on the surface. As far as this…episode…goes, it made its way to the newspaper through some other channel. So, if it's not me, and it's not Josh…who else do *you* think's been talking?"

"I don't know it's not Josh," he challenged, a festering grudge laced his tone, "and neither do you. But it is possible that Frank Deacon in my office has a hand in this. There were only the five of us—you, Greg, Frank, Dustin Weaver, and myself."

"Let's read what the article says." She turned to the

paper. Not knowing who to trust in the situation made sticking to the facts advisable.

WILD WEST HANGING OF HORSE THIEF REPORTEDLY TOOK PLACE LAST FRIDAY NIGHT

The Sentinel *has received word of a strange event that took place along County Road 22, either last Friday night or early Saturday morning, April 18th. Straight out of the pages of yesteryear, a body was found hanging from a crossbar, with Horse Thief emblazoned on a paper duct-taped to his shirt. The identities of both the victim, and the perpetrator or perpetrators, have not been disclosed if known. Nor has confirmation of the event been made by the local authorities. Both the Sheriff and the Local Police have been contacted for comment, but as of this printing, no official response has yet been received.*

"Not good," she commented, "but I've never said anything to anyone about duct tape."

He eyed her close. "I believe you. But, no, word leaking out about this isn't good at all. And anyone who thought they saw something will be calling. In fact, it's already begun." The sheriff stood up.

Emory followed him with her eyes. "What would you like from me?"

"Hell," he said, scanning the lobby and back at the people eating their breakfasts. All five of them at that hour. "I halfway hoped that you'd just tell me that you'd slipped up and let the word out."

She halfway snapped back. "And I've been hoping all along that you'd keep me in the loop as far as information concerning the victim when it became available. But that hasn't exactly happened, either."

The sheriff sat back down. "Greg and I have nothing personal against you. I did a bit of checking. Yours, and your family's, ability to keep quiet has never been questioned. Not for the last hundred and forty years or so." Followed by a decided twinkle, "Nor has your aim, Calamity Jane."

That provided her reason to scowl, and a sad flinch followed his words. Just another reminder. "Go easy on the Calamity business," she cautioned. "My new boss claims my past history is locked tighter than a drum, but obviously that ain't so."

The sheriff rose for the second time. "As usual, he ain't asking the right questions of the right people. And from what I've heard, Annie Oakley might be more accurate in your circumstances, but Calamity Jane sure has a ring to it."

Great. Now he felt free to give her shit. Of course, that implied acceptance on a certain level. She could always invent a name for him, too. Something that would irritate him every and any time it crossed her lips. It would just take a bit of thought and experience with his opinions and tender spots.

But back to the matters at hand. "Shall I keep on asking around about missing or stolen horses, or do you want me to knock that off? It's not exactly like I'm getting anywhere."

"Keep on asking and see what you get. If nothing else, believe it or not, it probably calms people down. Even in this day and age, I'd guess that few people out here would actually feel disposed to coming to the defense of an honest-to-goodness horse thief. A *hanged* horse thief."

"I take your point."

"Other than the novelty of the crime, it's doubtful that many would sympathize with him as presented.

Then again, I can't vouch for everyone." He scanned the breakfast room, and out the glass doors, wrestling with a decision. "Come by the station at 1:00, if you can. I'll share what we've got. With your promise of confidentiality, of course. You break this, and you're done out here."

18

DUSTY MIKE KNOWS PLENTY— HE JUST AIN'T SAYING

*N*OTHING GOOD *NOTHING GOOD NOTHING GOOD* KEPT playing through her mind instead of the radio on the ride over to the office trailer—the copy of the paper abandoned, but certainly not forgotten, on the worn seat beside her.

Hard to believe, but horses might end up proving the lesser part of this tangled equation.

Perhaps she should have told the sheriff about Dirge. The biker's appearance offered a harbinger of problems —but whether it meant drugs or other biker illegalities remained undetermined, and she hadn't seen him since. The Territorial Sons were no social club of weekend warriors. No matter that she had a soft spot for him, he damned sure wasn't out there to take in the scenery, or for an over-due vacation. But, for now, one problem at a time.

The comparison with Annie Oakley held an undeserved compliment. Annie Oakley never missed. She had. Hell. Calamity Jane her ass, but somehow it fit just a bit better.

And the sheriff dug up information on her that Josh

hadn't been able to find. Likely the sheriff operated through the law enforcement channels.

All of which stirred her up a bit, as did Josh's parked truck, of course, waiting—proving that once again, he beat her into the office. His early starting hours sure gave the impression that he was a far sight more dedicated than her in comparison, waltzing in at 7:00. Maybe she'd get in there at 6:00 on Monday. Just to see for herself when he truly arrived.

No one liked him...but was that entirely fair?

She snatched up the newspaper, folded it to the article, and entered the trailer.

Already seated at his desk, one hand rested on his hip as he already stared at his own copy of the newspaper.

"Is that what I think it is?" Emory asked, holding up her folded edition.

He slowly nodded. "Guess Hammond doesn't have as much control as he thinks he does."

Obviously, the dislike, or distrust, ran mutual between the two men. "But watch out. Blame will be headed our way as sure as the sun rises. Hell, that's part of the reason I left the DEA and came over here."

The DEA? Just another oddity staring her in the face, right there.

She held her tongue...for a moment. "What's on the roster for today?"

"More of the same. Everything is close in for you today." He handed her the clipboard. "All cattle."

"Fine." She never asked what his roster held. In fact, she started to doubt that he even had one.

"More than fine. Cattle's where the money's at, and I'll stick to them, when I can."

"I don't know about that," Emory frowned. "I take it you didn't grow up around horses."

He grinned. "That obvious?"

"Pretty much," she replied, a little flicker inside of her warming toward him.

"In that case, let me tell you a brief story. My cousins had a farm about twenty miles away. And on that farm, they owned a stallion named Sargent, or some dumb thing. Anyhow, I hated that horse, and he hated me right back. My cousin dared me to try to ride him one time..."

"A *stallion?*" Emory interrupted, incredulous.

"I can tell that you see where this is headed," he nodded. "Anyhow, my cousin bet me five dollars that I couldn't stay on one minute, and I took the bet."

"Oh no..."

"Oh yes. First, he tried to scrape me off along the side of the barn. When that didn't work, somehow we ended up in the corral—don't ask me how—and my cousin closed the gate. Ol' Sargent and I went around and around. Him bucking, me holding on for dear life, and finally I came loose, sailed through the air, and broke my arm. I got my five dollars, though."

"Did you beat up that cousin?"

Josh reared back a bit, shocked at the suggestion. "Beat him up, what for? We had a deal, and those five dollars tasted sweet. But trust you me, I've never gotten on another horse again. And that's the deal Ray and I struck. I'd stick to the cattle, and he'd tend to the horses."

"Horses can often be more valuable than cattle," Emory countered, "but we can make that same arrangement if you like."

Josh smiled, wide. "I'd sure appreciate that, if you don't mind."

Emory found the friendly tone of exchange odd. Decidedly odd. "No problem at all."

"Ray did cattle, too, obviously, but toward the end he

wasn't so good at climbing fences as fast as he needed to, if a bull came charging. The arrangement worked out for both of us." Again, that same smile.

A smile that any used car salesman would be proud of.

She did a double-check to see if he played her for a fool, but if he noticed, that grin never faltered.

"Where did Ray go, anyhow?"

"I think he said Arizona. Isn't that where all the old folks go?"

Emory quirked her head. "I haven't a clue. Anyhow, perhaps we should talk about what hours you'd like me to keep. You've beat me in here every single day this week."

He pursed his lips, assuming a superior expression. Either that, or she was well underway toward developing one hell of a chip on her shoulder. She eyed him closely and decided that he didn't come across as too terribly hungover either, but it wasn't always obvious. Not when the player held his cards close to his chest.

"When it's busy, the hours get longer and start earlier," he said, unconcerned as he searched his desk for some random object or paper. "Don't worry about it for right now." He abandoned the search, stopped fussing, and gave her his complete attention. "What was that bit about Myra Brandt?"

Emory held out yesterday's clipboard for his inspection.

He took it, skimming the contents.

"Unfortunately, she's missing papers on a horse she wants to sell. She says that she bought the horse back in the spring of 2021 out at the fairgrounds, but she's fuzzy on the details. She claims the event, hosted by some sort of horse rescue operation, has since gone defunct along with the charity. You don't happen to know anything about an outfit or operation like that, do you?"

He blinked a few times, searching his memory. "That happened a while ago when I first took up this post. I do recall something about a rescue group holding an adoption sale at the fairgrounds—but I sure don't remember their name. She didn't either?" He scrunched up his face with a theatrical concentration.

Emory knew, if she were personally involved, that she would recall at least some of the details. She kept her expression neutral. "No. Maybe it will come to her. She wants to ship the horse into Utah."

Josh shrugged. "I take it you didn't sign off on the paper for the undocumented horse. Of course, she can get a copy of the brand inspection…"

Emory wondered if he meant to test her.

"How could she get a brand inspection without a bill of sale? Sure, the horse has been branded with her brand…but that's not enough. I'd guess the thing to do is locate the records of that rescue group."

He laced his fingers, placed them atop his head, and leaned back in his chair. His eyes, once again, switched over from neutral to hard. Stone cold and hard. "I guess. And I guess I could make a few calls on her behalf. But none of that sounds suspicious. That's the overriding impression I've come away with after our limited conversations. Suspicion."

The way he eyed her wasn't casual and felt almost like a dare. Emory made no move to claim the seat in front of his desk—nor did he offer it to her.

She stood ramrod straight in the tight space in front of his desk. She'd remain standing, too.

"Do you want to discuss this, or not?" Emory acted oblivious to the hostility.

Do not back down. Do not give him the upper hand.

"Not really but go ahead, I guess."

"Initially she pretended that she handed me his papers, but they were only old vet reports on the other horse whose papers she has in her possession. At first it seemed that the papers got mislaid or misfiled at the sale, but she eventually admitted that she knew she needed to get title papers from that group, but never did. She didn't really explain why. What's more—according to her—you were the brand inspector overseeing the sale."

"The one that she doesn't remember the date for."

"Yeah. That's the one."

He scratched his neck and started searching through his computer files. He didn't deny a damned thing but left her just standing there with nothing to do, other than watching him search. Acting as if she didn't belong.

"She can't transport that horse to Utah without proof of ownership," Emory reinforced, knowing that she risked annoying the hell out of him. Stating the obvious proved one quick way to piss most people off, so she hopped onto the next subject. "Do you have a roster for today?"

The back of his neck turned reddish above the collar. He scratched and bothered it out of what she gathered a nervous habit, ending up ruffling feathers of hair at his neck. A vein in his jaw throbbed, but neither his expression nor his tone changed. He handed it to her, without meeting her eyes. He just kept typing and staring into that damned computer.

Emory, clipboard in hand, left the trailer.

"See you later, then," she said, halfway out the door.

Josh Tucker grunted in her direction but didn't even bother to look up.

Not exactly how she wanted to start her day, but she'd

make do. She was more interested in what the sheriff had to tell her. She'd decide, if and when, she would clue her new boss in.

A FEW ROUNDS of butts and brands later, Emory travelled through the main part of town and Mike's Rusty Spur came into view. Emory checked her watch—11:30 a.m. leaving an hour and a half to kill.

Certainly enough time to shoot the breeze in the name of goodwill and friendship.

Although spaces were open in front of the bar, she parked the brand inspector truck a block away for propriety's sake and walked over to the watering hole. Pulling open the door, she stepped just inside and allowed her eyes a moment to adjust to the dim interior. A few men hunched over their beers registered, one or two eating, and not a whole lot of conversation going on at that early hour.

The radio, and not the juke box, played country and western in the background.

A middle-aged woman came over to her. "Are you here for lunch honey, or just drinking?"

That question actually shocked her. "What do you serve?"

"Hamburgers, chicken strips, bar food..."

Emory glanced around. Dusty Mike worked behind the bar, his back toward her. "Sure, I'll have lunch. I also hoped for a word with Mike, there."

The woman didn't seem in the least surprised. "Mike! This young lady wants to talk to you."

The man turned, a smile lighting his face when he

recognized her. "It's the newest brand inspector, Rose. What can I get you to drink?"

"Do you have iced tea?"

"Umm…"

That amounted to a *no*. She changed her order and offered a smile to show it wasn't a problem. "Diet Coke, then."

"That I can do. I'll bring it right over to you. Did you see today's paper?"

"I did," she admitted, the pleasant bantering tone fading. "That's part of the reason why I'm here."

"Terrible thing," Rose's voice came from behind her.

"Yes, ma'am."

Rose pressed in, dead serious on the matter. "Is it true?"

"I'm not at liberty to say, one way or another."

Mike came out from around the bar, carrying the soft drink. Other customers sat along the bar rail, but Emory chose a table in the middle of the room and away from the regulars.

"I can see that you're busy, and I don't want to take you away from your customers." Emory apologized as he set the drink on the table.

"Everyone is fine for a few minutes. Shall I sit down?"

She gestured for him to take a seat. "Please do. Do you know Josh Tucker? He's a brand inspector, too. My temp…I mean my boss, in fact."

"Sure."

Emory removed the straw from its paper casing. "I called him after 4:00 yesterday, and I got the feeling he was in a…social setting."

Mike just laughed, his eyes twinkling. He wasn't about to say another word along that line of inquiry. Just like she wouldn't say another word about her part in discovering the hanging.

She tried the direct approach, with the proper respect paid toward boundaries. "So, knowing that you aren't about to betray confidences on that matter, did you hear anything about the horse thief hanging before it turned up in the paper?"

Mike shook his head. "No. I said that I'd call if I heard anything about horses. I'd guess that would extend to horse thieves, although I never thought about that one before."

"*If* you heard about them."

"If I heard about them. Correct."

Rose came over. "You're keeping her from studying the menu," she scolded.

Emory scanned the offerings. "What do you recommend?"

"People like the cheeseburgers," she replied.

"Sold," Emory announced.

Dusty Mike still eyed her. "He didn't say a word about horses. But he did say a few words about his new *temporary* brand inspector."

"Anything I want to hear?"

He stood up slow, like his recollections weighed him down.

"I don't think so," he replied, his voice sounding like a father's. "And, come to think of it, it was last Saturday that he said something off. No one believed him at the time, but likely they do now. Remember, you didn't hear it from me."

19

POSTMORTEMS—IN MORE
WAYS THAN ONE

AT 12:55, EMORY PULLED UP SQUARE IN FRONT OF THE sheriff's building for all of the world to see. Make that all of the world concerning Vermillion; and that didn't expand too far as population counts went, but it still covered plenty of square mileage. Checking the street traffic up and down, very little stirred about on a weekday afternoon, as it hadn't for the last quarter century or so.

Probably even longer.

The circumstantial evidence pointing to Josh, still in the process of sinking fully in, as having likely leaked the story to the local newspaper, hit a whole new litany of concerns. As her boss, she normally would have felt a marked measure of loyalty toward him. But as her superior...that loyalty to him just wasn't there. She did, however, remain loyal to the badge. As a result, for a split second she hesitated to expose the law enforcement/brand inspector connection.

Did parking a marked BRAND INSPECTOR truck

implicate them all in some way that she didn't yet fully understand?

She caught hold of herself. While their truck might hint of a relationship with law enforcement, most people wouldn't put two and two together. After she told the sheriff what she had learned, the sheriff's office might not think that the brand inspectors were much of an asset at all—at best, they'd be considered a liability.

At worst, the next best thing to traitors.

Emory Cross had never acted the part of a liability, and she didn't plan on starting.

Of course, the news about the hanging spread like wildfire, but nothing linked her or the office to any of it.

It took all of about three seconds to decide.

"To hell with it," she settled, climbing out of the truck, and swinging the door shut with a satisfying thud.

Checking that her shirt tucked into the back of her jeans and her hair didn't fly out in band-free whisps like a crazy woman, she strode forward like she belonged.

Glancing at the door—featureless beyond the block letters spelling SHERIFF—she entered the dated and utilitarian building.

The sheriff's office confirmed the apparent deep-seated bias against rural and remote Colorado. Plagued by a cookie-cutter mediocrity, a disproportionate number of the public offices emerged as by-products of a civic building boom from last mid-century. The Vermillion sheriff's office proved absolutely no different and came off even a shade worse than some.

Cynical, perhaps. But who could say whether the local governments hadn't received a price break on architect's plans, or maybe a long since dead governor had a nephew who couldn't find a job on his own. Graft and favors, although rare, were not unheard of in the hinterlands.

She hesitated just inside of the entrance like some sort of junior building inspector.

The linoleum floored waiting room smelt of burnt coffee reduced down to a lethal strength on overheated warming plates. Avocado green leatherette chairs and a dusty, brown-edged rubber tree plant lurked with a misguided hope, shoved back into a corner and away from sunlight. Emory glanced into its pot—dry as a bone and ready to croak.

Off to the side, a desk guarded the front entrance, an old steel affair that probably weighed one hundred pounds if it weighed an ounce. The nearest thing to an acting reception desk, there sat Frank Deacon, jackass at large.

"Can I help you?" His eyes sparked with a recognition that he failed to entirely conceal while he pretended that he'd never seen her before.

Emory stared him down. "No, but that plant could sure use some water."

"I'll get to it," he scowled.

"What's this—the budget version of *treat them mean to keep them keen*? That probably doesn't work well in your case, and you know damn well who I am and ought to be able to figure out why I'm here."

Muffled laughter came from the back of the room, out of view. *Just another one of Frank Deacon's fans*, she figured.

The deputy colored at the exchange but didn't have the balls or the wits for a successful comeback.

"I'm here to see sheriff Hammond," Emory added, stating the obvious to propel the exchange forward to a hopefully swift conclusion.

"Is he expecting you?"

"Doesn't he let you know everything? Oh wait, probably not. But yes, he is expecting me."

"Wait over there," he snarled, indicating the leatherette chairs.

The coroner entered as she halfway lowered into one of the seats. She caught herself and straightened at his entrance.

"Hello there!" He held out a strong, thick hand. "If it's not our new *temporary* brand inspector. How are you settling in? Thinking of making the position permanent?"

"I guess one never knows."

"Come on back," he said, perfectly comfortable and accustomed to the surroundings.

Deputy Deacon interjected himself into their conversation. "I've instructed her to wait until the sheriff is ready for her,"

The coroner literally waved him off and motioned to Emory, arm outstretched to indicate the general direction. "It's this way."

Together they passed down a dismal, narrow, dark-paneled hallway—the monotony alleviated by various civic awards, black and white photos, and a few framed commendations hung at intervals. At the end of the hallway, and presumably the end of the building, a door cracked open twelve inches wide, promising a larger office beyond. The plastic nameplate read *Sheriff Joe Hammond*—its holder the only permanent fixture in a plastic world where names could easily be changed and replaced: sliding in and out as the need, or elections, arose.

Just another hazard of a low paying position, Emory figured. Every position had its downside. But some, as in elected sheriffs, had to display a sense of confidence that they might not feel at all times. In such a position, they would always have to make do.

Getting by and *making do* didn't always make the best of poker hands.

She thought of Josh's mention of upcoming elections.

The sheriff, seated behind his desk, abandoned his reading at the sound of their footsteps and took off his glasses.

He leaned over to see who approached. "Come on in."

"Don't want to interrupt important police business," the coroner claimed, without breaking his stride. "But then again, I've got a plane to catch tomorrow." He glanced back at Emory following in on his heels. "Going to see the wife's mother in Arizona for a long weekend. Four days of supposed paradise is about all I can take."

"Shut the door behind you, d'you mind?"

Again, the 1970's paneling dominated the office, but this time it only went halfway up the walls. Wainscoting, she believed the proper name. She shut the door behind her, noting its lightweight, hollow construction.

"Someone could put their fist right through this," she mused as the door latch clicked into place.

"Don't think I haven't been tempted," the sheriff replied, dry and not entirely kidding.

The coroner, already seated, chuckled. Emory took her place in the visitor's chair right alongside his.

The sheriff's eyes bore into the pair of them. "Not one word of this discussion leaves this office," he cautioned, voice low.

"Agreed," Emory spoke aloud, while the coroner simply nodded. "Before you start, I ought to tell you that I just heard that it might have been Josh who spilled about the hanging."

"Son of a bitch, I knew it!" Joe Hammond spat out the words. "How'd you hear that?"

Emory shifted in her seat. "Rusty Spur banter, but I'm not supposed to tell—so please, don't you either."

"Damn it. I knew he couldn't be trusted. I knew that all along. And you didn't know about this connection this morning?" he pressed.

"No, sir, I did not," she replied.

"Damn and double damn."

The coroner cleared his throat.

The sheriff eyed him. "Oh, hell. Greg, go ahead."

The coroner opened his file, scanning the results as if they might have changed since his last consultation.

"This man didn't die by hanging," he pronounced. "The toxicology report came back that he died from fentanyl. A lethal fentanyl overdose."

Emory blinked a couple of times. *But did that preclude him from being an actual horse thief?*

Probably not.

The sheriff twisted his chair a bit to the side, chewing the inside of his mouth and staring off into the brush and sage distance beyond his lone office window. "And we still don't know his identity. We've combed through the missing persons reports and are no wiser than when we started."

Tired and resigned. "I guess in that case, it was all just a matter of time," he concluded.

"You mean on account of the drugs?" Emory asked.

"Of course," he replied. "What else?"

Emory glanced over at the coroner, then to the sheriff, and back again. "He didn't come across like a hardcore drug addict to me. I've seen a few out on the eastern plains. And isn't there some sort of law against tampering with a corpse?"

"There is," Sheriff Hammond said. "Just as soon as we catch whoever did this."

"He had a lot of tattoos," the coroner added, frowning, "and was aged between twenty-five and thirty. Physically he wasn't in bad shape at all. Also, he didn't have the markings of habitual drug use. Perhaps he just tried it a few times, and this last time, he took a lethal dose or got a bad batch, which ended up killing him. That's tragic enough right there. Judging by his body composition, he did physical labor or worked out at a gym. Haven't received confirmation on the fingerprints yet."

"So, no known criminal history or missing persons report," Emory echoed. "But why? Why go to all the trouble of stringing him up like that, and what about the sign?"

"No idea," the sheriff admitted. "It's odd. The whole thing is *very* odd."

Dead end. Then, uncomfortable, she thought about Dirge. And felt even more uneasy than before.

"Problem?" he asked.

Dirge likely amounted to little more than a shot in the dark. She didn't want to bring him up to the sheriff. Not up front, and not until she had definite proof. She felt that she owed the outlaw that much.

"This entire event bothers me, that's all. Won't it be next to impossible, if he hasn't left behind records, to ever get him identified? Beyond hoping that his employer calls for a welfare check, or his landlady or mother gets around to wondering where he is and calls for missing persons? Don't suppose he had money in his pockets or more drugs, did he?"

The two men exchanged glances. "He had thirty-four dollars on him and some loose change. Why?"

"I'd think that if he were homeless, he wouldn't be carrying anything like that amount," Emory explained.

"We can take a picture of him postmortem, and circulate it," Hammond expelled, unhappy at the prospect. "Not sure I like doing that, but I'm not sure we've got a better course, either."

"Still, why hang him up? Literally." It flat-out didn't make sense, and Emory stuck on that detail.

"Someone with a sick sense of humor?" the coroner speculated, but the question posed didn't require a real answer.

"Either way," Emory mused, "that had to be one hell of a lot of work to get a dead body strung up like that, and living people had to do it."

"And that, my brand-inspecting friend," the sheriff sighed, swiveling back around to face them, "is where the detective work comes in."

Her mind snagged upon the crime scene. "The ranch roads. You said you were going to go talk to the people who lived back that way."

The sheriff nodded. "We did. I handled the main ranches, and Frank handled the lesser travelled roads. Neither one of us found out a damned thing that we didn't already know. None of which involved this incident. The ranchers hadn't heard anything unusual or out of place."

"You didn't tell them about the man hanging from their crossbar…" Emory pressed.

"Hell, no! That would have gotten everyone up in arms. And Frank didn't find anything at all. Just an old house where transients, or kids hung out to party, along with old ranch structures about ready to blow over in the next strong wind, or heavy snowfall. I took the left road, and he took the right."

Emory chewed on that information. "Maybe people use abandoned buildings to shoot up drugs. Do you trust Frank to assess the situation accurately?"

The sheriff sat up a bit straighter. "Maybe I'll just take a drive out there, to see for myself. Probably there's nothing to be found, but no harm in a second set of eyes making sure."

She shrugged. "Look for drug paraphernalia as evidence…maybe the sign of a struggle."

"Do you want to ride along?"

She could do detective work as well, and wanted to drive out to the scene to search for further clues to be found. Something about that splitting ranch road still troubled her. However, concrete items first. She needed to locate Dirge—and locate him fast. Provided that he even remained in the vicinity.

"I have something pressing that I need do first, but I would like to join you. Can it wait a few hours?"

"Don't see why not, since it's waited this long. Remember, no offense and once again, don't mention this to anyone and especially not your boss Josh Tucker. What an ass."

"Trust me, I won't."

The coroner nodded. "She's not the problem, Joe."

The sheriff tilted his head in agreement. "My personal cell is 970-476-4392."

Emory punched the number into her phone, and let it ring.

"And now you have mine. I'll call you just as soon as I've finished up," Emory said rising, and nodding at the two men as she left.

Passing back through the main office, she noted Frank Deacon's empty chair and the deputy missing from his post.

What a piss-poor guard dog, she thought, leaving the building.

20

IT AIN'T AUSTIN CITY LIMITS

A SEEDY WATERING HOLE LURKED ON THE EDGE OF TOWN, just over the boundary beyond city jurisdiction. A beacon for the shady and the shiftless, and those that didn't take showers as a rule—it commanded a location bound to make law enforcement just that bit more interesting when push came to shove.

Emory noted the establishment before in passing, and like the majority of people with standards or common sense, didn't even slow down, but drove right on by. Hell, as far as she knew, it didn't even have a name —only a highway address. Such a place people either frequented—or they emphatically did not. Most people would naturally stay away out of a vague sense of self preservation.

Going past 1:30 on a weekday afternoon, she pondered the odds. On a danger scale of one to ten, she gave it an eight. Which meant it was the exact type of place that motorcycle gangs would hang out. And by extension, that included Dirge.

She drove toward the nameless watering hole, hands

gripping the steering wheel a bit tighter than usual—her bruised knuckles completely overshadowed and forgotten.

"If there are no motorcycles outside, I won't go in, it's as simple as that," she concluded, speaking aloud.

Not that it helped.

Not to mention the term 'motorcycles' came across as far too benign. The better description would be 'choppers', but using, or even thinking that word struck somewhere in her gullet as a product of that renegade lifestyle, behavior, or the one-percenter culture. The same that tried to cause her serious harm out in the land of the double-lettered roads. The use of the word *chopper* seemed four steps toward endorsing Dirge's bad-boy persona—that bad-boy persona which had saved her life.

Still. The use of the word chopper just felt plain wrong, coming out of a ranching mouth like hers.

She slowed as she neared the debated location, the building edged into view. Hunkered down and set back on the lefthand side of the road, it almost blended in with the trailer park surroundings directly behind. Rundown with rough plank boards, if the outside were anything to judge the clientele by, they wouldn't be pretty.

Sure enough, three choppers slung-low and menacing, listed outside in the dirt lot.

Icicles formed inside her heart and made her blood cool. Sure enough, one of them displayed the Territorial Sons emblem or patch, as they called it.

Understand that ambushes come in various guises. That lecturing voice echoed inside her brain in warning.

Yeah. She'd learned that lesson the hard way, and others had died as a result. But she still stood. These days that knowledge didn't make her feel a whole lot better.

She could have just as easily died as lived. She got lucky in a crapshoot, felt more to the point.

A weathered, hand painted sign boasted of pool tables, and seemed appropriate given the surroundings. A mid-century chalet-type orange slanted metal awning capped the doorway. A nicety preventing heavy snow from landing upon patron's heads. A misplaced thoughtful gesture, for what would likely prove a rough crowd.

Locating the nearest parking spot to the door for a quick getaway if needed, she pulled in and killed the engine. She debated whether or not to wear her badge and decided it would just piss people off and piss them off royal.

Climbing out of the truck, she eyed the toolbox in the back where a rifle waited, stowed, and locked away. Brand inspectors often carried rifles for the express purpose of putting down animals too far gone. If she carried a rifle into a bar, she'd likely get fired if not shot outright.

For the oddest reason she couldn't define, that thought made her mood lift and she smiled.

Ah, hell. She'd leave the rifle behind and take her chances.

She should have slipped her Smith and Wesson into the glove compartment, but she hadn't.

How did that old saying go? If wishes were horses, she'd have a whole herd.

And judging by the ragged, dated, and beer-sopped exterior, probably everyone in the bar packed firepower. Everyone, with the exception of her.

She sized up the building one last time and approached the entrance—a flimsy door punctuated by an ineffective narrow strip of diamond-paned glass best suited to a suburban home. Those diamond patterned mullions didn't have much purpose beyond decoration… other than as rifle rests. But the raunchy establishment remained just a bar, not a fort. Still, it might have come under siege at one point or another.

Grasping the flimsy doorknob, she took in the deadbolt higher up that provided the bar's best, and perhaps only, line of defense if one ignored the potential of gunfire.

Turning the knob and opening the door, she stepped on into the dark interior that smelled damn near the exact same as the Ace High in Stampede, the only comparison she could make with certainty. Darker than the Ace, she located the bartender who tracked her as she entered. A big, burly man wearing a plaid flannel shirt, his broken nose spoke of bar brawls and pool cues wielded as weapons. His shaved bald head added to the general air of menace, compounded by a long, dark beard streaked with two distinct lines of gray. His clothes crossed somewhere between biker and Jeremiah Johnson.

He reminded her of gristle—stringy, tough, and unsavory.

As the crude sign advertised, two pool tables hunkered down in the left side of the building. Pseudo-stained glass pool lamps hung suspended from the ceiling, individual colored glass panes missing at intervals like, no doubt, some of the clientele's teeth.

Coors and Schlitz had likely never appeared in worse shape.

Glancing around, the bar flies sparked her interest— but there weren't that many to go around. Not at that hour. Most of those flies at the watering hole occupied themselves by playing pool and drinking longnecks. None of them were Dirge.

The five men playing pool sized her up as fresh meat. One of the players, poised to take a shot, did so—the striking balls cracking and clacking, thudding as they found their pockets or banked off the felt rails.

The man who took that shot straightened afterwards, pool cue upright. Long, greasy, light brown hair, but she had never seen him before.

"Can I help you?" The bartender left no doubt that he found her presence an intrusion.

His hulk, backlit by mirrors reflecting muted bar lights, came across as pretty damn solid.

"This is a public bar, isn't it?" Emory simply refused to show a shred of weakness or doubt.

Her words had the same effect as a rifle shot.

"Maybe," the bartender growled. "Who wants to know?"

"You saw my mouth moving, didn't you?"

He placed both hands on top of the bar, and locked his elbows, making himself seem even larger than he already appeared. "Yeah—and who in the hell are *you*?"

"My name's Emory Cross."

"And what is your business in here, *Em-o-ry Cross*?"

"I'm a brand inspector."

A ripple of silent disbelief followed by shocked belly guffaws. "No cows in here, lady," one of the pool players snarked.

"Oh, I'm not looking for cows," Emory half-sang, allowing the insult to roll off, more interested in identities and checking into the dark corners than in trading insults.

At least now that she had everyone's attention.

A man came out of the head and leaned against the door frame.

She caught sight of him out of her peripheral vision. He aimed his voice up into the ceiling to make sure that his exasperation bounced back down and carried—and carried clear. "You know, *Emory*, sometimes a fellow just wants to have a drink by himself, in a bar, where most women would have enough damn sense to stay away from."

Bingo. Dirge.

He acted like they had just seen each other, and his tone conveyed a continuation of an earlier grievance. Acting as if, somehow, they were a couple.

Bully for them.

"I just wanted to talk to you," she played along, but remained within leaping distance of the front door just in case. She had no intention of jeopardizing her position by moving further in without a good reason. A *damned* good reason.

All movement in the bar stopped in anticipation of the fight about to unfold.

"Maybe," Dirge droned, "I don't want to talk to you. You ever consider that?"

Snickers came from the men as Emory waited, biding her time.

"There's still a few things that need to be said," she countered.

"Damn it all to hell," Dirge exhaled, finally propelling himself forward. "Since you've already caused a scene, you might as well come out with whatever the hell it is that you want."

"Outside," she said. "This isn't a public conversation."

"Fine," he growled, like expecting a knock-down drag out fight.

Turning on her heel, Emory banged back out through the door. Someone bleated like a sheep, the insult clear, but it didn't matter to her. She paused outside in the open, breathing a bit easier. Out in the open proved a far safer bet than being trapped within four hostile walls.

Dirge lumbered on out taking his own sweet time about it, wallet chain swinging and belt holding up sagging pants—a Confederate belt buckle emblazoned, oversized.

"After this is done, I think I'm going to kick me some ass," he threatened, then his blue eyes locked into her. "You know, either you're stupid or stubborn. Which one is it? I would have thought you'd have learned your lesson by now."

"It's in the middle of the day," she answered, finding her words a stupid defense and they both knew as much. "Anyhow, I wanted to talk to you."

"About?"

"About why you are out here. The *real* reason."

He lifted his eyebrows like he found that funny. "It's a free country."

"And one that still has laws."

"And outlaws, too. You find another butchered calf?" He puffed up a bit at that latest round.

"No. Something else. Is Cade dealing drugs up here?"

His head snapped back a fraction, surprise rippled. "No. What makes you think that?"

"You sure?"

"If he is," Dirge spoke slow and deliberate, "he hasn't said."

Something in his posture and the way he shifted his weight from one foot to the other said he wasn't entirely certain on that count.

"What if I were to tell you that some guy OD'd?"

"I'd tell you that's the way of the world," he said, expanding his arms wide, voice sarcastic.

The memory of Dustin Pruitt lingered along with other ghosts and tragedies.

"Is someone in debt to the Territorial Sons up here?"

He chewed on that a trifle too long. "Not that I am aware of."

Which meant someone held a debt. However, that line of smoke-and-mirror questioning was designed to get her nowhere, and nowhere fast. "I know you aren't here for the scenery, Dirge."

"You know no such thing. But I'll tell you what. This bar ain't for the likes of you, unless you want to go asking for trouble."

"I'm trying to solve a problem," she said.

"Hell, ain't we all? Now, if you don't mind, I'd like to go in there and finish my drink." Her eyes travelled to the tattoos on his arms.

"Where's Cade?" she persisted.

"He should be in Stampede with those jet-setting assholes and running through a string of girls who just can't wait to land themselves a Colorado cowboy. Or at least, that's where I last left him."

"Shit," Emory scoffed, but that all sounded true.

"Exactly," he replied, and turned.

"Before you go, there's one other thing I want to ask you. How did a farm boy like yourself wind up with so many tattoos?

He paused and turned back toward her. "Is that a real question?"

"Actually, it is."

"I got my first one at sixteen. The Colorado one." Laced with doubt, he answered plenty cautious but despite himself, he still warmed to the topic. "Once you get one, there's no reason to stop, as they say. A lot of these mean something, and I got them with other Territorials. It's kind of a list of accomplishments in a way."

She deposited that information with a manufactured appreciative nod. "Which is the newest?"

"This dagger." He pointed at a thin-bladed knife—the curved edge done in red ink with drops of blood falling. Fairly menacing, all said and done. "Now, don't you have work, or something more official, to do?"

"I have work to do indeed," she said, "but isn't your tattoo actually a fixed-blade bowie knife?"

He guffawed. "I'll be damned. And what would you know about a thing like that?"

"Plenty. Does that design mean anything in particular?"

He stiffened his neck, with no intention of answering. "Nice try. I've got a smaller one on my butt, too. From back when I was a prospect. Wanna take a look?" he leered, only partially kidding.

"I'll pass."

"Uh-huh. Never figured you for a knife and tattoo chick anyhow," he remarked, unconvinced as he returned into the bar.

Emory watched his back as he entered into the darkness and shut the door.

Let him think whatever he wanted. She had latched on to something, and that something concerned him.

21

SHOOTING GALLERY OR STANDING TARGET—TAKE YOUR PICK

As Emory stood alone in the unprotected open, an uncanny sense stole upon her.

Rough voices raised and carried, but they weren't the source of her worry. Feeling distinctly in someone's crosshairs, the hair on the nape of her neck prickled from a whisper of a long history of rangeland violence—and today the distinct sense of being watched and assessed.

Her palms itched to take up that rifle from the locked box. More than anything she wanted the scope over the firepower, but she'd take both. But if whoever tracked her carried arms, showing a rifle in the current situation amounted to an invitation for target practice.

With her body providing the target.

Bare-eyed, she scanned the setting, turning around slowly in place a full three-sixty, but still couldn't locate the threat. Music started up in the bar—the sound of the bass thudding and reverberating. Cars drove by at intervals, engine sounds approaching, then fading in the distance as she stuck out like a sore thumb in that damned seedy parking lot.

Most certainly, someone watched her, waiting.

Standing there out in the open like that, she knew that she took a chance—a chance for no real reason. Maybe she wanted to test her nerves. That steel-spine pride held her in place, not wanting to give anyone the satisfaction of catching her flinch—or of acting afraid.

She eyed the clear plate glass windows, marveling that they remained intact and in good shape. Wondering how many bar fights resulted in someone getting thrown through those very same panes. But on that day, from the vantage point of the parking lot, the run-down bar revealed nothing more ominous than neon beer signs.

No one bothered enough to check on her from what she could tell.

If someone tracked her, they possessed enough smarts to stand back, deeper into the dark interior. A nuance which made them that much more dangerous.

A small, steel-grid vent perforated one of the outer walls near the roof and snagged her attention as an excellent place for someone to keep watch…

Who cared if Cade sold drugs? Who cared why Dirge rode into town?

Apparently, *she* did.

Taking stock and noting two pickups and two battered cars, one of which appeared like it hadn't run in a very long time, the three choppers listed and menaced. Beyond the immediate set-up, a down-in-the-heel trailer court backed up along the periphery didn't have much to boast about either. Beyond the trailer park and further out, the ever-present flattops rose from the landscape creating natural vantage points…for surveilling or shooting. Take your pick.

Trees, leafing too early given the probability of springtime snows, offered scant coverage and were easily dismissed.

Swinging her gaze across the road, a few RVs parked in a sprawling campground surrounding another low-slung building that served as the office.

Trust your instincts, a voice inside her head cautioned.

Crack! A single gunshot rang out.

That did it. Those instincts told her to get the hell out of Dodge in no uncertain terms. She flung open the door and dove into the truck, noting how the shot sounded like it came from the direction of the trailer park, or out of the bar's backdoor for target practice—maybe shooting bottles or cans—maybe something else. That *something else* got to her, and she had no reason to stick around to find out what it amounted to.

Gunning the engine and slamming the pickup into reverse, small rocks crunched and spit up under the tires as she spun the truck around. Adrenaline surged. She shifted into Drive—the tires spinning in the dust before gaining purchase and peeling out of the dirt-patch lot.

So much for that steel spine—all it took was one single shot fired, and she fled.

They'd call her chicken shit. And that notion didn't sit well at all.

Shame stinging cheeks faded as she settled down a notch or two once the tires reached the solid pavement of the county highway.

That gunshot most likely wasn't aimed at, or near, her. Of course, she had no proof to back that conclusion, one way or another.

She'd taken a spooky turn, no argument on that count.

Memories of that remote sand wash biker party

flooded back, unbidden, and most certainly unwanted. And carrying a distinct message.

Rough men play rough. A lone female holds a more precarious position than a lone man. Men in groups turn ugly in groups. She was responsible for her own survival.

———

THE FOUNDING FATHERS of the town of Vermillion liked their civic parks. Rattling back into town like hell itself chased her, she pulled over into one such hamlet to regroup.

Her hands trembled and her stomach stayed clenched.

"Hells bells," she muttered, resting her forehead on the steering wheel while still hanging on for dear life. She panted.

No, this time she'd just spooked herself, but as most horse people knew, spooks served a purpose and often happened for a reason. She took a few deep breaths to rein in her dented pride.

She always used deep breaths to calm horses. And it always worked. If it worked for them, it would work for her.

A sudden comparison came to mind. That's how she'd acted...the same as a boxed-in, spooked horse. Shying away from an undefined, invisible threat. She'd never taken to riding in arenas for that exact same reason.

Danger lurked in confined spaces.

Thinking back, like so many other ranch kids, she had picked up an after-school job at a local dude ranch where the "last of the line" horses ended up—on a string for trail rides. Emory worked with the horses bought on the cheap, ones that had been standing around too long. That remained one fundamental basic about horses. All horses needed riding and handling, or they forgot (or pretended to forget) everything they'd ever known—

Wait.

A group of high schoolers drew her attention.

Standing around a picnic table far past the lunch hour, they should have been indoors in classrooms or in the library studying. Upon closer inspection, Emory noted their hands—first deep in pockets then darting out and fidgeting.

They acted both suspicious and guilty, all at the same time.

Small items passed, palmed between an older kid wearing a denim jacket, and the others. The suspicion came from the way they kept glancing around and checking over their shoulders. Even from the distance, she gathered that money changed hands. A drug deal transacted, right before her and the rest of the town, all in the broad daylight.

In downtown Vermillion, Colorado.

Shit. Transactions concluded, they parted—the denim jacket going one way, and the three boys and a girl drifting back in the opposite direction, and toward the school grounds.

Responsible adults needed to figure out a way to stop the drugs from spreading in this town, and that included her. That outskirt bar sure might have something to do with it. As far as Dirge played into the mix...chances looked high.

She thought about decisions and choices—decisions and choices that she herself had made. One thing held certain, she might not be all that fancy, but she always got the job done.

Emory just needed a boost of confidence.

Digging out her cell from her pocket, she scrolled down and located the programmed ranch number. It rang on through.

"Yo!" her father answered.

"Hello to you, too," Emory replied.

"Anyone else get hanged?"

"No…and that's not funny."

"Yeah, actually, it kind of is. Did you all get that sorted out? I'll tell you what, it even made the newspaper here. Someone at the gas station claimed it made national news. Did you know that?"

She guessed with such a sensational story, the fact that it travelled and made the rounds couldn't be all that surprising, considering.

"National news. Oh, man. No, but I guess it stands to reason. They still don't know who the hanged man is. But I'm not supposed to talk about any of that, or they will boot me out of this county. Trust me. What I'm calling about is a different matter. Do you know where Cade is?"

"Not that again," he snarled. "What in the hell are you asking about Cade for?"

"Drugs."

"Oh, is that all." The relief in his voice flowed clear.

"Isn't that enough? I believe I just watched a teenaged drug deal go down."

"And you think Cade is behind it?" For once, he sounded gobsmacked. "You have GOT to get your mind off of Cade Timmons."

"Dad. My mind is not on him."

"Whatever you say, but I don't need you getting sweet on him again. And he just ain't smart enough to be the source of all this state's ills."

A longer pause. "What if he, or his kind, are the best we can hope for to keep the Lost Daughter running?"

Silence. She could sense the struggle in her father's mind as he formulated a response. "Is *that* what you're thinking?" He nearly spat the words out, incredulous. "We need Cade Timmons in this family like I need a hole in the head. Speaking of which, maybe you have holes in yours! Now I'm thinking about hanging up this phone and pretending that this call never happened…"

"Dad! I called you for a reason."

"Yeah—apparently to piss me off major league."

She pressed three fingers to her forehead right above her eyebrow where the throbbing threatened. "I need to know what Cade is up to. Seriously."

"Well hell," her father thundered. "I don't know! What do I look like? His social director?"

"Now you're starting to piss me off…just let me talk to Monty instead."

He didn't even bother to answer. Their two male voices conferred in the background. Indistinct, other than she heard her name, and a few swear words besides.

"Hello?" A bewildered, wheezy voice came on the other end. "Is this Emory?"

Those two men possessed the very distinct ability to drive her insane.

Exasperated. "Yes, Monty, it's me."

"You've managed to piss your old man off pretty good. He's snorting and rearing like he might start breathing fire any minute now…"

"*Monty*. Ignore Dad for a minute and pay attention to me. I made the mistake of asking Dad if he's seen Cade Timmons."

"Oh. Yep. That's what set him off, then." In no rush,

he sounded like he hadn't a concern in the world. Or a brain in his head.

"Yeah, I already know that. You still go into the Ace high, don't you?"

A pause. He sensed a snare. Or at least he thought he did. "Ever' now and again," he replied, guarded.

It amounted to more than that, and they both knew as much.

"*Have* you seen Cade?"

He held the phone away as he asked Lance, but she heard him all the same. "What am I supposed to tell her? She wants to know if I've seen Cade."

"The truth," her father's voice snapped, voice coming from a distance.

"She ain't going to like it none," he replied, holding the phone away. Then back into the speaker. "Rumor has it that Cade's got some girl pregnant, and he's likely to pull a runner. *If* he can manage it."

Hell's bells, but she shouldn't have been all that surprised. A pregnancy was bound to happen, sooner or later, figuring by the way he carried on.

"What about dealing drugs?"

"I thought we weren't supposed to talk about things like that on the phone…"

She squinted. "Why not? Have you been watching too many of those true crime shows again?"

She imagined that he hitched his pants up at that one. That's what he did when things didn't go his way and he needed to regain composure.

"I have heard that he's on some sort of supply line. The anything-you-want-we-can-get-it type…as long as they can pay."

"That sounds about right. But why wouldn't he be

able to leave Stampede? It's not Mandy that works at the hospital, is it?"

"Now, how the hell would I know?" Exasperation rippled as he tired of the conversation. "No, wait a minute…no…it couldn't be her. No one would think twice about that. I think she's one of them wealthy twists. She's gonna clip his wings—and clip them good." Monty crowed that last part.

"Let me know if he leaves town and you catch wind of it, will you?"

"Sure," he agreed. "But I have to say that I take your father's point. We don't want him around here. It might have been OK before he started dealing drugs, but he's crossed one of them there lines…"

"Can I talk to Dad again?"

It's your daughter, she heard him say to her father.

"I know who the hell it is," he grumbled. And into the phone, "What."

She wanted to tell him that she loved him. "You know that biker Dirge—Cade's cousin? He's here. And that can't be good. That's why I asked about him."

"Yeah, ok then, if that's really the case. Cade's an asshole. Next time, I'm shooting him in the knee. That all you need from us?"

"If Cade's dealing drugs to high schoolers, I'll shoot him myself. And I'm aiming higher than his kneecaps. I don't need anything else from you two right now."

A chuckle from her father before the line clicked over, dead.

22

ABANDONMENT TAKES THE EDGE OFF

THE TATTOOS MIGHT SIGNAL A COMMON LINK, BUT SHE didn't want to keep the sheriff waiting any longer than necessary for her call.

What the hell, abandoned properties held clues, too.

She selected his number from the list of recents.

"I'm ready when you are," she said. Just like nothing at all had gone wrong.

"Meet you at the old crossbar," the sheriff replied. "I'm heading out now."

Emory drove in that direction, admiring the vastness of the steel blue storm sky that made the world seem almost insignificant below. Shafts of light penetrated the cloud cover, painting the mountains and valley in an everchanging canvas of contrasts and shadows as the sky flowed.

An urgent, northern wind buffeted the clouds and brushed down against the earth in an unchoreographed dance. A dance that preceded a veil of driving snow.

Spring storms could turn deadly, like the snapping of a bear's jaw waking from hibernation. The unwary often learned such lessons the hard way. But Emory, lured by the show of the deep tumultuous sky, felt her spirits lift as they danced along with the song of the wind, her blood thrilling by the untamed wildness carried within.

A familiar song sung over the years—a primal song beyond time and man.

The old, weathered ranch entrance and crossbar came into view along the right side of the road, mercifully bare and unadorned this time around. From her approaching angle, the wooden poles stood defiant against the sky, against the land. Subjected to, and worn down by, those same storm elements gathering force and amassing into dark cloud banks. Out of ingrained habit, she scanned the higher elevations and the nearest rock outcroppings.

Sure, there were places to hide and take aim. But they'd hung the man instead. Although she couldn't put a finger on it, that notion wouldn't ease up and troubled her deep down.

It also allowed for a longing to steal in, unbidden. It turned her thoughts toward home, one hundred miles over and pretty near out of reach. Damn.

Homesickness seeped in, and she brushed it away, concentrating instead upon the age of the wood. Wondering about the original inhabitants who erected those old lodgepole pines to mark their boundary in the wilderness. To carve out a place in rugged land and make it their home. Had they been honest and upright, or had they danced in the shadows along with the Crosses?

There was no way to tell.

The wood split into chinks along the grain, wood checks and fissures developing through the years and occurring from widespread temperature fluctuations. When those poles were felled and stripped a century or so back, the knots would have protruded like talisman eyes—ever watchful and ever present.

A lot of those old ways died hard, as people forgot about the fight it took to hold a ranch against all comers.

Those knots smoothed and gaped, battered by the heat, the cold, and the elements over the years.

Nothing more deadly at that moment than the slate blue snowstorm gusting in.

Alighting, one cowboy boot after the other, she hopped out and stood on a stranger's ranch road. A ranch that might hide its secrets well. She dragged on her jacket as an afterthought, far more intent on the hows and the whys of the very strange horse thief story than by the dropping temperature.

Tire tracks patterned the dirt in places, but no telling who they belonged to, or their motives in the first place. One thing for certain, people used that road and recently, too. As she'd noted that first day, the road split off into a sweeping Y further in. Taking in the slopes, contours, and the lay of the land—basins and meadows hinted that they waited beyond.

Natural barriers fit in perfectly with their type of ranching. The trick would be, and always had been, where to place the buildings defensively—both against man and the weather.

A painting of a landscape once wild. A scrub-covered land for ranching, and not good for much else. Other than raising families that grew as tough as the mountains that spawned them.

And further out, the wild horses roamed.

The wind blowing in her hair, the steel blue of the clouds fringing rain reached down like fingers toward the earth made her knock off her unfettered musing. Rain and snow meant the destruction of precious evidence. Emory scanned the sky, judging how much longer the storm would hold off. Debating whether to call the sheriff to find out if he'd been detained.

Sheriff Hammond solved that debate by pulling in right alongside of her. She eyed the building clouds.

"Looks like we'd best get moving," she said by way of a greeting.

"Follow me," Joe replied.

His tires didn't kick up all that much dust, but he wasn't wasting any time. At the branch in the road, he veered right at the cut. The road curved and hugged the sloping khaki contours, opening into a wide basin at the far side of the foot of the hill. Exactly as she had figured. Near the opening of that basin, the road trailed further in, passing a large decrepit structure standing alone, and strangely without outbuildings. Of course, maybe the outbuildings had been pulled down, or lost in other ways to time. Or they had never existed at all. Perhaps they approached the front of an old stage stop—a distinct possibility. The sheriff halted in front of the house, and Emory pulled up right behind. Together, they each studied and assessed the tracks in the dirt in reference to the abandoned building. Gap-toothed boards slipped or fell away, windows busted out, sharp sharded and glistening in their casements—the front door ajar, held in place by a single, rusted hinge that threatened to give way like everything else.

That gray, weather beaten structure once held someone's hopes and dreams. On the other hand, it might have held their nightmares. It never served a purpose to go all star-eyed and sentimental about the past.

The past could prove just as messed up as the present.

"Don't look like much," the sheriff remarked, toeing

some detritus lodged in the ground. A gust of wind hit, banging the door with a sharp staccato crack.

She shied ever so slightly at the sound, glance darting to the source.

Emory covered her nerves, shrugging them away. "There's tracks in the dirt, but those could be Frank's... or anyone's for that matter. I take it that people live further back and use this road as well as the other?"

"No. We can drive it to make sure, but the Connell's use the lefthand road, and I think this links up behind in a circle. I spoke to them myself the day of the discovery, and they flat out wondered why I was even out there in the first place. I told them that I was just making the rounds, but they didn't buy it. They've got two boys in high school, involved in sports and that type of thing, but I guess they hadn't driven the road that morning."

"Don't suppose those boys hold parties out here?"

"I suppose anything is possible, but I'd be real surprised if they did."

Emory nodded. "Shall we?"

Walking toward the door, each scanned the ground for signs of anything out of place or out of the ordinary. Only old discards and fractured glass shards were embedded into the ground in places, filmed over and cloudy from time.

Emory kept her eyes open for the deputy's footsteps and found none. "I don't think Frank got out of his truck."

The sheriff only grunted as a few snowflakes swirled.

"Sneaker prints," he said, pointing down to the ground. Emory walked over. Sure enough, but for the moment, that had limited value. Still, the sheriff snapped a picture while they still could before the storm hit. He pulled the flashlight from his belt, shining it into the

building's interior. Dust coated the remaining floorboards and revealed recent footprints. The odd thing
about the tracks remained the positioning. They only
went in as far as the center of the room, where a wider
area brushed clear of dust stopped in front of a gap in
the floorboards. For people used to investigating, it
marked the position like a roadside sign.

"Looks like they were kneeling down to get at something," the sheriff said, taking photos with his cell.

"It's a decent enough hiding place," Emory concluded.
"There might have been, or be, something hidden
beneath the floor. No offense, but I'm lighter than you
and can look if you want."

He handed her his flashlight. "Be careful where you
step—the wood might be rotted. And shine a light down
there before you go sticking your hand in. Rattlers might
be waking any day now."

She edged forward, testing each board as she
progressed, anxious to avoid any more accidents
involving wooden impalements. The flooring, what
remained of it, felt solid enough under her weight, but
all it took was one false step. She knelt where the
disturbed dust had rubbed away, leaned down, and
shined the light underneath the flooring. The dirt might
have been hollowed out and scooped away at one point
—it wasn't a snake hole, and there weren't any animal
droppings. Now whether that hole had been intentionally made, or simply covered over during construction
would likely never be known. But as for this current
century, the ground remained more than half frozen and
might have been disturbed, but then again might not.
Certainty about the ground's condition proved elusive,
just like everything else in this case.

"It's an old dirt subfloor," she told him. "The plank

floor came once they got money and time. I can't tell if it's been touched. You want to come see for yourself? It'll hold."

She shined the light again. Nothing definite.

The sheriff came over to inspect. "No tracks anywhere else."

Squatting back on her heels, Emory scanned the building and shrugged. "Let's walk the perimeter. If we don't find anything there, I guess that's it, don't you think?"

"Any number of places could be a hidey hole," he said, nodding toward the floor opening. "But we'd have to get real lucky to find it. Even more lucky to catch someone in the act."

"Yeah," she replied, peering upwards through the holes overhead, and catching a glimpse through a gap in the roof of the sky above. "That likely won't happen."

Backtracking where she'd already stepped and returning out into the open, she long-legged it around the perimeter of the house's foundations going toward the right, while the sheriff veered to the left. The building claimed the small rise allowing the downhill land sloping away to act as the discard dump. Old, rusted tin cans, broken beer bottles, modern-ish pop cans, and old rusted mattress springs faded in their slow decay back into the ground. Give it another century or so, and all traces might completely disappear as the earth reclaimed what it could.

A wall of pale weather approached from the far end of the valley.

To the left, an old two-seater outhouse listed. He inclined his head in its direction.

"We'd best get moving, and I'll do the honors," he said, stepping toward the outhouse, flashlight held high.

He didn't go all the way in but stayed on solid ground. Shining the light upward, he paused.

"Lookee here," he exclaimed.

Emory joined him, peering overhead into a gap between the outhouse walls and roof. There, a small bundle waited, stashed, and hidden from sight—unless someone knew exactly where to focus. In that case, the wrappings were easy enough to find.

More evidence pictures taken, before handing her his flashlight.

"Hold this," he said, pulling on a pair of gloves. Setting first one foot and then the other up onto the plank outhouse seat, he tested the wood's strength as he quickly reached up, snatched the bundle, and set one leg back down on the flooring.

Wrapped in butcher paper, he unfolded the package, to find a plastic zip lock bag filled with white powder.

He pulled out an evidence bag from his back pocket. "Can you open this?"

She did, and he dropped it all in and sealed it. "I'll log this in as evidence."

"I still think we're missing something," Emory said, the weather pressing in.

"In the outhouse?" He didn't sound thrilled but remained willing. They both noted the holes.

"Might as well," he claimed, taking a breath.

"Oh, for goodness sake," Emory chided, still holding on to the flashlight. "It'll all be dried down there anyhow."

Crouching, she aimed the beam into the pit, where the darkened bottom revealed recent usage—nowhere near as dry as it ought to be.

"Somebody's been using this." She aimed the beam

under the edges of the holes to see if anything had been taped underneath.

Just plain old ordinary wood.

"Let's take one more look at the dump before the weather turns," she said. "Say, does this ranch attach to the BLM or another outfit?"

He eyed her. "Myra Brandt's place backs up to this one, or maybe there is a strip of BLM land. But that's a ways away."

That nugget captured her attention right there. Emory stared at him hard, shoulders square to his. "Are you ever going to fill me in on the story there, or do I have to figure it out for myself? Whatever the case, I can sense the undercurrents running swift and deep."

The sheriff shuffled a bit, deciding whether or not to trust.

She waited as the insistent wind blew colder.

He eyed her. "She never filed a formal complaint."

There it was. The other side of Myra's story. "But…"

"But there was a problem there. Seems she sold some horses to a kill buyer. Under false pretenses, of course. He claimed something like he wanted to put them on his ranch to keep each other company, or some other line of bullshit."

"Why didn't a complaint get filed? I would have raised holy hell."

"Oh, I'd guess due to cost. Her word against his in a court of law can get mighty expensive. No one, well almost no one, has money like that to throw around out here. We tend to save up for squabbles involving water or mineral rights."

"Yeah," Emory said, thinking that logical enough in the given circumstances. "And when did all of this supposedly happen?"

"I'd guess about four months ago. Definitely during the winter. Dustin Weaver probably knows more about it."

Dustin Weaver.

"I don't like the sounds of that story," Emory admitted.

"Probably no one does," he offered.

In the meantime, she had some sales records to check. And maybe she'd rustle up Dustin to see what he had to say.

Together they moved over to the top of the old dump and peered down what they could of the slope, the sheriff now carrying a bag of drugs at his side.

"What are you thinking?" he asked, staring downhill at the varied refuse.

She pulled up her collar, cold. "If that young man died of a drug overdose, as stupid as it may sound to say, he had to die somewhere. I mean, was there a fight, or did someone just find his body and hoist him up? And why this particular crossbar? Why any of it?"

The sheriff side-eyed her. "Want a job in my department?"

She cracked a grin. "I think I'd get in too much trouble. But seriously, all those questions need answering. Sure, it's a warning. But a warning of what?"

"I don't see any signs of a death or a dragging here. They'd likely have had to drag the body if he were already dead. Shall we drive down that road before heading out?"

"That would be good," she replied, thinking that even if all she learned confirmed that she knew how to read the land, it would be time well spent.

THEY CONVOYED along the dirt road as the snow really began to fly. The dirt tracks curved around a sage covered slope to reveal another empty pasture as the sky turned gray. Probably a hay meadow come summer, and a nice one at that.

Her phone rang. *Sheriff.*

"Ready to call it?" he asked.

"Might as well. Thanks for letting me tag along."

At least she established to herself that she could read the land—a fine thing.

Nevertheless, she needed to figure out how to read a few more signs besides.

23

OLD WEST BAIT AND SWITCH

Monday rolled around, and Emory arrived in the parking lot at 7:00 a.m. on the dot, Josh's pickup already parked and waiting.

She glared at the stationary pickup, resisting the impulse to feel the hood to check if the engine remained warm.

Uncertain what kind of reaction to expect—each day could be a new experience on that front—her nerves chanted a low, jangling kind of hum with each step she took.

Half of her felt like knocking on that damned door, but she pushed on through.

"Why, there she is!" He exclaimed all nice and enthusiastic, although it remained only the two of them.

She plastered on a smile. "Good morning."

"I planned on having you stay in the office today and field calls, but now that this has come up...I guess I'll change the plan."

"What's come up?" she asked, feeling like she ought to hold onto her wallet.

"An opinion piece on the wild mustangs. While it doesn't directly involve us, we might get calls and I want to be on top of it. So, I'm going to give you a choice. You can either familiarize yourself with the brands and the stock growers in the area if you want to stay inside, or you could go out to check on the wild horses." He scanned her notes from the week before. "You can consider the offer a reward for doing a *damn fine* job last week."

He grinned.

Something in that *damn fine* sent the warning bells ringing—and ringing loud.

"Wild horses or brands?" he insisted.

Dealing with Josh and his ups and downs sure felt like a strange rollercoaster ride with no logic applied—or end in sight.

"I'd have to say the wild horses," Emory replied, already on guard for having a choice in the first place.

"*Outstanding.* Now, what you are looking for with the wild horse herds are any branded horses that have joined into the bands…and while you're at it, pay attention for any signs of a wolf population. Make sure that you take a pair of field glasses. They're over there."

Fine.

"One of the ranchers last week alluded to the threat of wolves, but they haven't had any problems themselves yet."

She realized she offered him an olive branch, but why she felt the need to seek some sort of truce didn't feel right or normal. Yet, she continued down that path. "Have you fielded any reports of them killing livestock?"

"Not yet," Josh replied, returning to his computer screen, ostensibly occupied by searching. That man spent a whole lot of time and effort staring into the depths of his computer—in her mind at least. "It's likely just a matter of time. They're on their way down from Wyoming, or so I hear."

Wolves would likely have very little to do with wild horses in the natural scheme of things, at least from what she knew. Maybe if an old mustang was downed already. Broken leg, or some type of injury that rendered them unable to move.

Another olive branch, laced with a hint of need-to-know. "Did you ever find record of who officiated at that rescue society sale—the one where Myra found her mustang?"

That question provided a close brush with a fundamental disagreement.

She really didn't want to embark upon yet another "suspicion" lecture. The suspicions, of course in his mind, being hers and hers alone. But she just couldn't let it rest.

"No, but it just doesn't sound like the kind of mistake that I would make. But I'm on the trail of something else. Something more important than ancient history."

If he wasn't going to say, she wouldn't ask.

Another not-entirely-pleasing expression flitted across his face, one he almost hid as he stared into the computer. Only one week in and she already recognized the traces.

"Either way, you'd best get headed out. That is, if you are going." He didn't even spare her a glance.

Grabbing a pair of binoculars off the shelf, she scooted back outside, with the wry realization that she'd never even had the time to take off her jacket.

SHE CONSIDERED what she knew of the famed stallion Picasso, excitement mounting. Poster boy of the wild mustangs, one of his claims to fame were his unique coat markings, and his three-toned black, white, and cream mane flowing in the breeze. Not to mention his many accumulated battle scars. The embodiment of the wild horse herds and of a rare freedom, from the pictures, he offered a type of unfettered beauty seldom seen. He also, from what she'd read, hadn't been seen in recent times. And so the cycle of life continued. No doubt he'd have offspring around—pinto mustangs with those same fancy manes. While she would have loved to watch the stallion...well. Every living creature had to die at some time and that included her.

A voice inside of her chided, *that included Hugo as well, although far too young.*

For once, she didn't slam the door on that feeling. Instead, she let it open ever so slightly—a crack allowing brief investigation. The truth didn't sting as it once had, but no, the hurt still lingered.

Damn either way.

Enough, and she shut the door on that, having a job to do.

No sooner had she driven about two miles down the road, than the first question hit.

Before she lost coverage, she veered off to the side of the road.

"Josh Tucker," he answered.

"This is Emory, and I've got one quick question. Have any recent stray or stolen reports come through? If I can't make out the brands from a distance, but the horses are branded, what's the plan?"

Dead silence.

She blinked a few times. Waiting.

"That's two questions," he criticized.

She hated being corrected over stupid stuff, and his response surely belonged in that category. "But no, there haven't been any recent reports. Just if you locate some domestics, make note of it and describe the horse as best you can. Then if someone out in that direction files a report, we have a decent idea where they might be. It's called being *one step ahead of the game*."

Yeah, right. And odd. Definitely odd. "Will do. Just wanted to make sure. Thanks."

She ended the call and tapped the edge of the cell against her chin and lower lip.

Should she, or should she not, call Terry and Dave?

Dustin Weaver might make a better first call, following the sheriff's advice.

She placed the call through.

"Sheriff's Office." None other than Frank Deacon, and she didn't feel like sparring with him.

"May I speak to Deputy Weaver?"

"Who's calling?" Suspicion laced his voice.

"Emory Cross, brand inspector."

He didn't even bother to put her on hold, but called over to the other deputy, "It's that eff'n brand inspector."

A momentary pause, and the sound of approaching footsteps.

"This is Deputy Weaver. Can I help you?"

"Hi, it's eff'n Emory Cross."

"Sorry about that," he apologized, with a slight and tired laugh.

"Say, can you go somewhere that Weasel Junior can't overhear? The sheriff suggested that I call you about the five horses Myra Brandt sold to a buyer in Nebraska."

She could have sworn that he suppressed a groan—

but his voice remained professional. "Sure thing. Let me put you on hold. Be right back."

Emory waited.

"I'm here."

"Thanks, Dustin. I was out at Myra Brandt's place, and she's trying to transport two horses to Utah–a different, yet related, issue. I spoke with her, and she told me that a few months back she sold five head to a buyer in Nebraska. She claims she felt kind of strange, called the buyer and he told her that they all died from equine flu."

"Yeah."

So, he was a typical guy with one-word answers. "You heard about all of that?"

"I did." *Great, now he worked his way up to two words.*

In all fairness, she sensed him struggling.

"I know that your cousin knows Myra—who came by while Kai settled in last week. She bought some hay from her. Hay that Myra no longer needed."

Silence.

She proceeded. "I asked the sheriff, if the Nebraska buyer misrepresented themselves, why she hadn't pressed charges. Worse than that, I can't even find record of the sale and shipment."

He cleared his throat, and a chair scraped.

He lowered his voice. "Myra is a touchy subject."

Waiting, she gave up after a few moments of dead airspace, and decided to try again—verging on a white lie. "I'm going to call the Nebraska brand inspectors, but thought I would try to solve this locally, if I could."

"Um…we'd appreciate that…"

"But I really can't, you see," Emory pressed the advantage. "Everyone knows that something happened, and I heard that she hires ex-convicts. She told me she fired the guy who recommended the Nebraska outfit."

"That's the story."

"So, you don't know the person who she fired?"

"No. Don't think so. But that's the thing. We never know who she's got working out there." Dustin paused. "To the point that it's kind of strange."

"Patty, your cousin, seems to like her well enough."

Emory could feel the wall go up.

"She feels sorry for her," Dustin claimed, making it sound final.

"Because…"

"Because she's having a stretch of hard years. Her husband died, the bank is pressing for payments she likely doesn't have…and she's outside the circle, as it were."

"Because of how she runs her ranch?"

"That accounts for a lot of it, sure. No one is saying that she is doing anything illegal. She's very standoffish and she keeps to herself."

"She sure doesn't like me," Emory half-complained.

"Maybe so—and you're probably asking too many questions. She wouldn't like that."

"I saw two young men I think that she's got working for her. They were arriving as I left. We literally passed on the road."

"Those would likely be her new batch of hires then. They don't seem to stick around long."

Emory nodded at that last piece of information. "Thanks, Dustin. I'm headed out to visit the wild horse herds today, in case I'm out of range and anyone wants me on your end."

"Noted. See you around," he said, and clicked off.

Abrupt.

What the hell. She had intentionally told him where she headed in case something went wrong. She wondered if he latched on to that part. That remained a prevalent concern in the wide-open empty. People could, and did, go missing.

Either way, she didn't plan on being the next statistic if she could help it.

Towards that end, she clicked in the Greeley number. Since she had already pulled over...

"Terry Overholzer, brand inspection."

"Good morning," Emory said without identifying herself. "Are you in the office?"

"Good morning yourself. Now what are you up to?"

She bit back a wry smile. He evidently didn't feel *too* sorry for her. "Going to see the wild horses out here."

"That sounds nice. Day off?"

"No. That's my point. The plan is for me to drive out there, see if I can locate any of the wild horse herds, and if I find any to check whether there are domestic animals running along with the band."

Silence.

"Yeah. That's about my reaction. So, I have a pair of binoculars, and I'm headed out."

"Is your cell phone charged?"

"Yes."

"Do you have water?"

"Look, Terry," a glimmer of humor flashing. "I don't have a water problem, and I've gotten better at charging my phone."

"Every night before you go to bed..."

"Got it. The reason I'm calling is that I need another set of eyes. Do you mind searching for any reports of stolen, missing, or strayed horses in this area? And, when exactly did Josh Tucker take up this post?"

"He started out under Ray Thompson."

"Was Ray good?"

"Yes, but on the older side for computers. Not sure how well he did with them and the forms, but he knew brands, animals, and the entire business, while upholding the letter of the law."

"People out here don't seem to think much of Josh."

Terry made no comment as he pecked away at his keyboard. That man pounded the keys hard. While that used to annoy the hell out of her when she shared the office with him, she now found the loud tapping a type of reassurance, a sound now causing her to bite back a smile.

"Three estrayed horses returned to owners Sam Livingston and Michael Craig back in 2021. Ray filed the report and closed the report. Josh worked there then…but nothing on horses since. A few transportation permits…"

"See anything for Myra Brandt?"

More pecking. "No. Should there be?"

"Right. Yes, there should be. According to that rancher, a couple things are going on. She said that she transported five horses into Nebraska, but she won't state where or to whom she sold those horses. That would have been four to five months back. According to her, she called the buyer to check up on them, and he said they all died of equine flu. I'd sure like to check with the brand inspectors out there just to make sure that they haven't had any incidents reported…but if illegal horses are being shipped around, it's unlikely that they'd report any outbreak. Do you have any friends over in that direction?"

"I can certainly do some checking for you."

"Now she wants to transport two horses into Utah,

but she has no proof of ownership on the one…and it's a mustang, I'm fairly certain. A mustang without the freeze brand marking from the BLM. She says that she bought him at some rescue sale, and they didn't give her the papers. Now Josh is digging into that one, because according to Myra, he officiated at that sale."

Terry whistled through his teeth, low.

"And I'll take it that you read about the hanged horse thief," Emory concluded.

"Hell, everyone has heard about that. Just thought you'd slip that into the conversation, did you?"

She cleared her throat. "I'm the one that found him."

"That doesn't surprise me much." The senior brand inspector sounded a bit pained more than anything else.

"Next question, what do you know about mustanging?"

"Precious little. That's not a plains thing."

"Yeah. Obviously, I've never run into it before either, but there are whispers and hushed conversations. Something is passing me right on by—something the ranchers know but aren't saying. I did meet an old guy who considers himself some sort of local historian. I'll stop by his place on the way back from my field trip."

"I'll have a few conversations and get back to you, Em."

24

THE COLD DESERT OF THE
SAND WASH

THE ROAD LEADING TO THE WILD HORSE BASIN REMAINED largely untraveled. The outpost ranches and structures, never prolific to begin with, grew wider apart until they vanished altogether—the land holding sway and rendering man's attempts at permanency both insignificant and unworthy. The unending sky shone brilliant blue with skittering clouds buffeted about by the currents of the geostrophic winds. Resulting shadows travelled and played on the earth, dancing upon the jutting claystone buttes rising from the flats. Standing apart and defiant, those claystone formations taunted the higher ranges where winter remained. Spring, always slow in coming at altitude, hinted its intentions in khaki, struggling toward green-and-tender. Tender insistence pushed, rising as winter's brittle brown grasses yielded and gave way.

Everything turned according to cycle.

The young pushed the old aside, claiming their place in the nature of all things. Those old, dried grasses would yield—overrun in time—knowing that young and tender green never lasted long out in the dry.

The sun playing hide-and-seek from behind the dappling clouds created the painted valley canvas of rolling sage-covered hills.

A patchwork quilt of a landscape.

Mottled shades of slate ebbed and flowed in a tide of wind that promised no rain.

THE BEAUTY of the ever-changing light and landscape spoke to her without a voice—capturing her soul and making her breath hitch.

For that moment, she understood the stirring call to freedom, but couldn't fathom, deep down, what it truly meant.

She came from this land that had the ability to humble and to make her feel small.

Unfettered vastness. A vastness that created a surge in her heart. A surge she hadn't felt for quite some time.

All in the quest to locate wild horses.

TURNING off from the pavement onto the BLM land, she rumbled along the rutted road, uncertain as to how or where she'd find the mustangs.

Having done her homework beforehand, she noted that the Sand Wash Basin covered in the region of 246 square miles of rough terrain. Taking the road called the Wild Horse Loop, her first destination was the Two Bar Spring. Anything mentioning water offered a decent beginning in the cold desert that would turn hotter and drier by the month. She drove along the isolated road, scanning the horizon searching for any signs of the wild horses.

A dust cloud hung low on a distant rise.

Stopping dead in the center of the road—since she assumed she was the only one out there—Emory grabbed the binoculars to scan the rising dust along the top of a slight rise further down the road.

Nothing. Just the wind kicking up the dust.

She scanned the terrain. Limited by the truck to the rough and rutted road, horseback offered another possibility, but a more dangerous one. Kai would probably handle alright, and she'd have a better chance at finding the mustangs in the outer washes where the roads didn't reach.

But she didn't know the terrain. And they'd need to pack in plenty of water with her. Shaking her head and discarding the notion, she'd need a very specific reason to track if she were to take all of that on.

A dinged-up diamond shaped sign had tattered and faded red pennants to get its point across. *Roads Impassable When Wet or Muddy.* Sure enough, the road dipped into a draw, chiseled by mud gouges where tires had fought. Sucking clay mud that dried up as quickly as it formed, proved no one's friend. The hard evidence stared right at her.

Sagebrush, bunchgrass, saltbush, and scrub—the arid land wouldn't take prisoners, and only the most foolish would assume otherwise.

But back to the mustangs.

Wild horses would stay near whatever water they could locate, and since April fell in the wet months of spring, they would have more watering holes to choose from than during the hot, dry summer months.

Another dust cloud rose up and she tracked it travelling toward her. Before long she recognized a BLM truck approaching from the opposite direction. Pulling up alongside her vehicle and pointed back toward the way she came, the man's glance flicked over the lettering proclaiming *Brand Inspector*.

He rolled down his window, and she rolled down hers.

"Hey there," he said by way of a greeting.

"Hello," Emory replied.

"Is something wrong?" He nodded at the lettering on the side of the truck.

She halfway laughed, trying to find the right words without sounding utterly ridiculous. "Umm. No. Nothing's wrong. My boss sent me out here to inspect, from a distance, the wild horse herds. Maybe he's doing me a favor since I'm new to the area."

"He is doing you a favor! This is a great place. At any one of the springs you may find horses gathered."

"Actually, I hope you won't think that we're completely insane, but there's an idea being bantered about that some domestics may have joined up with the wild horses out here."

Startled at that last part, his head jerked back a fraction in surprise. "Really? I've never heard of anything like that."

Thinking about it further, he cocked his head in disbelief. "Domesticated horses are actually a far cry from the true wild mustangs. Especially the stallions. Not sure what a gelding would do out here and survive, for example. Mares would be a different story."

Emory certainly didn't disagree with his assessment. "Beats me, but it probably wouldn't turn out well for the gelding. At the very least, it's awfully rough and dry."

He blinked a few times, as if trying to recall something applicable. "Don't exactly know where a horse would wander *in* from. You know, if anything, I'd say it would be more of a problem of gates being intentionally left open, if you catch my drift. As far as legalities are concerned, if a wild horse wanders off and away from the basin, they are no longer protected. That means they are then subject to removal."

"Dog food?"

"That'd be my guess. So, if you happen to find any gates open around the perimeter of the basin—not that you'll be out along there—please take a picture and close them. Then send the location along with the picture to us, and we'll investigate."

Emory realized that she must have frowned, because the man tried to read her expression, studying her. "Something bothering you?"

"Oh, a few things. My name is Emory Cross, what's yours?"

"Peter Latham. Nice to meet you."

She nodded. "Don't suppose you've had reports of any missing mustangs or that type of thing."

He inhaled and tilted his head. "Missing wild mustangs would be a really hard thing to prove. Horses do die, and there's no guarantee that we'll ever find the bodies, as you can imagine. But sure. I wouldn't be entirely shocked to learn that horses were let out through those gates I referred to. Some people in this area believe that the wild horses, or mustangs, are a type of public property that they have every right to. Their families have taken wild, or feral, horses from this range for the last hundred or so years. They are considered by some as "free" horses…although gentling them is no easy task."

Like Myra's mustang.

"Not sure I like the sounds of any of that," she admitted.

"Stealing, or taking, the horses? Me neither, and that's the straight truth. Nothing good usually happens, I'm pretty sure of that much."

She thought about it. "You know, that makes the mustangs a kind of a ghost horse in a way. Like those ghost guns without serial numbers. If they leave these confines and are taken, there is no registration, travel papers, bill of sale or anything to document their existence in the first place."

He nodded. "Never thought of it in those exact terms, but yeah. I guess that makes sense. Those mustangs that are legally rounded up are freeze-branded with the markings at the base of their manes. That's what we use to keep track of them."

Emory nodded. "I've seen those brands."

"You probably know this, but when a mustang is adopted, after one year passes successfully with their new adopters, they get paperwork, which means the mustangs are no longer undocumented horses at that point. Of course, they pay the $125 up front as an adoption fee...non-refundable if the experiment doesn't work. But when the year passes, they contact us, and we release the paperwork. At that point, I'd assume most would register with the brand inspectors. You know, we'd have a record of that horse."

She nodded, but although simple enough, the practicalities presented a lot to take in. "I'd need to think about all of this. Here, let me give you my card in the meanwhile. My home office is out in Greeley, but the cell works just fine. I'm assigned to Vermillion for a while, helping out."

He grinned and took her card. "Call us at the office if you need anything or have questions. Closer ties between the agencies and departments might do wonders out here."

"I agree," she smiled. "But just to ask again, you do not know with any certainty of horses gone missing from here."

"I do not," he replied. "But every now and again, we get a report of a gate being left open. An occasion that doesn't give me the best of feelings, should we say. A person would have to go well out of their way and through rough territory to get to one of them. They wouldn't happen upon it for no reason."

With that, he patted the side of his truck door, and headed off—travelling back in the direction toward the County Road, as she drove in further.

———

THE TRUCK JOLTED and bounced along the dirt tracks of the loop road for a while longer.

As she neared the location where she suspected the springs might be, again she crested the road, stopping on top and able to see down into a depression.

And there she found them—a band of wild horses.

Thrilled, she grabbed the binoculars, and alighted from the truck—unrealistically afraid that the horses might simply disappear into the distance like a fleeting mirage.

The mustangs, for their part, weren't troubled by her in the slightest. A grouping of mares and foals with one mature stallion grazed. *A harem.*

Knowing that horses possessed a tremendous range of peripheral vision…she also knew that their straight-ahead sight proved weaker than humans'—they needed to be closer to an object to see the same level of detail as a human. Beyond that, however, she wondered why the horses were not interested in her presence. Domesticated horses always stared at people or new objects nearby. Prey animals—they had to pay careful attention to any perceived threats.

Normally, she should be considered a threat, despite her distance.

Puzzling, Emory then located what claimed their attention. One black mustang with two white rear feet called coronets—stopped all movement and stared at the harem in the distance—holding out his black tail, rigid.

A sure sign of high alert on his part.

A grullo mare with a flowing black mane came up to him, blowing and nudging before moving onward to another approaching stallion with a white blaze down his nose. The white blaze-face proved to be a bachelor stallion, drawn to the dark stallion's mares. All three mustangs leaned into each other—the grullo, blaze-face and the dark stallion entwined their necks, rubbing. They broke apart in an instant of horse communication rippling—the blaze-face hind-bucking the grullo away.

The commanding black stallion trotted away and out of reach, seemingly uncaring.

But it amounted to an act. All just an act.

The blazed-face mustang then approached the stallion, and turned his rear to the herd stallion when he got within range—a clear sign of horse aggression. The blaze-face hind kicked at the dark stallion.

The dark herd stallion circled back around and charged.

Clashing, the high-pitched squealing of the horses fighting proved they weren't playing around.

After the initial clash, the blaze-face approached the mares, then doubled back to charge the black stallion and, raised up on his hind legs with teeth bared, locked into him.

The herd stallion equaled the charge. More high-pitched squeals that carried and sliced through the wind.

Rearing, clashing with their front legs and teeth, when they returned all four legs down to the ground, they pawed. Willing and ready to engage in another skirmish to win the battle contest.

The older stallion charged again, driving the bachelor off.

The bachelor would try again another day, until the time he succeeded in his attempts to breed. Today's dominant stallion would weaken, until he too, was driven off and banished.

But on this day and for this day, the band resumed grazing as if nothing at all had transpired.

Through the binoculars, she noted that the black stallion's coat had the marks of previous battles and encounters, but he came through this latest bout unscathed.

Needless to say, she thought with a chuckle, there were no domestic brands identifiable within that band.

Emory took her time and watched the wild horses for a long while. The temperature shifted and dropped as the wind strengthened.

In time, she turned away.

What did they say about mustangs? Oh yeah. *American as hell.*

She'd have to agree with whoever said it—they'd got that part right.

And so she drove through the ever-changing landscape that danced in the light, serene and untroubled with a profound sense of privilege for witnessing what such a sight.

No wonder her family fought so hard for what they had. No wonder they came west and stayed. There were no go-backers in her family.

No wonder some of the horse's hearts broke when they were removed from the land. She developed an impression there and then. One that she would keep, and guard close.

25

GOSSIP, UNDERMINING, AND ALLIES IN STRANGE PLACES

EMORY PRACTICALLY FLOATED BACK TOWARD VERMILLION, enamored with the wild mustangs and thinking of very little else. But with each mile that passed, a tethering sensation pulled her back down to the here and now. As civilization approached, so did a lot of unanswered questions—all with loose ends that needed tying. The Crawford Ranch fast approached on the eastern side of the road. She slowed her speed. It wouldn't even involve a left-hand turn, but an easy right.

Casey claimed that old Mr. Crawford would like nothing better than to be consulted on the area's history and current rumors.

If the older Crawford didn't know anything of use, it would be easiest to find that out straight away, and without having to drive back in that direction for nothing.

Internal debate ended, Emory took the right onto their ranch road, rumbled across the wash boarding and pulled up into their yard. Completely unexpected, she hopped out of the truck and made it halfway to the house when the door opened.

Typical ranch behavior, the old rancher remained alert to noises and quick on the draw.

"Why, if it isn't Ray's replacement!" Old Mr. Crawford called out by way of a greeting. "Did you forget something the last time?"

She nodded and smiled. "No, sir. But I thought about something that Casey mentioned when I came out before…"

"Should I call him for you? I can get him. But here he comes now. He must have seen your dust travelling in. Casey!"

Casey came striding across the yard, with a smile plastered on his face.

Emory felt an unwelcome blush arise. Dang.

"It's the brand inspector," the old man said.

"I can see that, Grandpa."

Emory smiled, careful not to laugh at their exchange. "Sorry to bother the both of you now, but actually, Mr. Crawford, I'm here to talk to you."

"To me! Well, that's a nice surprise. Nobody usually wants to see me anymore…"

"Gramps…"

The old man completely ignored his grandson, practically beaming. "What can I do for you?"

Emory flexed her shoulders. "I drove out to the wild horse herds, and Casey mentioned last time about how you are a regional historian and authority, not to mention knowing most of the folks who've been out here a while."

"He said that did he?" He smiled over at his grandson, tickled. "Well, I'm guessing he is right. What would you like to know?"

"It's kind of a delicate thing, really. I guess maybe the starting point is the wild horse herds and the people who break and train horses. I ran into a BLM ranger, and he said that the herds are protected, but sometimes gates are left open, and the horses might wander out and become someone's cow horse...or words to that effect."

"Yeah," the old man exhaled. "There's plenty to what you just said. And you know, with those round-ups, there is a prevailing feeling that the government is coming in to take what is ours. Now I'm not saying that I feel that way, but the ranchers often had the wild horses on their properties—some say they are feral horses—and they would let them graze and claim ownership of them so that they were kept safe."

"Kept safe from who?" Emory asked, gaze darting between the old man and his handsome grandson. *She wondered if Casey might be a bit too old for her and decided he wasn't.*

"The mustangers."

She furrowed her brow. "What does that mean exactly out here?"

The old man's eyesight proved good enough to catch her uncertainty. "The people who used to round up mustangs for either ranching work or slaughter. That's caused a lot of mighty hard feelings along the way. But now the mustangs are protected, except for the federal round ups. It's not ideal...but I guess it beats the alternative. It gets mighty political, mighty fast."

"I have a mustang named Outhouse. He came through the prison program, but I haven't had much of a chance to work with him yet. He seems a very sound horse—and an honest horse from what I can tell."

"Mustangs can make fine companions, sure footed and hard workers. But say you come from a family that trains cow horses and you need money. Say your family has always taken horses from the wild herds to train up for free. Some of them might not like the new rules and ways."

"I can understand that," Emory answered with care, "but laws are laws."

"And I'm not saying that they aren't."

Emory exhaled. "What a mess."

"Are you talking about anything in particular?" the old fellow piped up, blue eyes sharp and alert.

"Oh, there's a problem with a rancher and a possible unmarked mustang that I haven't quite figured out yet."

"Myra Brandt?"

"Grandpa!" Casey exclaimed, positively shocked that his grandfather admitted as much.

"I shouldn't say," Emory demurred, "but it's not a bad guess."

"In that case," the old man said, sparking, "I wouldn't worry about it overly much. I saw her travelling with two horses west on this road. Likely she's heading into Utah."

That felt like an icy cold slap in the face. "What time did you see them?" Emory kept her voice level.

"Oh, I'd say about seven in the morning. *This* morning. They're long gone by now. You won't catch them."

Emory's watch read 2:13 in the afternoon.

"No, I guess I won't." Emory replied, mortally unhappy at the development.

"Before you go getting all upset," Mr. Crawford said, "there's a couple of things maybe you oughta know, and I'm only telling you because of who your family is. If you were coming from Ohio or someplace like that, you'd have to drag it out of me...and maybe not even then."

Emory glanced over at Casey, who appeared plenty

worried and more than a bit bothered about what his grandfather would divulge next.

"Myra sells horses that she may not exactly have legal title to. It's a lot of smoke and mirrors that doesn't set too well with most out here. No one enters into agreements with her, beyond buying her hay. She runs some cattle, and that appears to go a bit more on the level, but once she was left for widowed, she's had a tough time making ends meet. Most of us look the other way, but we try to keep our distance at the same time. Hay buying is one means of trying to help, and not getting involved all at the same time."

That sounded about right for most rural areas Emory figured. "I heard she sold five head to a kill-buyer by mistake, or under false impressions."

The two men locked eyes—Casey came across clear that he wanted his grandfather to stop talking about that subject.

The two of them locked eyes for a long moment. In the end, Casey backed down and spat.

His grandfather started back up. "I'm not going to say a lot about that, because I don't know. What I do know is that she hires what hands she can find, on the cheap. If I planned on poking around, I might start there. Casey, you got anything you'd like to add?"

"Nope." He chewed over a notion. "But grandpa's right enough. They're all outsiders or deadbeats, anyways."

He tipped his hat in Emory's direction. "I'd best get on with what needs doing." He turned and walked away without a backwards glance.

That solved that, she figured.

The old man took her measure, eyes shining with conviction and certainty. "I only told you because you're

Chuck Cross' granddaughter, and I figured to save you a bit of time. Hell, you'd figure it out on your own in the end."

Emory nodded at what amounted to a compliment. "I appreciate it, really I do. I need to tell my father that I've met you. Lance Cross. Here's another question, less volatile I hope. You haven't heard of any regional or local horse thieves lately, have you?"

He eyed her—eyed her close. "You mean like the one in the newspaper?"

"Yeah, that's the one."

"I'd say start working on what I already told you. This is outlaw country, and some things never change."

"I appreciate it, Mr. Crawford."

"Give my regards to your father," he replied.

SHE FELT on what amounted to a roll. A roll of the dice that could quickly change, and she decided to go for broke.

She'd head out to Myra Brandt's to ascertain whether she truly did a runner, feeling darned near convinced at what she would find.

When she came within range, her cell phone bleeped and displayed waiting messages.

She pulled over to listen at the side of the road.

Message one: Emory, this is Terry. Call me back when you can.
Message two: Joe Hammond here. Give me a call when you're back within range. I saw your boss in town.

Shit.

Both were equally important in the end, but the sheriff's felt the more threatening of the two.

Sighing, she called him.

"Joe Hammond."

"Hi Joe, this is Emory."

"Yeah, I need to get you in my contacts. Thought I recognized your number. Anyhow, how do you get on with Josh Tucker?"

"Hard to say. It seemed like he liked me well enough this morning, but that can change."

"That's what I was afraid of, and it already has. He does not like you in the least, and it's best that you know that up front."

Her stomach sank. "Why, what did he say?"

"He said that you're somewhat useless and are taking advantage of a cushy situation."

"How's that?" Her blood pressure surged, anger rising.

His voice held dead calm. His official voice. "Didn't you go out to watch the wild horses today?"

That took her aback. "Yes. He told me to."

"Did he now?" Emory could feel the weight of his surprise. "Well, that's not the story he's peddling. He's also gone back to a couple of the ranchers you've done inspections for, just to make sure that they were satisfied."

"You have got to be kidding me."

"Wish that I were."

She rubbed her forehead, mind whirling and temper rising. "How'd you hear about this?"

"My cousin is Alberta Jackson. They bought some cattle, and you signed off on the papers last week. They said you're just fine, and they don't like Josh Tucker. Anyhow, they said he made sure to try to undermine you. Said that you were on probation, or some other such shit."

"Probation? Probation from what? Jail?"

The sheriff chuckled. "Don't know. Most people don't give him the time of day but watch out and watch your back while you're at it. What reason did he give for sending you out to the wild horse herds?"

"This is irritating, not to mention stupid." Her blood pressure most certainly rose by that point in their conversation. "He sent me out to the herds as a 'reward for a job well done', and that's a quote. He also wanted me to check if any domestics joined up with the wild herds. Which is unlikely at best, but I guess one never knows. Son of a bitch."

"Yeah, pretty much."

She took a deep breath so that her words came out in semblance of sense. "Joe? I talked to Dustin this morning before I headed out. A lot of innuendo and some straight-out talk doesn't paint Myra in a great light. One other thing that's been bugging me as well. When the coroner gets back, I want to check the tattoos on that boy's body. They might give us a clue as to his identity. I spoke with a guy I know who claims that some tattoos carry meanings and mark events."

Silence on the sheriff's end. "I guess it's an idea, but I'm not holding out much hope there. I have pictures in the office. Will that do?"

She blinked. "Yeah, it should. I'd like to stop by to take a look once I get this current mess wrapped up. My old boss called, and I need to call him back. But I want to tell someone *local* where I'm going since I can't trust Josh any further than I can throw him. *Apparently.*"

A muffled laugh from the sheriff. "Makes sense to me."

"I'm going out to Myra Brandt's place to follow up on what she plans on doing with the undocumented horse."

A note of caution crept into his voice. "Any particular reason?"

"Yeah. Someone who shall remain nameless, thought they saw her driving with two horses towards Utah this morning. I'd like to see whether she and her horses are there, because that would dispel one rumor. And frankly, I'm not sure that she might not go off."

His chair squeaked as he changed position. "Want company?"

"I don't think so. I actually plan on just driving a ways down her road to where it crests. Out of rifle range, most likely."

"Don't like the sound of that," he cautioned.

Emory hadn't meant to complicate matters, but she had. "Let me call Terry and get back to you. The good news is that most people don't shoot at brand inspectors."

"Uh-huh," was all he said.

26

SPRING STORMS COME IN
DIFFERENT FORMS

Next in line came the call to Terry, along with the realization that she'd forgotten to ask the sheriff how the investigation portion of the horse thief case proceeded. Nor had he offered anything. She'd have the chance to ask if she wanted the sheriff's help with reconnoitering Myra Brandt's property.

For now, the Greeley Sale Barn's number rang through. "Hey, Terry! I didn't expect you to call me back so soon. I just got off the phone with the sheriff. Not good."

"What's not good?"

"Josh Tucker. He went back out to people that were on my rounds to check up on me, told the sheriff's cousin that basically I'm incompetent, AND that I'm slacking off because I was out chasing at the wild horse herds around, WHICH HE TOLD ME TO DO." She realized her voice came close to shouting.

"Settle down, Tiger," the senior brand inspector said. "I told you that there were problems out in that direction."

"Yeah. You ain't kidding. Not to mention I stopped by at a rancher's who told me that he saw Myra Brandt transporting two horses toward Utah without permits, because the paint is UNDOCUMENTED."

"Still sounds like you are yelling," he commented.

"Sorry," she offered, settling down a notch, although she didn't exactly mean it. "Anyhow, that other rancher knew about the sale of horses to the kill buyer. No complaint reports were filed anywhere that I can locate. The sheriff said it's likely a case of his word vs. hers type of thing, but everyone knows about it. Well, probably everyone but Josh, and flat out, I haven't asked him. Don't think I'm going to either—the way things are shaking out. I'm now on my way out to Myra's ranch to make sure that she and her horses aren't tucked away on their spread before I figure out the next step there."

"You finished?"

"Guess so. Well, unless you want to talk about mustanging and wild horse roundups. There's still some more follow up to do there."

"I spoke to Ray," Terry said, his words carrying plenty of weight.

"Oh, down in Arizona?"

"No," Terry dragged the single syllable out. "In Vermillion…"

Emory frowned. "Josh said he moved to Arizona."

"Josh was wrong. Ray's in Vermillion all right. It might be a good idea for you to meet up with him. To compare notes, and that type of thing."

"Sure," Emory replied.

"He's got some things that you might find of interest."

"I'll give him a call. Do you have his number?"

"I do, but that might scare him. Just go into the Rusty Spur and ask for him. You'll likely find him there."

"Barfly?" Emory asked.

"Didn't use to be," Terry replied.

EMORY'S LIST of items that required thought and attention grew and kept growing.

Call ended, Emory still held the cell in her hand, tapping it absently against her lower lip. While she made a mental list—a growing mental list—maybe she would just check the call log to figure out what held Josh's attraction out in the direction of Agency.

No matter what the other brand inspector said.

After checking on Myra. After looking at pictures of the tattoos on the horse thief. After trying to locate Ray Thompson, then she might finally have a chance to run through the call logs. Oh yeah. And they needed to check with the Nebraska brand inspectors as well.

Lazy, her ass.

She really wanted to check on Kai, but in all likelihood, that wouldn't be happening until the next day.

She redialed Terry. "Yes?"

"Terry, you didn't have a chance to call Nebraska yet, did you? I can do it if you want to point me in a direction."

"I knew I was leaving something off. No cases of equine flu reported in western Nebraska. So, unless we provide the specifics of the ranch or persons she sold those horse to, that's a dead end."

SHE CALLED JOE HAMMOND BACK. "I'm headed out to Myra's now. You don't need to follow or anything, but I don't think it would be the best of ideas to let Josh know my activities."

"I'd say that was smart on your part. Anyhow, he's probably drinking already. You know, that's another interesting thing there. He used to hang out at Dusty Mike's Rusty Spur, but he doesn't anymore."

"What happened?"

"Don't know. I've heard that he's spending his money at the VFW. But back to Myra Brandt. The rule I have with my guys is that they check in with me after making calls. I'll put you on that same arrangement. You report in when you arrive and provide analysis of the situational aspects, and you call back when the business is finished. Think you're agreeable to that? No lone agents on my watch."

Actually, she felt grateful that he cared enough.

"That works for me," she replied.

EMORY STOPPED the pickup at approximately the same crested location where she stopped the previous day—scouting out the ranch below. No sign of Myra's pickup truck, and the round corral waited empty. But that didn't mean the horses couldn't be in a paddock, or already in the barn. Emory snatched up the binoculars and scanned the scene below.

"Damn," Emory swore under her breath.

At that moment, out of the barn stepped Myra Brandt carrying two buckets.

She hopped back in the truck and called the sheriff. "I've located Myra, but not her truck or the horses. I didn't take a good count of the horse trailers last time, so

I can't say for certain, but it's possible that one is missing. Anyhow, I'm going down to talk to her."

"10-4," came his voice.

Placing the truck into gear, Emory drove down into the ranch yard.

Myra, predictably, frowned at her arrival and behaved put out at what she considered an intrusion. She set the two buckets down like it cost her.

"Hi, Myra," Emory said as she approached the rancher.

"Remember what I said about *overreach*?" She emphasized the last word to make sure her point got across.

"I do. Let's just say I passed by in the area. What are you going to do about the mustang's papers?"

"Nothing." No expression passed on the woman's face.

"Speaking of which, where is he and where's the bay?"

Barely a missed beat. "Oh, I loaned them to my hands to go trail riding." The woman smirked.

Emory nodded as if she believed her. "What are their names?"

"The horses?"

"Your two hands."

The rancher toyed with her. "They're part time."

"That doesn't mean that they don't have names. What are they, please." Emory did her best to stay level.

"Rick Briscoe and Jack Stuart. Why, are you keeping tabs or a list? Because if you are, let me tell you right now that they are products of our fine prison system. They worked with the mustang program. As such, they're decent horse handlers. Anything you got to say about that?"

"That program's good. They'd certainly have to be

decent handlers when they graduate," Emory replied, as agreeable as she could make it sound. "But I'd bet a fair amount on the fact that Oliver doesn't appear rideable yet, and probably isn't even saddle broke."

The woman's eyes narrowed. "Maybe you're just not a very good judge of horse flesh."

Emory bit back her initial response. "Fine. Have it your way. I'll be back in the morning to check on those horses."

"They won't be here," they woman spread her fingers wide, showing her palms. "They've all gone on a camping trail ride."

"Uh-huh. In this weather. It'll be cold for them, I'd guess" Emory remarked. "Ranch hands and horses alike."

Myra hesitated, flashing like she wanted to say something else—something far less pleasant than what she settled on. "They'll manage."

"Hope so, because the weather's moving in." Emory pulled up her collar as gray cloud banks clashed overhead, driving the wind to pick up speed and strength.

"See you later, then," Emory said, stepping back into her truck.

"I'll be here," Myra replied, eyed narrowed.

UP AT THE MAIN ROAD, Emory called the sheriff.

"She says she loaned the two horses to her two part time hands, and that they've gone camping."

"Actually," he said, "I hope that is not the case. Looks like we're expecting snow overnight."

"If they're camping, they could be anywhere on the BLM land. On the other hand, if they've transported the horses out of state, that's a $750 fine per horse. The unbranded one will be next to impossible to enforce. Guess I'll be contacting the Utah brand commissioners in the near future. I told her that I'd be back tomorrow. She said they'll still be gone. I guess that I out to visit her operation daily for a while, just to get my point across. Shit. It sure would make things easier if Josh did some field work."

He ignored her gripe against Josh—which remained the patent truth. "Utah should know—unless Myra's guys really have gone camping and get themselves into trouble with the weather."

"Time will tell. The plan is to go to the BLM Office, and then I'm headed to the Rusty Spur."

"All this excitement made you thirsty?"

She laughed at the ridiculousness of his question. "Ray Thompson frequents there, apparently."

"Yep."

Emory blinked. "You knew that and didn't tell me?"

"Hell, I didn't know you were looking for him," the sheriff said, none too worried. "But now that you mention it, that makes sense."

"What makes sense?"

"That you're looking for him."

Right beneath her nose all the time. "I'll talk to you tomorrow."

"Sounds like it," the sheriff replied.

EMORY TOOK A LEFT BACK toward town with the plan of visiting the BLM office, purpose twofold. Although she wasn't feeling sociable, she could fake it. And no doubt, those people were the ones who knew how the ranges worked in the Vermillion area, and how many head or units of stock they had registered for grazing and that type of thing.

How many head of cattle did Myra Brandt run? She didn't strike Emory as a horse person, but she did strike her as utilitarian.

Emory searched for the office address, and it pulled up no problem.

Nothing stood that far away from one place to another in town, and it didn't take long before she pulled up to the BLM office at the exact opposite end from where she travelled. In fact, it only took seven minutes to reach the building, which still came on the high side of a typical jaunt. All on account of how she hit the two of the streetlights wrong.

As feared—yet another low-slung '70's throwback.

Good heavens.

Feeling a wry smile tugging at what she considered to be the absurdity of it all, she went through the double glass doors. The two uniformed BLMers noted her entrance and smiled—a young woman about her own age, and a man likely in his mid-forties.

"Hello there," she said stepping up to their counter. "My name is Emory Cross, and I'm the new t— brand officer helping out in this district. I thought I'd stop by and introduce myself."

Surprise rippled. "That's nice of you. We don't get many introductions here. I'm Lynette Ruston, and this here is Dennis Corbett."

Handshakes all around.

"I'm permanently assigned to the brand inspectors out of Greeley, so this is a change of pace for me." A slight chuckle. "I'm afraid if you run my name through your database, I might just turn up."

"Really?" Lynette asked. "What for?"

"Under reporting. And that, as the story goes, is how I became a brand inspector."

"That must be some story," she replied with an easy smile, leaning down on the counter.

"You picked a hell of a time to turn up," the man named Dennis remarked, wry.

"Didn't I just. Bad timing with the hanging and all."

"Crazy," Lynette said. "Just like something out of a movie."

"I'll say," Emory agreed, making sure that she came across as friendly. "All of which got me to thinking about a couple of different things, of which you both may be the keepers of that very specific knowledge."

"That sounds like a promotion to me," the man joked. "Don't know that we've ever been referred to as 'the keepers of knowledge' before."

Emory laughed. "First thing. I wanted to ask about the wild horses out in the basin. I did some reading, and I'm not quite sure how that all works so thought I might run it by you. Oh, and I met Peter Latham out on the basin."

"He's our range rider." Lynette smiled at the term. "Anything specific we can help you with?"

"I'm afraid it's a case of I don't know what I don't know. When there are round ups, the mustangs are processed for adoption, correct? And the person adopting the horse comes pays the stated fee…"

"Upfront, and whether or not the adoption works out. One hundred and twenty-five dollars as it currently stands."

"Ok, and then they have a year to work with the horse, at which time they receive some sort of title from the BLM, correct?"

"Yes," Dennis said, now resting his arms on the counter and settling in.

Emory thought about how to phrase the next part. "How do you know the intentions of the person, or people, adopting the horses?"

The two officers exchanged glances. "Practice, to a large extent. The prospective adopters fill out adoption paperwork, which is reviewed. We also talk to them to determine what they *say* they want with the mustangs. Some think they're going to train them for their kids to ride, and I can tell you upfront, that is generally a bad idea. A supremely bad idea unless they know what they are doing and have loads of time to burn."

Emory laughed at the notion, scratching her forehead with sympathy and empathy all rolled up into one. "I've got a mustang special I need to work on, now that you mention it. Came out of the prison system."

"That system works and is a win-win, in my opinion," the man named Dennis said, warming to his topic. "All the horses and the inmates are trained the same, and the training rehabilitates those that work them in the program. Some of the incarcerated men turn to ranch work upon their release, on account of their experience in the training program. But back to the adoptions. I mean, the mustangs are *wild* horses. *Wild animals*. You'd be surprised how many people seem to overlook that fundamental fact once they gaze into the mustang's big brown eyes."

Emory laughed again. "Those eyes get me every dang time. I've heard some people claim they can see into their souls, but I'm not so sure I'd go that far...at least not all the time. That and their tangled manes. I didn't play with dolls as a girl, so I practiced on horse manes and trails. Anyhow... back to business. Let's play devil's advocate. I'm used to horses and have been around them all my life. Say that I want to adopt one during the next sale that comes around. What's the process?"

"You'd fill out paperwork, go to an adoption event, fill out more paperwork, and get matched with a mustang. After one year of successful management, the adopter receives a title from the BLM. Then, at that point, the animals are no longer undocumented."

The light went on. "And they can apply for transportation documents from us, if they want to take them seventy-five miles or more away. I guess they get branded at some point…"

"They'll already have their freeze-brand from us on them, so that should take care of that part. But sure, they could get branded again, I guess. So that ownership is clear, and so is the ranch or owner where they belong."

Emory nodded. That all made perfect sense. "But you don't want people just going out into the wild and taking horses, do you?"

Both appeared genuinely shocked at the prospect. "Oh no. That's not how that works at all. Roundups are coordinated.

"But what if someone just took some horses?" Emory persisted.

"It's illegal for one, but in truth, it would be hard for us to ever know."

Emory nodded, halfway reluctant, but still pressing. "Do you think that happens?"

Uneasy glances passed between the two of the uniformed employees.

Lynette stiffened, wary around the eyes. "I'd, unfortunately, not be all that surprised."

"You know," Emory began, as if making idle conversation, "didn't that newspaper article say the hanged man had a sign that said horse thief?"

"Yeah," Dennis added. "We were just talking about that. Hell, the entire town is talking about that."

"The thing is," Emory offered, "is that we haven't had any reports of missing or estrayed horses. I take it that all of your grazing leases are for cattle, right?"

"Sheep, too," Dennis offered.

Somehow, she always forgot about sheep. "How big of a district are you talking about over here?"

"About 3.15 million surface acres."

"Holy cow," Emory exclaimed, truly shocked. "That's huge. How on earth..." Her voice trailed off.

"Precisely."

"My hat's off to all of you. If you run into anything that I can assist with—here's my card. The cell's good. If you call the Greeley number by mistake, they'll just give you my cell."

She handed them each one.

"It was nice of you to come in and pay us a visit, Emory. Not too many people bother," Lynette said. "You'll be a welcome addition."

Reading between the lines, that meant that her new boss never bothered, or they didn't like him. To date, she hadn't found one person who professed to even respecting him.

Emory hesitated. "You know, one other thing. Not to be talking out of school or anything, but I ran into a woman who said she adopted a horse but doesn't have any papers. Frankly, I haven't run into that situation before."

"Meaning she lost them?"

"Meaning, she said, that she never had them. At the

sale, they never turned them over. There's no brand either."

"I'd say that is mighty odd," Dennis replied, "not to mention likely illegal."

"Yeah," That's what I thought," Emory said. "I'll take care of it, but you might be receiving one mustang back, for re-adoption."

Emory felt bad at the prospect. Moving horses unsettled them something fierce.

DISGRUNTLED RETIREES

LEAVING THE BLM OFFICE, EMORY STUCK TO HER PLAN. She dropped off the brand inspector truck, switched over to hers and drove to the Rusty Spur for beer time. Not that she held much with the habit of drinking, but a couple of beers or those White Claw cans couldn't go amiss. Especially if on a mission where she picked up something valuable. Knowledge amounted to a type of currency in the ranching communities, and the potential of learning something of use pushed her forward.

She had every intention of listening to whatever Ray Thompson had to say—Terry thought well enough of him, that message came through loud and clear.

Emory pulled up and parked right in front of the establishment. She eyed the front door and figured it couldn't be any worse than going into the Ace High. She intended to walk on in like she belonged. Hell, she could even have dinner there, if they were still serving.

Music hit her as she pulled open the glass door, but it wasn't the wall of music that slammed in your face at the Ace. Country and Western played low and melodious—

unlike Stampede as of late. The volume allowed for conversation, at least at that earlier hour. The possibility that the atmosphere turned rowdier after 8:00 pm remained, but somehow, she had her suspicions on that part. Upon her entrance, people gave her the customary once-over as she approached the bar, but they weren't unfriendly, and they weren't sizing her up as an easy target. Rose, serving drinks, glanced over as she took a barstool.

"Hello there, honey. What can I get you?" she asked.

"Do you have White Claws?"

"Just got them in. Haven't tried one myself. Don't know what flavors we have. Any one in particular that you want?"

"Whatever you've got is fine by me," Emory replied, stretching a bit and glancing around to determine who hung around. Not that she knew a single one of them, but it remained good practice to always take the lay of the land.

No hide nor hair of Josh Tucker, and for that she felt inordinately grateful.

Rose set the drink down in front of her. "You want to start a tab?"

She reared back a bit at the notion and Rose smothered a laugh.

"I'll pay as I go, if you don't mind." Emory pulled out her wallet in a flash. A bit overeager if anything.

"Four seventy-five, then," Rose replied, eyes twinkling. "How are you settling in?"

Emory took out six dollars and laid them on the counter, like the other people sitting at the bar did.

Hmmm. She supposed she just learned something right there.

"You've got a lot of territory to cover out here," she

said. "I've been doing a fair bit of driving. Still need to find a place to live, but as crazy as it sounds, I haven't had the time to make much progress there."

"I'll bet." She gave Emory a loaded expression that read, *horse thief*.

Emory cocked her head in unspoken acknowledgement. "My Greeley boss said I should introduce myself to Ray Thompson. If I should get the chance, that is. Do you know him?"

"Ray!" Rose hollered.

A silver-haired older man wearing a bolo tie and sitting in one of the back booths raised his eyes up from his drink, completely taken by surprise.

"This nice young lady wants to talk to you," Rose hollered through the bar, then leaned in to whisper. "Consider that an introduction."

She winked.

Shocked, Emory grabbed her drink and headed to the man's booth, barely noticing the two younger men who entered the bar.

As she crossed the worn plank floor, it sure seemed a farther distance than it truly was.

"Hi, Ray. My name's Emory Cross, and I believe you spoke to my boss, Terry Overholzer?"

She stood about two feet away from the table, not wanting to crowd the man.

"Oh, so that's you, then. I wondered what a 'nice young lady' like you would want with an old geezer like me."

"Can I buy you a drink?" she offered, still feeling a little too eager, but it was too late to cover that up now.

He held up his half-empty glass. "Not right now, but thanks. Take a seat."

"I thought you were in Arizona," she said by way of a beginning, and she slipped into the seat across from him.

The man chuckled, humorless. "Is that what Tucker told you?"

"Pretty much," Emory replied. "Maybe I wasn't paying close enough attention. To be honest, I thought that he frequented this place, but I don't see him in here. Just as well."

"Just as well is right. He got 86'd."

"86'd for what?"

"Casting aspersions, and I'll say no more. Let's just say he doesn't have too many friends, and he ain't welcome here any longer."

With that, the older brand inspector tightened down and would not budge further on that topic. She could sense as much, and gathered the clear impression that events boiled down to a case of territory, and Ray won out. Hands down.

Well, she'd leave him to his victory.

"Ray, did you read the newspaper?"

"The one about the horse thief?"

"That's the one. Anyhow, I'm not finding any records of missing horses, estray horses, or that type of thing. In fact, the last recorded mention of estrays was a report opened, and closed, by you. Do you find that odd?"

"Not so much," he admitted, eyes not dulled by booze, but plenty sharp. Sharp and appraising. "And you're thinking that he was a real horse thief?"

She hadn't expected his answer, nor the question.

"It's a possibility, isn't it? But the lack of records has me more than a bit baffled. I know there's not the volume on equines that we process on cattle, but still. Something strikes me as not quite right."

Another dry chuckle as he took a swallow from his

drink, the color a watered-down amber that caught the lights from the jukebox and refracted them. "Terry said you were smart."

"This time around, smart isn't exactly working."

He also found that admission amusing. "Maybe I will take that drink," he said. "Scotch and soda. Then I'll buy you dinner. Fair trade?"

"Fair trade," she replied.

SHE WENT UP to the bar, this time both Dusty Mike and Rose moved back and forth, waiting on customers. The two younger men, this time grabbing her attention, were seated at the bar, huddled somewhat together and not exactly approachable. One of their drinks, tinted red, struck as kind of frilly for the location and for the drinker.

"Scotch and water, please. For Ray," Emory said.

Dusty Mike poured a stiff drink, a little worried at the order.

"We'll be having dinner, too. If you're still serving that is."

He smiled and relaxed a mite. "Glad to hear it. The kitchen is open until 7:00. You could learn a lot from Ray, but he can get prickly at times."

"We all can," she smiled. "My boss in Greeley said I should meet him. I thought Josh Tucker drank in here as well."

"Not anymore," Dusty Mike replied, shutting the book on that option, handing her the drink. "He's migrated over to the VFW. Feel sorry for them over there, but they can handle him as they see fit."

Emory raised her brows at that piece of information,

but Mike offered nothing more on that line of conversation.

Returning back to Ray's table, Emory sat the drink down and reclaimed her seat. "The kitchen closes at 7:00," she said. "I ate in here the other day. The cheeseburgers are good." She smiled. "For the record, I'm not doing so well with Josh myself."

Ray surveyed his first glass—contents reduced to little more than half-melted square ice cubes—and laughed a kind of a hangman's laugh. "In the rest of the world, that'd be considered a point in your favor."

Emory waited, took a sip of her drink, and decided to tell him a bit more. "He sent me out to the wild horses, to see if any branded ones had joined the bands—as far as I could see. That amounted to one big old a wild goose chase."

"Sounds like it," he nodded.

"Let me ask you straight. Aren't people buying or selling horses out here?"

"Not so much nowadays...but yes, they still do. On occasion. Horses, as you know, are expensive, and no one's got a lot of money to be flashing about buying fancy horses these days."

Emory thought about what he told her, knowing that sounded about right. "What's the story with Myra Brandt, if you don't mind me asking."

He cleared his throat like it pained him, and he sounded like an old motor struggling to turn over. Then that noise faded away into a growl. Emory frowned, hoping he wasn't having a heart attack or something akin to it.

"Phlegm," he explained.

She did her best not to wrinkle her nose. "I take it you don't like this conversation."

"Let's just say that it's a loaded one." He eyed her, blue eyes cold and clear. "Those two Dimwas at the bar are her latest hires."

Emory's glance darted over her shoulder to note them again.

Ray didn't pay them all that much heed. "I got pushed out. Had no intention of retiring."

Tilting her head at the conversation change, Emory wondered how drunk he actually might be. He seemed sober enough…odd. Except for that abrupt change of conversation. Still, she went with the flow.

"Then why did you leave, or retire? However the case may be."

"I got pissed off one time too many."

"Because…"

"Because of changed reports. Claimed lack of ability. Hell, I was working my ass off, and he just stared into that damn computer all day. Worse than that, he acted like I didn't know how to do my job."

That account provided Emory's turn to chuckle. "I hear you on that count."

The older man warmed to the topic. "Not to mention his lack of attention to what is going on out here. A lot of it comes down to the type of fellows who ain't from around here, and who don't do a whole lot of talking."

Maybe like those released from the prison programs.

Emory would have laughed, but she smothered it. Everyone in this locale, at least where she was concerned, spoke around the important topics leaving her to form her own theories and conclusions.

"So, what is it about the wild mustangs that people are talking around—I can feel it, and I know it has to do with them."

"What do you think?" he challenged.

"If I were to make a guess, I'd say that every so often a wild horse gets taken illegally."

He raised his glass in a toast at her conclusion.

"But what I can't figure out is why. The BLM has those adoption events—why not just wait to go to those? For the price of $125, it doesn't seem worth all the risk to me."

"It's absolutely not. Not if you think of it in that way. You see, the people from out in this area have always taken horses from the herds. They were settled here before the laws came out. As a result, there's an ingrained belief that the laws don't apply to them. They're just doing the same as their fathers, and their father's fathers before them."

Man, that refrain sounded damn familiar. She felt her ancestors mocking her down through the ages. "I understand," Emory said, "but that doesn't mean that times don't change."

"Josh Tucker has a hand in it, mark my words."

Now that claim struck Emory as unlikely. "He told me he's basically afraid of horses. That you handled them. Taking that into account, I'm not sure what he's supposed to be doing with them."

"Maybe he's paid to look the other way and let people sort out matters as they want."

That amounted to quite the accusation—or drunken ramblings. "Paid? Who would be paying him, and why?"

The man took a sip of his drink, bothered. "Don't know. I'm just talking out of my butt—but maybe so. It's all I can figure."

"So that strung up horse thief could be a real one?"

"Hard to say, and probably not in the literal sense," the old brand inspector replied. "But I wouldn't rule it out entirely."

None of which sounded right. "But if someone called in a theft, no matter my feelings about Josh, I think he would certainly record it—don't you?"

"I do. He lacks the imagination to do otherwise."

"Then no stolen horses," Emory emphasized.

"Nope. No insurance either, because they'd need the reports to file."

Emory's can of White Claw stayed where she had set it, barely been touched. She took a long sip to slow the conversation and the accusations down. "This may have nothing to do with anything," she began at length, "but Josh spends a fair amount of time in the Agency. Do you have any idea why?"

"Not really, but hell. I'll make a few calls for you." He eyed her again. "You sure ask a lot of questions."

"And you sure have a lot of thought invested in Josh Tucker. Besides, questions are all I've got. It's the answers that I'm hunting for."

For some unfathomable reason, the older brand inspector seemed to find that amusing.

"So why did you leave the job—anyhow? You seem to miss it and sure haven't quite let go of it."

"Did Terry tell you that?" Again, he growled. *Fairly touchy on certain topics.*

"No. Just an observation. You could come back, you know. I'd say you're younger than Terry, and he's not going anywhere any time soon."

"I got pushed out, and I don't want to let that SOB win, and that's the long and short of it. Josh didn't want me nosing around…but I could swear he changed entries after the fact on my reports, and then said I didn't know how to use a computer right. I mean, how hard is it to fill out forms and save them?"

Indignant, he took a drink. A long drink.

"And that's another thing," he said before she had even formed another question. "Haven't you wondered why he's always at work before you are, and our hours start at 7:00? Bet you don't have a key to the office, do you?"

"Now that you mention it. Did you know that he worked in the DEA?"

Again, a mirthless chuckle. "No, I did not know that…but that might be mighty handy. For a fellow who drinks a fair amount, doesn't he seem in remarkably good shape in the mornings to you?"

"I wouldn't know about that," she admitted. "But I do know that I don't get many straight answers from him. Have you heard any strange bar talk about the horse thief?"

"All bar talk is strange. Now, how about that dinner?"

HE AIN'T GOING ANYWHERE—
HE'S ALREADY DEAD

ONE DAY LATE AND ONE DOLLAR SHORT, EMORY CALLED the sheriff.

"I'm ready to review the horse thief's photos," she said by way of a greeting.

"Hey, Emory. And good morning to you, too."

"Sorry."

He laughed. "Call Greg—he should be back by now. Today's turning into a pile of shit, and I don't want to wait on anything having to do with that damned horse thief. The sooner we get that solved; the sooner things return to what passes as normal. Call me if you need something specifically from me," he said.

And hung up.

"Dang, he must be busy," she said into the air.

She searched for the coroner's office and pressed connect.

"Coroner's Office," a male voice answered.

"Greg?"

"Yes."

"This is Emory Cross. Welcome back from vacation.

Say, I'm sorry to bother you, but where is the hanged man right now?"

"In the cooler," he replied, guarded. "Why?"

"The sheriff suggested that I call over to you. I don't mean to sound ghoulish, but do you suppose that I could view his body—or do you have pictures of his tattoos? I'm settling on a strange idea that maybe there might be a clue in them."

Dead silence on the other end. "Interesting," came the one-word answer at length. "Come on in. We've got pictures, and the real deal."

"It may be nothing at all. But it's something worth pursuing. At least, on the surface it is."

He chuckled. "Tattoos are on the surface, get it?"

Oh man, not him, too.

She didn't respond.

"Sorry, coroner humor. When are you coming?"

She'd already been in the office for her day's assignments—which were light. "How about now?"

"No time like the present," he agreed. "So how do you want to go about this? I'd suggest we start with the pictures first. Easier that way. Failing that, he's in the back in the morgue."

"Fine," she agreed.

He hesitated, and she could feel the pause. "Have you viewed a dead body before?" While he sounded all business-like on the matter, underlying concern leaked out anyway.

Another stab travelled through her. "Yes, unfortunately I have." *Hugo.* "I'll be OK."

"Never thought otherwise," he replied. "See you when you get here."

"On my way," she replied.

Emory high-tailed it over to the coroner's before the momentum left her and doubts crept in.

Another 1960's building to park in front of. *Easy in and out*, she thought with her own gallows humor, followed by a grin. *Although it wasn't exactly funny, it still kind of was.*

She pulled open the glass door, and stepped on in. The floors and walls gleamed a meticulous medical white. The interior smelled of cleaner and antiseptic, but maybe the scents comingled and were all one and the same.

The coroner waited for her, sticking his head out a door at the sound of her entrance.

"How was your trip?" she asked for politeness' sake. Not to mention it sounded a bit plastic.

"Visits to my mother-in-law are always their own special kind of hell, I'll grant you that. Arizona's weather is really nice this time of year, company withstanding. My office and the files are back this way. So's the body, for that matter. We'll deal with that after you see the pictures, and if we need to. What are you looking for in particular?"

She sighed. "It's kind of like I hope I'll know it when I see it, type of deal."

"Fair enough," he opened the door to his office.

Emory wondered if he'd have preserved body parts in specimen jars—but it turned out he didn't.

"Let me get you the photographs and the file."

"I thought your office would be more…interesting," she mused.

He cracked a grin. "Like Frankenstein's laboratory, is that it?"

"Something like," she smiled.

In fact, he had a normal desk with framed pictures of

his family, a baseball and some small sporting tokens, and his window had venetian blinds.

"Your job strikes me as a hard one," she said, taking inventory of his office contents, and trying not to appear too obvious as she did so.

"I like it because it's challenging, but that doesn't mean that I don't see disturbing scenes. For example, I used to hunt. Maybe it's the job, but I don't do that anymore. I've seen enough death, and I do enough gutting. What did Nietzsche say? 'When you gaze long into the abyss, the abyss gazes into you.' I'd say that this young man, whomever he was, gazed into the abyss too long, and it got him in the end."

Not knowing what to say to that, Emory sat down on a chair to wait. The coroner pulled out a file from a cabinet.

He sat down at his desk, papers and files stacked haphazardly. He, however, located the file he sought without much trouble.

He flicked open the manila file folder and scanned the contents. "These were taken while his body remained intact. He doesn't look the same after the autopsy; I've got to warn you in case you decide that you want to view the actual body."

He removed the photos and handed them across the expanse of his desk. Emory took the stack. The first photo on top showed his face and neck. His skin had turned more greyish-purple than she recalled out in the open. Then again, maybe she hadn't assessed him as closely as she thought.

She put that behind the rest.

The second photo showed his entire body, taken from afar.

The third were of his head, neck, and chest. Across

his chest *Old West* written in old-timey, gothic script stood out bold and oversized.

"What in the hell?" She muttered. "Why would anyone do something like that?"

"Beats me, you young kids. There's no accounting for what some people think is a good idea," he offered, consulting the picture she viewed. He read the question in her eyes. "What we see in here are the unattended deaths, the suspicious deaths, and those that require some sort of explanation of various kinds. For example, in accidental deaths, we often don't know whether, say, a person fell off a cliff, or was pushed. That's where the law investigators come in."

"Like this one," she said.

"Like this one," he agreed, more interested in her reaction than in the tattoos.

She stuck that photo behind the others, unconvinced and giving the entire situation a shake of her head.

Next up—a photo of an arm. She peered even more closely. Chattering skulls and a Celtic band that caught her fancy.

On the other arm, the photograph recorded a lone wolf howling. Nothing that matched Dirge's.

"I'm not seeing what I'm looking for," she murmured. Maybe it had been a crazy idea after all, and here she lingered, wasting a busy man's valuable, and important, time.

Legs and feet next. One tattoo on one of his calves—a bucking bull.

Next came a picture of his back...plain skin.

"Is that it?" she asked, handing back the stack of photos.

He rifled back through the file, moved aside a piece of paper, and located a couple of additional photos.

"These somehow got in the wrong place." He consulted the two photos and handed them over without saying word one about them.

The top photo revealed a butt cheek. And on that butt cheek a partial outline and the beginnings of a small bowie knife inked yet left unfinished.

A miniature version of Dirge's, unfinished and without the drops of blood.

"Wonder what happened there," she said, thinking those missing drops certainly carried some meaning. Fights or deaths or times the owners had bled for the club?

"Looks like he changed his mind, halfway through," the coroner remarked. "Considering how small it is in comparison to the others, well, it seems odd."

Yeah. Maybe. Then again, maybe not. She didn't know much about the Territorial Sons practices, and felt glad enough, considering.

"I sure don't know anything for certain, but that partial tattoo is exactly what I sought. But you're right—it's awfully small."

He sat up a bit straighter, his eyes locking into hers.

"Yeah," she said admitted. "I've got a connection."

"Think we better call Joe?" His hand hovered over his desk phone.

"He's having a bad day, but yeah. I think we had best."

He picked up the phone from its cradle, holding it midair. "Better to waste his time now, and save time later," the coroner said, and punched a speed dial button.

"Emory's got something she wants to tell you."

CONFESSIONS MEAN MORE IN SOME PLACES THAN OTHERS

THE CORONER AND EMORY EXCHANGED GLANCES OVER HIS desk. "I don't know that it's worth him coming over," she said.

The coroner shrugged. "He wanted an excuse to get out of the office and a slight change of scenery. The deputies were likely getting to him—and one deputy in particular. This'll give him a valid excuse to stretch his legs."

Emory pursed her lips. "He's not going to be happy with me. I've already received a bit of a lecture before."

The coroner pulled his neck back a little. "On?"

"Oh, on coming clean with what I know. Not carrying secrets. This might be a bit of one."

"But you just saw the tattoo now…"

"Yeah, but it's more of how I put the two and two together."

The way he quirked his mouth and head she took as a sign of sympathy…but she couldn't be certain how long that would hold out.

"Want to check out the morgue while we're waiting

for him to arrive? I can offer you the twenty-five cents tour."

Emory smiled and rose to her feet. "Might as well. Curiosity gets me every time, I'll swear."

The coroner rose to his feet and headed for the door. "Me too. That's how I got into this line of work; I reckon. Do you still want to see the body?"

She frowned, uncertain. "Not really. I think I've got the general idea. Is it possible to just take a peek inside of the autopsy room? Like I said, morbid curiosity."

Across the hall, the coroner opened the door to the room labeled AUTOPSIES in no uncertain terms.

"If you just want to stick your head in, you don't have to suit up," he offered. "Or just step inside the door."

"Stepping just inside of the door it is.

Together they crossed the threshold, hesitating inside a cinderblock-walled room painted white. A large industrial circular floor fan hummed, and she sniffed. Although masked by disinfectant, the room retained faint traces of bodily fluids. A wide built-in steel door covered most of the wall to the left.

"Is that the cooler?" Emory asked.

He chuckled at the term she used—straight out of a TV show. "Yes. We've got room for six bodies, but happily we've never had need for that many at the same time in recent history."

"Oh?"

"Let's save the history lesson for another time," he grinned, "but something tells me it is right up your alley."

Two stainless steel examination tables waited, again, scrubbed meticulously clean, they still gave her the heebie-jeebies. Each had wheels attached to the bottom of the legs, and each trolley backed up to individual sinks.

"I guess I don't need to ask what the overhead scales are for."

He nodded. "Body parts," he deadpanned. Probably trying to take her mind off of the tongue-lashing she would certainly to receive from the sheriff.

She nodded. "I guess I've seen enough for now."

They stepped back out into the hallway, and he shut the door on the room. "We bring closure to a lot of grieving families by answering their questions. I just wish I knew this horse thief guy's name."

They both knew that it would be discussed in a matter of moments. He didn't press her for details—a consideration offered that she didn't take lightly.

"How did you know that he didn't die from hanging?" She asked.

"No hangman's fracture. That would have been expected if he dropped from a height, meaning the crossbar. Additionally, there are no cervical injuries in his case. There were vertebral dislocations, but that could have happened after death, and when he got strung up. Anyhow, most modern hangings are suicides, and this isn't one of those. Not directly, at least. The result is the same."

"The drugs."

"Yes. The state mandates five categories that each death has to fall into. Natural, Accident, Suicide, Homicide and undetermined. This one is a puzzlement."

"How are overdoses classified?"

"Usually as accidents, but this one, because of the hanging, is classified as "undetermined" for right now. If we just listed it as accidental, that would be the end of it, except for the identification part. It would get swept under the rug, and we can do better than that for the man. There's more to that here, anyhow. Everyone deserves their final truth to be told."

"Yes," Emory said, voice trailing off. "I hope I haven't wasted your time, Doctor."

"Call me Greg. After all, I call you Emory." He paused, eyes travelling past her and out the glass door.

The sheriff had arrived.

"Hang in there, Emory. Whatever happens in this conversation. There's a lot of subsurface stuff going on right now, but no one is doubting you. It's important that you know that."

She took a breath, willing herself to stay calm. Imagining cold water flowing through her veins. Just the same as when she aimed an important rifle shot.

Unarmed, this time it would be her words that counted.

Damn it all to hell, she thought to herself as the sheriff walked in through the door.

Of course, he scowled.

"I thought we had this part straight," he said, coming right up to her. Hands on hips standing tall and looking down his nose. Trying to make himself bigger and her smaller. That's what men did when they assumed their authority at the verge of falling under fire.

She showed him her palms in a gesture of surrender. "That's why I'm here now. I had to be certain."

He eased down. A notch. "Shall we take this into the office?"

"Hell," Greg said. "Let's just sit down in the waiting room here and talk about this like normal people."

He received another of the sheriff's scowls for his efforts, but he didn't back down.

"We can see anyone coming in, in the unlikely event I

get a visitor" the coroner said—and the first to immediately take a seat.

That left Emory and the sheriff standing, and without waiting for an invitation she claimed a chair and sat down as well.

"A tattoo got me thinking. So, I came in here to see the pictures taken of the body...and sure enough, one matched."

"Start at the beginning," the sheriff said, none too pleased.

"Where in the beginning?"

"The *very* beginning."

Damn. "That goes back to the Calamity Jane part."

The coroner's eyes shifted, not having the slightest idea what she talked about. But the sheriff sure did. "Go on."

Emory took a breath, trying to figure out the best way to go about it. "The Territorial Sons are a biker gang that I ran into on the plains. One of the members, a man called Dirge, is a member of that gang...and he saved my life."

"So?" the sheriff prompted.

The coroner held his head slightly to the side, like he were eying a rattlesnake that he didn't trust not to strike.

"He has a tattoo of a bowie knife on his arm."

"And you know this because?"

"Because I saw it. Anyhow, and this you won't like, is that I saw him up here the other day."

The sheriff offered only a pure, soundless laugh of exasperation.

"Anyhow," Emory continued, "some of those guys run drugs. I asked him the reason why he was here and couldn't get a straight answer out of him. But here's the thing. While I spoke with him, I asked about his tattoos.

He said they were a visual timeline, and how some of them were related to his biker buddies. I'd say that partial tattoo links the corpse to the Territorial Sons."

She intercepted a glance shared between the two men. They were impressed, but she wasn't out in the clear. Yet.

In their silence, Emory shifted. Silence, as a rule, didn't bother her, but this time ...

"Where I'm going with all of this," she started back up, "is to tell you about the Calamity Jane part, for lack of a better way to explain it. We, meaning the Greeley brand inspectors, took a call for a butchered calf, which turned out to belong miles away. The calf turned out to be a warning to a rancher's son with a drug problem. To make matters worse, the son owed a drug debt to the Territorial Sons."

The sheriff cracked a half-cocked smile of admiration. "Damn, girl. Trouble follows you, or you follow it. That's a—"

She cut him off. "I'm not done yet. On the day I drove out along the backroads, and I smelled a fire. I figured, at the time, that some rancher had a trash fire burning or something to that effect, but it was dry. The last thing we needed was a wildfire. Anyhow, I went down a draw and, unarmed, stumbled upon a makeshift biker party with a lot of drinking going on. One of the fellows recognized me from court, where I testified against them. Dirge happened to be riding along, saw the truck and pulled over. He likely saved my life that day."

Puzzlement settled in the wrinkles around the sheriff's eyes.

"Testified...?"

"Oh, that," she winced without meaning to, immediately sorry that she had. "I shot one of them and he ended up arrested. That happened at the Greeley Sale Barn on my first day at the job."

A guffaw escaped from the sheriff, and the coroner leaned forward.

Emory frowned, now exasperated herself. "I was exonerated, I'll have you know. But he, and maybe a couple others, recognized me from the trial when I testified against their buddy. Anyhow, Dirge rode up as they were closing in on me. He fired warning shots, which caused enough of a distraction that I could escape. Then we got chased on the road, and I ended up killing one of them. That's when the Calamity Jane stuff really started circulating."

Silence. Dead Silence.

Shocked glances passed between the two men, and the sheriff's expression looked like he had made a sucker bet gone bad.

"I heard about the killing. Damn, I should have searched further back."

Emory frowned. "That was self-defense."

"Yes, so the report says," he agreed.

"But that's why I'm protective about Dirge—the biker—as much as I can be, within the law. He helped hold them off, then he risked his life for me, when we were being chased. At the end, he could have disappeared before the law arrived, but I asked him to stay to give a statement. Although he didn't want to, he did. You see?"

The sheriff sniffed, eyes still beady and locked into her. "Loyalty is an admirable quality...I guess even if it is questionably placed."

"I knew I should have told you, and I am sorry. For that part."

The sheriff finally took a seat, although he leaned

forward. He wasn't about to let her off the hook so easily.

"The upshot, I take it, is that this character might know the body we have in the cooler."

"Yes, sir. I believe there is a connection. Of course, I could be wrong, but I don't think that I am."

Again, the sheriff and the coroner exchanged glances.

"I'm fairly certain I'm not going to like this next part, but let's go for it anyhow," Joe said. "And where did you see the man with the knife tattoo?"

"At that crappy bar by the campground on the way into town."

The coroner spluttered. "You went in there?"

"I saw choppers outside, so I had to check it out. Dirge is here for a reason. But, like I said, he's not going to tell me. And I don't like just bringing him in for the hell of it, unless he's wanted on suspicion with proof to back it up. I haven't got anything on him. Except…"

A sigh. "Except that I thought I saw a drug deal in the park. High schoolers."

The sheriff rubbed his forehead as if it pained him. "Yeah. That's been a part of my problem today. One of the kids got suspended, and they found drugs in his backpack. When did all of this come about anyhow?"

"About three days ago," she replied. "Today is when I saw the tattoos lined up."

"That's true," Greg said, vouching for her. "She just came in, and we called you immediately once we made the connection."

The sheriff scowled at Greg for his troubles.

Emory rushed to his aid. "For what this is all worth, I don't think Dirge or the Territorial Sons'd be dealing with school kids. But they might be dealing with the people who are dealing to them…if that makes sense.

Anyhow, if the hanged guy is known to Dirge—he could likely identify him. The problem is how to convince him that he wants to do that."

"And you know where to find him? Don't suppose you know his true name, do you?"

"Henry Alderson."

"Don't like the thought of motorcycle gangs rolling into town and dealing to kids." He nodded for her to continue.

"I asked Dirge about that point blank. The question surprised him, and I do believe that he would do some checking on that count. Anyhow, we might find him at that bar on the edge of town."

I DON'T WANT TO DANCE
WITH YOU

EMORY DIDN'T FEEL TOO INCLINED TOWARD RETURNING, much less entering, the nameless bar on the outskirts of town…but she'd do it.

Anyone worth their salt would.

The sheriff and his deputies took their positions scattered around the periphery…the sheriff in an unmarked car, the same as Dustin Weaver. Frank manned the marked pickup, parked and waiting off to the side of the campground. Out of the direct line of sight from the bar as instructed, he acted ready to jump out of his skin at the slightest cause.

Her mean side surfaced, finding a slight kick at his expense.

Emory drove the brand inspector truck, eyeing his location.

Once again, Josh had hightailed it out somewhere in the field, leaving no one to notify locally. True, she could have called Josh's cell, but their trust had never run anywhere near that deep. Instead, she called over to the

Greeley Sale Barn, just so that some of the higher-ups knew the lay of the land. Especially if everything went bad—and this one had the makings.

The cell rang a few times before Terry picked up.

"Hey there," Emory said. "I've got to make this quick. You know that hanged guy I told you about? You remember Dirge Alderson?"

A cautious "Yes…"

"It's all coming together here now. The hanged guy has a partial tattoo similar to one of Dirge's—an affiliation everyone is thinking. Josh isn't around, so I figured I'd better inform someone of my actions. You're the lucky winner."

"Hang on a second. I don't think that's a good—"

"I'm with the local law. It can't be helped. We need Dirge to identify the body."

"Em—"

"Gotta go, Terry. I'm pulling up now."

"Shit. Call me when you're done. That's one call I don't want to make to your father."

Yeah. No kidding. But she'd do better than she did the last time.

Emory pulled up and parked right in front where everyone inside of the bar could see her, if they bothered to peer outside into the broad daylight.

"I'll call you when it's over." Emory clicked off.

She located the sheriff and Dustin, careful not to show it. The sheriff sat in his truck in the dirt lot, and Dustin waited, stationed in a car along the edge of the trailer park. The best course meant making this visit fast —especially before someone noticed him waiting in the trailer park and called it in to the law…or worse, called it in directly to the bar.

Joe Hammond gave her fifteen minutes from entering the bar to come back out again. Anything longer than that, they would come in after her, guns drawn.

Emory took off her Stetson and opened the locked box in the back to stow it safely. She would leave the truck doors unlocked as a precaution that just might not work.

For the brief moment while the box yawned open, she longed to pick up the rifle.

But she shut the lid back down, put the lock in place and clicked it.

Damn.

Approaching the door with the lattice-paned embellishment, she thought for the second time how out of place it looked. Pulling open the door, she entered into the dark interior world.

"Will you look what just came in through the door," the voice from behind the bar drawled. "Dirge! It's your old lady!"

Dirge glared over the top of his longneck—empty shot glass nearby. "She ain't my old lady."

Laughter rippled. "Whatever you say, man. Whatever you say. How about I buy her a drink in that case?"

"She don't want it," he growled.

Emory eyed the bartender, and eyed Dirge. "I'm on official brand inspector duty."

Laughter rippled. "And I'm driving their truck," she added, like that would make one molecule of difference to that crowd.

"Take a look outside, will you Bones?" The bartender asked one leather-wearing biker.

He eyed her as he walked by to check out the parking lot. *Eyed her like a side of beef.*

There's a brand inspector truck, and it's parked right in front of the door. Hell. Anyone who's coming in will see it," he called over his shoulder. "

"I'll move it," Emory offered. "But I need to talk to Dirge for a minute."

"What are you drinking?" The bartender asked her.

"Nothing. Thank you."

"It wasn't a request," he corrected.

Dirge shifted, mouth set in a tight line. His eyes took in everyone's positions, and he wasn't happy about it. "Let her go, and you have my word she won't come back."

"That's just it. She's not your old lady, and you obviously can't control her, whoever she is. Jack and coke it is."

Dirge wagged his head. "I said, let her go."

"And I said she's drinking."

Emory laughed, and bolted for the door, hoping to catch them off guard.

A big bear hug enveloped her, lifting her off from the ground and trapping her. Her feet kicked the air and didn't make contact. The arms wrapped around her belonged to the man called Bones who verified her truck, but it didn't really matter.

She was trapped.

Dirge stiffened but did nothing for her. Apparently, this time he would let it all play out—whatever 'it' entailed.

The man set her back down—everyone knew she wouldn't get anywhere.

Standing on the carpeted no-man's land between the bar rail and Dirge's table, she didn't know which way to turn.

"It's against the rules," she told the bartender thug.

"Rules are meant to be broken," he replied with a leer. He set the glass on the bar. "Drink up."

With a casual shrug she certainly didn't feel, Emory clasped the drink, and made to go over to Dirge's table. A lightning-fast hand darted out and grabbed her arm. "You drink with the one who bought it for you," he threatened.

She pointedly eyed his fingers digging into her arm. He couldn't have cared less. She inclined her head, still deciding to pretend that she wasn't bothered by any of his actions. Taking a sip, she just about choked.

"That's practically all booze!"

The laugh he gave wasn't friendly in the slightest. "Drink up."

"I'll puke."

"Then you'll clean it up," he growled.

Emory stalled. Her exit still blocked by the gorilla who grabbed her in the first place and who showed no signs of going anywhere.

Her watch said nine minutes left to go.

She sat down on a stool at the bar. "I'm allowed to sit, aren't I?"

"Since you asked."

She eyed the bartender who eyed her back. "Why are you doing this?"

"Because I can," he replied. "Now. You can either tell me what you're doing in here, or you can drink. And when you've finished that one, there's plenty more where that came from."

"I told you. I want to talk to Dirge."

"What if he don't want to talk to you?"

"No idea. Why don't you ask him."

"Since you asked," the bartender inclined his head,

but this was no show of manners but intimidation, pure and simple. She hated to draw Dirge into it, but she had little other choice.

"Dirge. If she ain't your old lady, do you want to talk to her?"

"Not particularly," he replied.

"Maybe she's packing, or maybe she'd got a wire on her."

Shit. "I have no such things."

The bartender came out from around the bar. "Let me just make sure for myself. Stand up."

Reluctantly, she rose to standing. It wasn't a polite pat-down, for damn sure. His fingers lingered certainly where they weren't supposed to, and rough about it, too. But his prolonged actions killed more time.

"Satisfied?" Emory asked when he had finished.

"Are you?" He laughed.

She didn't want to look over at Dirge, but she did, all the same. His eyes bore into hers, none too friendly.

"Finish your drink," the bartender said.

She took another sip.

"Faster," he replied.

Glass halfway to her mouth, the front door burst open. Early. In came Sheriff Hammond, gun drawn.

A door in the back didn't prove much of a deterrent either, because in nothing flat, Dustin Weaver covered the back with another gun drawn.

"Everyone, HANDS UP!" Sheriff Hammond yelled.

Sirens approached, pulling up in front.

"Who wants to go to jail today?" The sheriff hollered, scanning the crowd.

In came another sheriff that she had never seen before.

"Emory, go get your gun and handcuffs, if you have them." The sheriff instructed.

"She's been drinking," the bartender objected with a sneer.

"Good," Hammond replied. "Maybe her finger will slip, and you'll go down. Cuff him," he ordered Deputy Weaver.

Emory jogged out the door, and hurried back in, now armed with a rifle, and feeling much better armed.

"No handcuffs," she said to the sheriff, "and we'll need that man at the table there." Emory said, indicating Dirge.

"Cuff him," the sheriff replied, holding out a pair of cuffs.

She hesitated, and Hammond caught it. "Sam, you do the honors."

The heavy-set sheriff waded in.

A biker, standing near one of those demoralized pool table lights in the back didn't follow instructions very well.

Catching the movement of his right hand toward the inside of his jacket, Emory lifted the rifle.

"STOP, or I will shoot!" She called out, slicing through the activity.

That biker must not have been so good at hearing, or he thought she didn't have the balls to pull the trigger.

She pulled the trigger, and the glass from the lamp exploded, flying everywhere.

"Next one is in you. HANDS UP NOW!"

He didn't.

In one fluid movement, she slapped up the handle, pulled it back—the spent cartridge pinged as it fell to the floor and she cocked the rifle and returned the bolt to the forward position, ready to fire again for round two.

The biker changed his mind about going for his gun. He raised his hands instead.

The unknown sheriff had Dirge, whose hands were cuffed behind him.

"Sam, I'll keep an eye on him. Take care of that asshole back there, would you?"

"Sure," he replied, already cutting his way to the back of the room.

Frank Deacon burst in. Gun drawn and held out straight, grasped between his hands. *Two minutes too late to be of any use.*

Emory would bet anything that those two hands trembled.

Sheriff Hammond's eyes narrowed at his entrance, but he didn't skip a beat.

"Deputy, go help the sheriff work his way from the back to the front." Then to the crowd. "None of you move unless you are told to do so. We're searching for guns without conceal carry permits, illegal substances, and anything else that we don't entirely welcome in this county. Next person that moves when they aren't supposed to, I'll have the brand inspector shoot. This time, no warning shots. Understand?"

"Want me to pat people down?" She asked in a low voice.

"No. I want you to cover our men."

The two deputies, Sheriff Hammond and the unknown sheriff worked their way through the eight people inside of the bar. Four were cuffed, the others were let go after a bit of jostling.

Dirge, the bartender, the guy with the concealed weapon and the gorilla guy from the door were all cuffed.

"Business is closed for today," the sheriff said. "Anyone here know how to lock up?"

"The keys are under the counter there," the bartender growled. "If you've busted the back door in, I'm gonna sue."

"Yeah, right," Sheriff Hammond said. "Sue away."

"Frank, you secure the back door. Dustin, you take the squad car, and we'll load these two in the back. The suing shithead bartender can ride behind Sheriff Marcuson and I'll drive the gun-toting knucklehead. Everyone out. Now."

BACK INSIDE THE brand inspector pickup, Emory called Terry back. "It's done, and four people are being hauled in. One of them is Dirge."

"What in the HELL are you all doing up there?" he demanded, genuinely angry.

She frowned. "Working. You're the one that sent me out here, don't forget."

"Shit. I'm not going to forget, but dang it—all I envisioned you doing involved getting the records cleaned up out there and the operation running straight. It did NOT involve hanged men, biker bars, sting operations or anything of the sort. It concerned LIVESTOCK. Do you get that?"

Dave mumbled in the background, likely taking her part on one of the finer points.

Terry turned to respond to him. "Yeah, Dave. I know it said horse thief…"

She bit back a smile at the two men and their bickering.

Terry's voice came back into her ear, exasperated and

clear. "OK, so you done good. But knock it off," he spluttered, and the line went dead.

Yep. He was mad all right.

But he sent her to do a job, and she did it. And did it well.

***

BACK IN THE county jail with everyone booked and processed, the sheriff separated Dirge from the others. Held over in a separate holding room away from the other arrests, she figured that didn't improve his mood any.

Emory waited in the non-descript reception room with the green leatherette chairs and languishing rubber plant until called.

When the summons came, she followed Dustin back to one of the holding rooms where Dirge waited. Dirge —handcuffed and irritated—oozed defiance. Seated in front of the sheriff, he glared at her when she passed through the door.

Based upon his newfound opinion of her, she felt that she had to say something.

She owed him.

"Dirge, the sheriff had to arrest you so that it appears like you're not any part of this."

He scowled. "I'm not."

Emory sat down. "Look. Dirge. Show the sheriff your dagger tattoo."

He shifted in his seat and stuck out his legs. Stared at the ceiling, eyes capturing nothing in particular.

The sheriff wasn't amused, but then again, neither was Dirge.

Emory tried one more time. For everyone's sake. "I

explained to the sheriff our past history, and how you saved me. Actually, I'm trying to do you a favor here. No doubt you read about the young man hanged from a ranch gate. You turned up about the exact same time. He died from a bad dose of drugs. He has a partially completed tattoo surprisingly similar to your dagger..."

"And this is your one shot to speak before this goes any further," the sheriff interjected.

Dirge eyed him. "Fine. Roll up my sleeve, I don't care. It ain't going to tell you anything."

"It won't, but you might," Emory countered. "Let's start with why you are out here. *Really* out here."

"No comment."

"How about you look at pictures and help us at least identify the victim. You wouldn't want a Territorial Son buried as a *John Doe*, would you?"

Dirge sprawled out a bit further.

The sheriff pulled out a couple of pictures of the man's face, and the dagger tattoo. "Do you recognize him."

Emory could tell that Dirge didn't want to help in the slightest, but that old human compulsion to stare death in the face rose within him. Despite his intentions, his eyes flickered over the photo.

A change registered on his face and in his eyes. He recognized him all right.

"What happened there?" he asked at length.

"We'll tell you," the sheriff countered, "after you give us a name."

"I ain't going to tell you."

"That's a pretty piss-poor way to treat a brother and all. Don't you lot have a vow of loyalty or some such oath that you take? Well, I'll go ahead and tell you. Strung up from a hangman's noose for the entire world to see, your brother was displayed for all of the world to see. How do you suppose that makes your *club* appear? I'll tell you. Weak. It makes *all of you* all appear *weak and pathetic*. Anything but badass."

That hit a nerve. He thought about the sheriff's words —not Emory's. She could tell that much, too.

"Spencer Hyatt, I think. Don't know for certain. He was a prospect."

"Thanks, Dirge," Emory said, but he just glared in her direction.

Any friendly bond they once shared had shattered with the arrest.

The sheriff took the lead. "What are you out here for? Your rap sheet ain't that long that we can't release you. Seems to me that you'd be doing better on your...club... business out free, rather than locked up and behind bars."

"What do you want to know?" He aimed the question at the sheriff—pointedly not toward Emory.

"What are you out here for? The real reason." The sheriff sat forward.

"We heard of a batch of bad fentanyl. Laced. We didn't distribute it. Wanted to find out where it's coming from. Told that shithead to stay away from the lot of it. Deaths drive away business."

"Did you know about the hanging?" Emory asked.

She thought he wouldn't answer but he did. Giving her the stink-eye while he did so. "No. Not until word circulated and he didn't make contact as agreed."

"Where'd the prospect come from?" Emory leaned forward, intent on the answer.

"How the hell should I know? They just come."

"Right, and you don't check them out. Must be pretty easy to get infiltrated that way." The sheriff laughed.

Dirge glared. Said nothing.

"Let's take you back and get you booked," the sheriff said, rising.

"He's from Sterling. He worked out here for a while, so we figured that he'd be able to handle the assignment. Apparently not. Since I've told you something you needed, tell me one thing. Where's his horse?"

"Horse?" Emory repeated, not understanding.

"Motorcycle. Bike. Hog."

Her eyes darted over to the sheriff for permission. "No idea. Any idea who killed him?"

Dirge wagged his head. "You lot just told me the drugs did."

"Where'd he *get* the drugs?" Emory pressed.

"How the hell should I know?"

The sheriff cleared his throat before the line of questioning descended into a squabble. "What are you out here for?"

"The prospect didn't report in as agreed. Like I said. I came out searching for him."

"Not to mention he got strung up like an advertisement or a warning. Where did he work before?" The sheriff eyed him sharp.

Dirge mouthed off. "You'd have to ask him."

Sheriff Hammond leaned forward, tired of the banter. "We're asking you."

Something in Hammond's tone reached Dirge's sense of self-preservation. "Don't know. Some ranch. He claimed he used to be a bull rider—before he broke his leg. Guess that finished it for him. Probably he spent his days loading hay and mucking out stalls. Isn't that how washed-up bull riders end?"

Maybe.

Something in the silence got to Dirge. "Said he was sick of cattle," he added.

"And club life appeared better," Emory challenged.

He just stared at her in response.

The sheriff cleared his throat. "I'll take it from here."

TROUBLE A-PLENTY

EMORY HAD CROSSED A LINE WITH DIRGE, PROVING THAT once and for all, they were on opposite sides of the law. Never should the two meet. But they had met, and she owed him. *Still* owed him, in fact. But that debt reduced with each snide comment and dagger-look cast in her direction.

The outlaw biker obviously now had an understandable and genuine problem with her and, much to her surprise, his opinion hurt. She knew that she'd acted the part of an informant, a role that never could sit well with any Cross. Certainly, her part in his arrest would never be anything she wanted to go around admitting.

But she had a job to do, plain and simple. And her actions were the only way she knew to gain a shot at identifying the victim. *Spencer Hyatt. Former bull rider.*

Spencer Hyatt who had worked somewhere within the area.

And her favorite rancher, Myra Brandt claimed to have recently fired someone.

Those pieces fell into place, nice and easy.

Even though she had just pulled away from his office half an hour earlier, she called the sheriff. "You still sitting with Dirge?"

"We released him already. The scumbag bartender, too. The only two we could keep were that big hulking slimeball and the none-too-bright concealed weapon carrier. They get to spend at least tonight in jail, and then we'll see what the judge says. One of them skipped out on parole. Go figure. My guess is that bar will be opened back up for business any time now."

She sighed. "Guess I'm not on Dirge's Christmas card list any longer."

"Who cares? Oh, wait a second. You two weren't an item, were you?"

She practically choked. "Oh man. No way. My dad would kick the shit out of him."

A chuckle from the other end. "Just checking. Anyhow, do you have a reason for calling beyond the Christmas cards you'll be missing?"

"Very funny. You know, Myra Brandt mentioned that she, and I quote, "canned" a ranch hand. Did you ever hear of any ranch hands looking for work?"

"No, but then again, I likely wouldn't."

"She hired two part-timers to replace him, she told me. You also said that her land backs up against the druggie outhouse we scouted. Have the results come back from those tests?"

"No. Not yet."

"You see where I'm headed with all of this."

"I sure do." Silence. "Whatever happened to those transportation papers Myra needed?"

It seemed an odd question coming from the sheriff.

"Nothing," Emory replied. "I can't do them. I meant to go check to see if those horses returned from the camping expedition—which I'm sure they didn't by the way— but then all of this came along."

"You sure you can't do the papers?"

He acted like a dog with a bone.

"Yeah, I'm sure." She wondered why he persisted, going against brand inspector protocol. "The group that was supposed to provide them to her went belly up. I checked that horse out...and it has no freeze brand or hot brand. Chances are, it came out of the Sand Wash, which is illegal as hell."

"Run it by your bosses in *GREELEY*, but I have a plan. Say, if you aren't doing anything in particular, why don't you come back here, and we'll call them together?"

"Am I in trouble?"

"No—not from my end. But it might help if we all spoke to get on the same page. Now, are you coming or not?"

"On my way," she replied.

Emory pulled a u-turn, knowing that maneuver landed the next closest thing to illegal as well, but figured it justifiable since she travelled on official business. She pulled up, hopped out, went straight through the front door, and didn't even bother to break her stride to deal with Frank Deacon.

"Hey! You just can't..."

But she could. And she did.

The open office door allowed their voices to trail out. It came as no surprise to find the coroner parked in the chair. Those two were a strange, but effective, alliance.

"Heard I missed some excitement," the coroner said eyes travelling over to her.

"I probably still stink like the booze he made me drink."

The men exchanged concerned glances.

"Don't worry, I don't think it was laced." That additional detail made the pair of them go more bug-eyed still.

"Let's call your boss," Joe said.

"How about the sale barn number, because that way we might get Dave, too. He's pretty good at brand inspector trivia."

"Is there such a thing?" Greg asked, incredulous eyes wide open.

She couldn't resist. "Of course. We play it all the time."

More blank stares. "Joking..." she said, locating the number, and switching it on to speaker.

"Brand inspectors, Greeley sale barn." The voice belonged to Dave.

"Hey Dave! Is Terry around?"

"What, I'm not good enough for you anymore? Yeah, he's here."

"I've got you both on speaker phone. I'm calling from the Vermillion Sheriff's Office. Terry Overholzer and Dave Worrell, meet the sheriff Joe Hammond, and the Coroner, Greg Foster."

The men exchanged stiff, long-distance greetings.

"I don't know what you know," the sheriff began, "but we've had some trouble out this way. One woman needs transportation papers to Utah, and Emory can't give them to her because she doesn't have any documentation proving her ownership."

"Fair enough," Terry hesitated, uncertain as to his point.

Emory didn't know the point he aimed at either, so sat there, silent.

"I asked her if there is a way around that, and she said no."

"She's right." Terry replied, chair squeaking as he shifted.

The sheriff cleared his throat. "What if I were to tell you that there is a high likelihood that the woman stole that mustang off of BLM land."

"I'd make that a *hell no*, in that case," Dave commented in the background.

"Did you hear about the hanging here?" Joe persisted.

"The entire state heard about the hanging," Terry's voice betrayed his growing impatience.

Emory piped up. "Dirge knew the guy's name. Spencer Hyatt. There's a chance he might have worked for the woman who wants to make the shipment. And I spoke to Ray Thompson. I found him at the Rusty Spur, just like you said."

"And?"

This time the coroner spoke up. "This is Greg. He didn't die by hanging, he died by a drug overdose. Word has it that Myra's become a bit unhinged about a bad sale to a kill-buyer that maybe this guy recommended. Joe— did you find any information on him?"

"In the ten minutes I've had since my office cleared out? Yeah, I ran his name through the database. Seems he has a DUI prior, in Nebraska. Also seems that he worked for one Larry S. Dewright, a known kill buyer. Anything more will take more time and additional tracking."

Frankly, since Emory didn't know what Joe angled at, she continued to wait, unspeaking.

The sheriff continued. "I thought that if we got Ray to sign a document stating that he worked at the adoption, then the BLM could provide a record for the mustang…"

Emory cut him off. "But I've been told the mustang

hasn't been freeze branded, so that can't be on the up and up."

"It's not," Joe agreed. "If we manage to present her with something that she thinks means she can ship, and which by extension allows her to assume that we don't suspect her of any illegal doing—"

Emory grew impatient. "I told you last night. The horses were gone yesterday, but old Mr. Crawford claims he saw those horses being transported in the direction of Utah."

The sheriff leveled his gaze at her. "He also said he saw Myra driving."

"Yeah," Emory groaned. He had indeed.

"Why not get Josh Tucker involved? I'm not sure I understand what we can do for you from over here." Terry inserted, although Emory felt pretty certain that he only tested the waters.

The sheriff, although seated, had taken on something of a bird-dog posture. "I'm calling over there because Emory trusts you. Now this goes no further than this office…"

"I promise," Emory sighed.

"We've got concerns about Josh Tucker and the distribution of drugs."

"*What?*" Emory gasped.

"What in the hell do you think he's doing down with those pipeline people? We're pretty certain that there a link and a conduit for the drugs getting into the high school. Organized crime is obviously behind drugs somewhere along the line, but that's someone else's problem and not mine. We'll handle what we can locally."

They could all hear Terry groan a little before he spoke, words slow and deliberate. "So, you think that if we doctor these papers so that they read like the transport of the two horses can go ahead, she will let her guard down. And you do what precisely?"

"Yeah," Joe said. "That's the part that I haven't quite worked out yet. But none of it will work out at all, if she can't ship. Then she'll just transport the horses over state lines in the dark of night, both horses will be gone, and we'll have lost this chance to learn something more."

"Like they already have, in all likelihood," Emory dug up the sore subject, which they all seemed to have forgotten. "Do we even know that the hanged guy worked for her?"

"Not yet," the sheriff replied. "But Emory could go out there, saying she figured out a work around...and by the way, what was that hand's name? Kind of a tit-for-tat arrangement."

"Spencer Hyatt. And if the woman doesn't fall for it?" Terry challenged.

"Then she doesn't get the papers."

Emory leaned down toward the phone. "All of which would mean that she still has to have possession of those two horses—which I'm not sure that she does. Beyond that, I'm pretty sure that she needs the money those horse sales would bring."

Terry groaned again. "I'll need to tell the higherups, so they don't think we've all turned bat-shit crazy. Josh is being watched from our group as well. I'm not at liberty to say more, nor do I know many additional details. The thing is, that we really don't want to spook him. Not right yet. Deal?"

"Deal," everyone in the room replied.

Emory drove out to Myra's property, certain that she would find nothing good. She turned on the dirt ranch road and crested the hill—this time not coming to a stop to survey the outfit below, but to try to approach in an air of friendly and open helpfulness. A friendly helpfulness that she didn't necessarily feel.

She pulled up into the yard, hopped out and noted the corral—as empty as expected.

This time, Myra opened the house door and glared out, displeased.

"Over-reach," she said by way of a greeting.

Emory inhaled and let her breath slowly release. "I spoke to my boss in Greeley, and he has an idea that should work in your case."

"My case?"

"The undocumented mustang. Everyone has been pulling out the stops, and we located Ray Thompson."

Clear relief poured from the woman, and she took a few steps forward, no longer hostile.

One hell of a turnaround act, from what Emory could tell. She wondered where the horses were at that precise moment.

"*Ray Thompson.* Josh Tucker treated him very poorly and drove him out," she said. "It is a pitiful thing to do to a man his age and with his experience."

Now Emory started to feel misgivings.

Stop it, she told herself.

"Several brand inspectors tried to locate the records from that outfit where you acquired Oliver. Upon talking to the BLM, you would have to file for missing papers for $40, and they would pronounce that the adoption "took" successfully."

"They'd do that?"

The woman eyed her without a trace of malice or

dishonesty from what Emory could tell. And that threw her off kilter even further.

"Yes, with Ray's assurance that he presided over the sale. He'll claim misfiled paperwork or pure clerical oversight. It ought to work."

That caught the woman. Clearly torn between what she wanted and what she'd told Emory, she balked. "But I told you. Josh Tucker worked the sale."

"Yeah," Emory said, uncertain what to say next.

Myra frowned. "I don't understand."

"Neither do I, exactly," Emory answered in all honesty. "There's bad blood between Ray and Josh. Ray is working with my boss out of Greeley to get this done."

"You mean that *you* helped me?" The woman held her head like a horse ready to rear.

Emory sniffed. "To a point. They sent me back out here to talk to you, although it hasn't been going well."

The woman had the good graces to appear ashamed.

"Where are the horses now? Still out camping?"

At that, the woman colored and cleared her throat. Her eyes scanned the landscape behind Emory.

"They're back in the far pasture."

"They are?" Unbidden, the words burst from Emory.

"Yeah," the woman said, mournful deep down. "I couldn't do it."

"Do what, Myra?"

"Sell to a questionable buyer. Oh, I thought about it, all right. But one of the men called me and said he had a bad feeling. Turns out I couldn't do it in the end."

Emory blinked. If that didn't beat all.

"I'm going to pretend I didn't hear the transporting over 75 miles part—although I shouldn't. Can I see the horses?"

"Sure," Myra said without detectable artifice. "Do you want to drive, and I'll do the fences?"

"Sounds good," Emory said, climbing back into the truck and Myra jumping in the passenger side.

The rancher pointed down a winding track. "Head out that way. It's not far. You just can't see them from here."

A zinging along Emory's spinal cords warned that her actions made her vulnerable.

"I'd best call Ray," she stalled. "Wait, I don't have his number."

"I do," the woman announced and pulled out her phone.

Just great.

She punched in the number as Myra read out her, hoping like hell that he wasn't in the Rusty Spur. The phone rang. "Hello?"

"Ray? This is Emory Cross, the brand inspector. Say, I'm with Myra Brandt, and we're going out to inspect her two horses that are in one of her back pastures. She's agreeable to filing for missing papers with the BLM."

Dead silence. Myra frowned. "Ray?"

She turned to Emory. "He must have gone out of range."

"Here," Emory said holding out her hand. "Ray?"

"Is that you, Emory?"

"It is. If you have any questions, will you please call Terry Overholzer? Do you have his number?"

"Do you need me to come out there?" Ray asked, concerned, and completely baffled by the call and exchange.

"I don't know," Emory replied, in all honesty.

"Give me back the phone," Myra said. "Ray Thompson, I could kiss the ground you walk on! This one here ain't so bad if one overlooks how young she is."

She handed Emory back her phone.

"Ray?"

"I'll make a few calls. Call you back in a few minutes. Ask Myra if there's cell coverage back there."

"Will calls make it through in your back pasture? Ray wants to know."

"No," she replied. "But it won't take any time at all to go get them. You can check them out, and we can meet him back at the house if that's OK."

"You hear that Ray?" Emory called out.

A small voice came through the phone's speaker. "I'm on it," he replied.

RIDING SHOTGUN

THE WOMAN DIDN'T APPEAR TO BE CARRYING A GUN. IN fact, even if she carried, she acted as happy as hell.

They turned round one bend, came to a fence, and Myra hopped out to open it. As Emory pulled through, she grabbed the Smith and Wesson from the glove compartment and stuck it down in the pocket on the door—out of sight.

Just in case.

Myra hopped back in, not noticing a thing. Another bend in the meandering track, and another gate. Again, Myra hopped out, opened it, and closed the gate behind them once Emory passed through.

The track led to an open meadow, and sure enough. There, the same two horses she had seen before grazed on the tender shoots springing forth. One blood bay and one paint.

Despite herself, Emory smiled. Those two horses, at the moment, hadn't a care in the world. They didn't know that they'd likely had a close brush with death.

"A couple of things," Emory began.

She received the long side-eye from the rancher, although not entirely hostile.

"Oliver's a mustang, isn't he?" Emory continued in a calm voice, finding that she gripped the steering wheel that much harder, "and he's missing the BLM markings. You know that, right?"

"Yes, I do," Myra made no bones about it.

"In that case, how do you want to explain that omission?"

"Just a bad day all around at the sale, and another ball got dropped." Myra offered her version of events with conviction, although they both knew that the likelihood of that being the case was low.

"Fine," Emory agreed, although it bothered her and tickled at the back of her throat. "But here's the catch. We don't want *you* on the witness stand, we want that Nebraska outfit for a variety of reasons. To do that, we need the name of the hand you fired."

Myra jutted her chin out, eyes angry and a bit wild. "That's the price, huh?"

"That's the price," Emory replied. "And no questions asked about these two boys here."

"That shit-head's name was Spencer Hyatt, but I don't even know if that's his real name. Canned his ass, like I said before."

Past tense used for part of the sentence threw a flag right there. "Was?"

"Was what?" Myra still scowled.

"His name. You used the past tense."

"Nothing. Once they leave my employment, I no longer care."

There rang a flat note in Myra's voice that Emory caught. Had she guessed that Spencer and the hanged horse thief were one and the same?

Emory didn't press any further, although she easily could have. But she would stick to the agreed plan. "I guess you don't need to bring them in unless you want to. Ray sounded like he'd be the one signing off. Actually, I'm not sure what the next steps are either."

Emory pulled out her phone. "You're right, no reception."

"I'll bring them in. It's about that time anyhow, not that they'll be all that hungry. You can wait for me in the yard, and you can leave the gates open, as I'll be coming right behind you. Their halters are waiting on that post."

And so they were. A red and a black halter. Waiting for the two horses.

"Sounds like a plan," Emory replied.

BACK IN THE RANCH YARD, Emory made a quick call to the sheriff. "It's working. Her former hand is our guy, Spencer Hyatt. Did Ray call you?"

"Terry did, after Ray called him." His voice came across bothered.

"Now what?"

The sheriff cleared his throat. "Ray's already headed out there to sign off on the transportation papers."

"She's not transporting anymore," Emory countered. "All we're doing now, is making it so that the BLM will issue replacement papers."

She paused. "What do we do about the hanged guy?"

"Ray's actually going to handle that one. To a degree."

That made no sense to Emory. "He is?"

"He is," Joe Hammond replied. "And the less you know, the better."

"Here comes Myra now, so I need to hang up. When can we expect Ray?"

"Ten minutes, give or take," Hammond replied.

"Fine," Emory said, clicking off.

She called out to Myra, all nice and friendly. "Ray's on his way. He'll probably be here in about ten minutes or so."

"I'll put these guys in the round pen then, to make it all easier. I sure am glad that Ray's making a comeback," she said with a smile that almost made Emory forget that she just might be the enemy.

Ray drove up shortly thereafter, as planned.

"You have the papers to sign?" He shot over to Emory before offering the rancher a smile. "Good to see you again, Myra."

The woman beamed approval. *For him.* "Well, look who's back in the saddle. Glad to see you, Ray."

"I heard you need an affidavit of a sort."

"Yeah, but like I told Emory…"

The woman's use of her name startled her—Emory shocked that Myra even recalled her name at all. The rancher, for her part, didn't notice Emory's reaction, but kept on talking to Ray.

"Josh Tucker officiated. It wasn't you."

"I ain't surprised at that," Ray grumbled.

Emory handed Ray the BLM papers that she had printed, and he wrote his explanation in and signed. He gave the paper over to Myra with a few words of advice. "I'd take a copy of that before you send it in. Just to be on the safe side."

She nodded, clearly relieved at how everything turned out. "I think I'll drive it in to town as well. What else do you need from me?"

Man, Emory thought, *that opened up a whole can of*

worms right there. "Nothing that I am aware of," Emory replied. "Ray?"

He shrugged. "Nothing on my end."

"That's it for me today," Emory claimed. "It's been a long one. I'll see you later, Myra."

"I'll follow you out," Ray replied.

Myra smiled and even waved, watching the brand inspectors pull out, affidavit in hand.

BACK UP AT the county road, both brand inspectors pulled over for a brief consultation. Emory climbed out of her truck for what felt like the hundredth time that day.

"I almost feel bad," Emory admitted as she reached his window.

"Yeah," Ray said. "But I've seen worse. I bet she'll stick to the rules from here on out. Anyhow, I'm headed into town."

"The Rusty Spur?"

He thought about it. "No. I'm going to go to the grocery, buy some food and cook myself dinner. Maybe I'll go for an after-dinner drink. I want to talk to her boys if they're in there. On a neutral ground where they might talk a little freer."

She nodded, halfway towards approving. "Don't drink on an empty stomach is what I've always heard."

"Hell, that would kill the buzz," he teased. "You want to come over for dinner?"

"Actually, I would like that, but not tonight. I need to go back to the sheriff and see what the next steps are. Then I'll likely go to the grocery store and get a microwave dinner. Then, with luck, I'll head out and ride my horse. There's an idea. Exercise Kai."

He laughed, saluted her, and drove off.

She walked back to her truck smiling.

And discounted the drone of an approaching motorcycle. In fact, occupied with the ins and outs of Myra's transactions, she never even gave it a thought.

Starting up the engine, she checked the road behind her as she pulled out. Clear.

She made it about a half mile down the road, the motorcycle growing louder. In the rear-view mirror, she saw him coming.

He approached closer and closer, gaining on her.

She kept watching, and decided she could either speed up or slow down—but that chopper travelled fast —poised to overtake her.

The body composition the mirror reflected sure looked like Dirge. In fact, it all likelihood, it *was* Dirge.

She slowed.

The chopper overtook her—pulling out into the on-coming road alongside.

Dirge all right.

He swung right in front of her in a dangerous and aggressive maneuver. Far too close for comfort and all but clipping the truck's front fender.

He pulled over to the side of the road, dust and rocks churning up as he came to an abrupt stop.

She pulled up behind him and jumped out, nerves jangling.

"What in the hell do you call that?" she yelled.

He dismounted in nothing flat, angry as well. Pulling himself up to his full height—bigger and bulkier than she ever noticed before.

A voice inside of her warned that she stood on dangerous ground.

"I trusted you enough to stop," He said it like it pained him.

"I could easily have hit you and killed you."

"You're right," he said, taking a few steps closer. "I shouldn't have trusted you. Shouldn't have trusted you at all."

His eyes narrowed, mean.

A cold whisper brushed against the back of her neck. She had never considered that she might need to protect herself against Dirge.

"I am sorry about you getting arrested, and I mean it. I'll own that. It was my fault."

"You're meddling in things you oughtn't."

"HORSE THIEF," she spoke the words in a half-shout. "I had to figure out whether it is true or not."

"And I'll bet," he said stepping even closer, "that you still don't have it figured out."

At this point, she could either take a half step back or hold her ground. She didn't move.

She could *smell* him. "The problem you have on your hands is bigger than what I've got on mine."

"You sure about that?"

"You've let it become known that there is a link between the Territorials and the fentanyl."

She became aware of the slow rumbling of a heavy truck behind them, but she wouldn't turn to look, embarking upon an important point.

"The sheriff let you go. There's nothing connecting you to any of it. Just that you were looking for a missing prospect. Come on, Dirge…"

Looming closer, he tried to intimidate her, and it worked. There was something in his eyes…

"Don't you touch me," she growled.

He didn't care. He grabbed her arm and squeezed it hard just to prove his strength—that he was the stronger of the two. Emory, reluctantly, crumpled down to kneeling from the pain inflicted, her arm locked in his vicelike grip.

She would not plead, even if he broke her arm.

"Don't you think you control me bitch, because you don't," he snarled.

The truck rumbled up to a stop behind them. Dirge's head turned and Emory shot a glance over her shoulder in response.

A large blue county road crew truck. And out jumped Jimmy Hudspeth wielding a shovel as a weapon.

"You let go of her now before I bash your head in," he threatened.

Dirge's laugh rumbled low and deadly, and he let go of her arm.

From her kneeling position, Emory could see his arm move toward an interior pocket. Despite the pain, she grabbed his ankle and pulled as hard as she could, knocking him off balance. He fell to the gravel, hard and with bones crunching.

Jimmy rushed over, holding the shovel above his head like he was going to bash in a rattlesnake.

"Jimmy, wait!" Emory's voice came out urgent, as she climbed to her feet, diving over to the Chevy and retrieving the Smith and Wesson. Gun cocked and pointed at Dirge, she approached.

"Hands away from your jacket, and you KNOW I'll shoot." His hands were held wide, away from his body.

"Jimmy, I'll cover you, but reach into his interior pockets and see what you find. Set the shovel down out of his reach."

He did as she asked, setting the shovel well away from Dirge. He reached into the biker's leather jacket and pulled out a gun.

"Back away from him, Jimmy," she said. "Pick up your shovel and come stand over by me."

"Is this your new boyfriend?" Dirge yelled from the ground. "A road grunt?"

"County maintenance," Jimmy replied.

Emory ignored the pair of them. "Request law enforcement backup," she said into the radio.

Josh Tucker came online. "Emory?"

"Need the sheriff out on Highway 22 by the Morrisette's place. Over."

"Stay on the line, over." Josh placed the call through.

She could hear him talking to the sheriff's department.

"They're on their way. I'd come out to help you if I could, but I'm about a hundred miles away…"

The sirens approached, Dirge still laying on the ground, Jimmy wielding the shovel, and her pointing a weapon.

One car passed the scene—fours eyes widened as they realized the severity of what they witnessed. Instead of stopping, they lead-footed once they truly understood the implications.

Emory's cell rang.

"We're on our way," Joe Hammond said.

"Good," Emory clasped her arm, realizing just how much it hurt. She would have one whale of a bruise, but if the sheriff didn't come soon, things could still turn a whole lot uglier.

ROUGH DAY ALL AROUND

Sheriff Hammond's truck flew down the road, arriving one minute after the call.

"Set the gun on the hood of my truck, please," she instructed Jimmy. "Before the sheriff gets here."

The sheriff pulled up, skidding. Followed by one of the deputies. Gun drawn, they both emerged from their trucks, barrels pointed at Dirge who remained on the ground like an upside-down tortoise.

"We've got his gun here, but didn't pat him down," Emory said, still holding her weapon and nodding at the gun on the hood of the car.

"On your knees," the sheriff barked to the biker.

"Need to roll over to do that," Dirge called back.

"Make it slow. There's three guns trained on you."

Dirge slowly rolled to his side, pushed himself part of the way into an all-fours position, kneeling in the dirt along the side of the road.

"Hands on your head." The sheriff's voice rang out.

When Dirge finally pulled himself up to kneeling with both hands atop his head, he might have not been happy with the sheriff, but he glared furious at Emory—his anger burning for all to see.

Hostility directed squarely at her, and only her.

"Cuff him," the sheriff directed Frank, who fastened one cuff on the first of Dirge's wrists, pulling his arm down behind his back before cuffing the other wrist.

"You have the right to remain silent. Anything you say can and will be used against you in a court of law…"

DIRGE, his bulk stuffed in the back of a patrol car, stared straight ahead, and no longer at Emory. The sheriff tipped his hat at both her and Jimmy, but he mainly eyed the young brand inspector.

"Do you know what this is about?"

"He's plenty pissed off about getting hauled in is what this amounts to," she replied. "I know you've got your hands full right now, but we're narrowing in on the other matter. Most likely. Ray's got an idea that he's following up on."

"Fine," the sheriff answered. "I trust him, do you?"

"I do. But then again, I trusted Dirge, as well."

The sheriff smirked. "Yeah. Most people would have warned you against that one."

Jimmy and Emory stood shoulder to shoulder and watched the sheriff drive off.

"I owe you a dinner," she said.

"How's your arm?"

"Bruised pretty good. But that doesn't mean I can't use a knife and fork. Are you free tonight? I sure could use a margarita. A strong one."

"That would be the top shelf," he replied. He side-eyed her.

"Meet you over there?" She asked. "And this time, I'm paying."

"After all of this, this time, I think I'll let you," Jimmy replied. "I actually thought he might really hurt you, bad."

MIDWAY THROUGH THEIR MEAL, Emory's cell rang. She pulled it out and recognized the number.

"It's Ray Thompson," she told Jimmy, "and I had better take it, considering everything that's going on. I'm sorry."

Then into the phone. "Hello Ray. Where are you?"

"Outside of the Rusty Spur for my evening constitutional. You'd better come over. Myra Brandt's ranch hands are inside, and they seem to be in a talking mood. Especially if you care to buy them a drink."

"I'm finishing up dinner—you would not believe it if I told you all that's happened since I saw you last. Buy them a round to keep them occupied, and I'll pay you back when I get there."

"Well, hurry if you can—but I'll get out of them what I can in the meantime."

Emory clicked off, thinking about this newest wrinkle. Jimmy eyed her as he finished his plate. "More trouble?"

"It's probably what you think I'm made of about this point, but maybe."

He nodded. "There seems to be a lot that goes with being a brand inspector."

"It's not like this usually," she said. "I hate to do this and cut the evening short, but I need to pay the bill and go over to the Rusty Spur."

"Do you want me to come along for back up?"

It wasn't the worst offer that she'd had. "Do you know Myra Brandt or anyone that works for her, or that ever has?"

"That crazy horse lady? No. I don't know her or anyone that's worked for her."

That caught her. "Why did you call her a crazy horse lady then?"

"I've heard that she breaks wild horses. You'd have to be plumb crazy to do that—and everyone calls her a crazy horse lady that's lived around here for any time at all. Something happened along the way, but I don't know the details."

He searched his memory and came up empty. "But I know that she took it real bad."

Emory signaled for the check. "What else have you heard?"

"Nothing." He shook his head, blue eyes wide. "I'll go over to Dusty Mike's with you, if you want."

The waitress came with the bill. "Here, it's mine," she told her, glancing at the total. She pulled money out of her wallet. "Keep the change."

"Is everything all right?" The waitress looked worried by Emory's abrupt pending departure.

"Everything's fine. I just need to catch some people before they leave. Jimmy, I'll see you later. It's just that this is kind of official business."

"I understand," he droned, then explained to the waitress, "She's a brand inspector. A temporary one for out here."

The woman nodded. "You sure seem to take your job seriously."

"Yeah, I do," Emory called over her shoulder with a smile, as she hurried out the door.

THE DARK INTERIOR of the Rusty Spur matched the night outside, and it was busier than she'd seen it the other two times she'd entered. It only took about a second to locate Ray sitting with Myra's ranch hands.

They looked rough around the edges, with shaggy hair and dirty clothes. They'd obviously come straight from work.

Dusty Mike, working behind the bar, raised his hand in greeting when he saw her.

Looking over at the men and making sure that they didn't notice her—she pointed to them quickly.

She sidled up to the bar for a drink. "Diet Coke, please," she said in a low voice. "But can you make it look like booze? Or anything. Just no alcohol."

If Mike was surprised by her order and request, he didn't miss a beat. "How about club soda and cranberry juice with a lime?"

"Much obliged," she said glancing over at the table where the three of them sat. "I think I'm picking up that tab as well."

"They're paying as they go," Mike said. "And I'll bet I know what you're in here for."

She tilted her head. "We'll see. How much do I owe you, then?"

"It's on the house," he replied.

EMORY APPROACHED the table with caution, since Ray and the two younger men seemed locked in deep conversation. They also came across as drunk or verging right at that door—especially the two younger men.

"Hi there," Emory began, sizing them all up while pretending to be friendly. "I don't think we've met before. My name's Emory, and I work with Ray. Well, part of the time."

Ray nodded. "I was telling these two that we were just out at Myra's today, but we didn't have the pleasure of seeing them. Take a seat, that is, unless you're meeting someone."

Emory eyed them all and sat down in the empty chair at the table. "I'm not meeting anyone," she said. "Myra claimed you both were out camping or trail riding the other day. Wasn't it cold?"

"Forget about that," Ray interrupted. "We were talking about tampering with corpses."

"Excuse me?" Emory did her best not to appear shocked, but likely failed. She had to hand it to Ray—if that indeed was the topic.

The seemingly youngest man also appeared the drunkest. "Man, I don't want to go back into Cañon," he slurred, then her presence finally registered with him. "I'm Jack. What'd you say your name was?"

"Emory. What about corpses?"

The slightly older ranch hand, stared at Emory flat out to the point it was almost disconcerting.

"I was just telling them how tampering with a corpse is only a misdemeanor," Ray explained to her, then to the others, "Emory can help."

That was news to her, but she did her best not to let on.

However, the older one piped up, believing Ray's lie. "He'd been dead for at least a day when Myra found him holed up in one of her outbuildings. Guess he came back there because he didn't have any other place to go. He had a spike in his arm."

"A spike?"

"Needle," the younger one helped. "Shootin' up drugs."

Emory checked with Ray, who nodded. That part of the story aligned with what she knew. *Spencer died from drugs. Tainted drugs.*

"So, you two are the ones that strung him up?" She felt her eyes narrow. "Why would you do a thing like that?"

"Yeah," the younger one whined. "She paid us two hundred dollars each."

Emory shook her head. "But why?"

The older one took over. "You'd have to ask her, but then there go our jobs."

Hell, Emory figured. If they were on probation, which they most likely were, there went their *freedom*. But at that moment, either she or Ray really ought to call the sheriff. "What's the story with the five horses Myra sold to the Nebraska broker?"

"Shipped 'em off for dog food, I guess. At least, that's what Myra said," the older one offered, still staring at Emory. "That dude that was there before us brokered that deal."

"Did he?" Emory did her best not to appear shocked. She also didn't understand why the two young men were so forthcoming with sordid details, and to strangers no less.

Chalk one up for booze.

"Do you know his name?"

"Don't know and don't care," the older one said. "My name is Rick Briscoe and I'm single."

Great.

"None of this makes sense," Emory told them, straight out. "Why put the horse thief note on him?"

The younger one wagged his head. "She said that horse thieves got strung up in them olden days. That he deprived her of her horses, but that didn't make no sense to me, because she got paid."

Well. Myra's positioning on the matter made plenty of sense to Emory.

"Let me buy you all a drink," Emory said, rising to her feet. "You've had a rough time."

Shit.

"Let's have a round of tequila shots," the youngest one suggested, perking up at the notion.

"I'll just have a light beer," Ray said.

"And I'll have a whiskey shot," The older one added, still leering. "Thank you," he at least added.

Emory scooted up to the bar, straight to Dusty Mike. "One tequila shot, one light beer and one whiskey shot. Then please call the sheriff. Tell him that I requested it and he'll need transportation for two."

A few moments later, just as the shots were going down, the sheriff and his deputies arrived. Lights flashing, they burst in through the door.

"NO ONE MOVE," Dustin Weaver yelled, leading the bust.

Emory noted that first, figuring the Sheriff eyed him for promotion.

Behind Dustin, Joe Hammond followed in on his heels. "Mike, turn on the overhead lights!"

The lights flipped on, partially blinding everyone.

Myra's two ranch hands blinked, stunned and drunk, their reaction times proved slower than most of the other patrons. Dustin and the sheriff came directly over to their table. "Hands where we can see them."

"Son of a bitch!" The younger one screamed at everyone and to no one in particular.

The jukebox music continued to play, twanging a happy song completely out of place. Dusty Mike killed it, and the bar descended into silence other than for a few shuffling feet.

Dustin cuffed the younger one, and the sheriff the older. Hands behind their backs, they were led out to the awaiting patrol car. Under his breath, the sheriff spoke to both brand inspectors.

"Wait here. I'll be back in a minute." Then he called out louder to the other patrons. "Sorry folks, it's all over now."

And down went the lights, and the jukebox turned back on.

Everyone sat there with their drinks, stunned.

Gradually conversations resumed, although no doubt the took different courses.

Emory brushed her hair back from her face and Ray took a sip of his beer. "This has been one hell of a day," she murmured.

The sheriff returned inside. "They're on their way to the jail. Hell, it's practically a full house." His eyes travelled from one brand inspector to the other. "Probably you two should come into the office. I need to take your statements, and Emory, I need to know if you want to press charges."

Ray's head snapped back.

"I had problems before I got here," Emory explained. "Problems with the biker."

"How's your arm?" the sheriff asked.

She cocked her head. "Still sore, but no. I don't want to press charges."

He sure didn't look like he approved of that decision. "We'll talk about it back in the station. Ray, if you've been drinking, let Emory drive."

THE TWO BRAND inspectors sat in the sheriff's office, waiting for him to join them.

Ray leaned forward, folded in half, forearms on his legs. "You want to fill me in?"

It had been a terribly long day.

"After we parted on the road, Dirge the biker rode up. I was already moving, and he practically clipped my truck. He's mad at me and grabbed my arm."

She rolled up her sleeve and showed him the coloring bruise, marks already visible.

A nerve in the older brand inspectors neck throbbed.

The sheriff walked in at that same moment; eyes glued on the forming contusion. "Like I asked before, do you want to press charges? Assault comes to mind, and we can probably toss in a few others for good measure. Deserved, too."

An angry flush rose up along Ray's neck and he pressed his lips into a thin line.

"I'm not going to press charges." Emory insisted, adamant.

Ray's exhale at that news practically exploded. "Why in the hell not?"

His vehemence took Emory by surprise. "Because I owed him...but I don't anymore. Not after this."

"You're kidding," Hammond spluttered.

"I am not," she replied.

"Well, I'm keeping him in overnight. You'll have a better chance to think about it. Now, moving on to the other two. I can't have you in at their questioning, and lawyers will be appointed for them. What did you get?"

"Ray got the most of it," Emory replied.

"They told me that they never knew Spencer Hyatt

personally prior to his death, but that apparently Myra found him in one of her out buildings, already dead and with a needle in his arm. Myra paid them two hundred dollars each to hoist the corpse in a hangman's noose. He was the one that brokered the Nebraska deal with the five horses that were presumably killed."

"That's it?" Sheriff Hammond asked.

"That's all they told me," Ray replied, "but isn't that enough?"

"Emory?"

"Like Ray said. Nothing more. But it's kind of under-standable, really."

"Come again?"

"She was mad. Livid, even. As far as she is concerned, Hyatt was a horse thief, and she wanted everyone to know." Emory shrugged. "In a way, she has my sympathy. She didn't kill him. He did that to himself. She just displayed him. What will she be charged with?"

The sheriff stretched out, somewhat incredulous. "Tampering with a corpse. Withholding information. Obstructing an investigation. I guess that about covers it."

That made one long list.

Emory cleared her throat, while everyone felt uneasy. They were all thinking the same thing.

Who would run Myra's ranch if everyone was stuck in jail?

BREAKING UP WITH THE PAST

THE NEXT MORNING AND NO PROBLEMS SOLVED, EMORY Cross's cell rang once, then twice—forcing her to turn down the radio as she drove along. At first, she figured it had to be the head brand inspector, but when she pulled the cell from her pocket, instead it read *RANCH*.

"Hello?" Sticking the phone between her ear and her neck, one hand remained on the wheel at all times. Still illegal, pretty much, but what the hell.

Her father cleared his throat and said nothing.

She waited a minute, but still nothing came through. That silence or hesitance meant whatever he had to tell her would be bad.

"What? Say Dad, I'm driving."

"You've got to tell her," Monty droned in the background. "She'll find out, sooner or later."

"Tell me what?" She demanded, abruptly pulling off alongside the road.

Another silence where she could feel his hesitation across the distance.

"I don't exactly know how to tell you this, honey…"

He never called her *honey*. Not unless something was really wrong.

He inhaled, and her heart leapt up into her throat as she waited for him to come out with it. "Hugo's father called this morning. He wants to visit Hugo's grave, and he's coming out from Texas. I know you've only been on that job a little while, but I really think you ought to be here for his arrival."

Tears pricked, much to her horror. Tears never did bring anyone in this world back. Not when they had already departed. "Damn." One singular word came out of her mouth, and about summed it all up.

"We always figured this day would come," he added.

So had she, but she had never figured it would come so soon. "I…I don't know what to say to him."

"He'll be here this Sunday, so that gives you some time. Guess you best try to get here before he does."

"How did he sound?"

"About like Hugo," her father made a strange bark at the end of his name. "Nice. Had a drawl."

Of course he acted nice with manners, and of course he had a drawl. He hailed from *Texas*. And they'd have to explain just how and why his son ended up killed in Colorado.

Barely had she recovered from that first call when her cell rang again, and this time it was her Vermillion boss.

"Hi, Josh," she answered, blinking back tears.

"I don't suppose you've found a place to live yet, have you? It's just that I got your expense report, and the plan was that you'd find temporary accommodation. It's all adding up."

"I'm sorry, and yes, I know. I haven't found any place yet, to be honest. Ray? I have to go home this weekend. I don't think I'll get the housing sorted out until next week."

A pause. "That'll be fine, I guess. Actually, it's not my problem."

He sure didn't make it sound fine. Not at all.

"What happened the other day that I had to call the sheriff about? I have to say, you sure get yourself in trouble."

"I was being attacked by a biker. If a county worker hadn't driven by, I might be in the hospital about now. Anyhow, where were you? Back out in Agency?"

"That's none of your concern."

"It is when you can never lend assistance," Emory countered, anger rising. "You're always one hundred miles away. Why is that?"

At least arguing was better than feeling.

"And have you voiced your concerns?" His voice came out tight and mean.

"I sure have," she replied. "To anyone that will listen."

"You know, Emory, it's like you and I have gotten off on the wrong foot. But let me tell you what. I'm leaving this post. I'm going back to the DEA. This is my last week. And I will leave all of this wild west shit to you."

SHE NEVER WENT into the office that day. If there were brands to check, Josh Tucker could just do it himself. What she needed to do was to call Terry, and then check in with the sheriff.

She called over to Greeley.

Dave answered. "Brand inspector, this is Dave Worrell."

For one horrified moment, she thought she would burst into tears at the sound of his voice.

"Oh, Dave…"

"Emory? Em? What's the matter?"

"Everything's the matter. If Terry's around, can you put me on speaker phone?"

"Yep. Sure thing." A moment passed, and he voice sounded a bit farther away. "There. Go ahead, Em."

"I feel hysterical," she admitted. "Dirge got arrested for attacking me, and we know what happened with the hanged horse thief. It was Myra, but we learned that from her workers. They're behind bars, and Joe is trying to figure everything out, no doubt. Then Hugo's father is coming out to see his grave, and then Josh is moving back to the DEA—I'm probably not making any sense."

"That's a lot, Em. One thing at a time, here."

"Well, I'm not going into the office, because I just got in a fight with Josh. This is his last week, or so he said. Did you know about that?"

"No," came Terry's voice. "But I talked to Ray because he's worried about you. Hell, we are, too. Don't go back to the office *at all* while Josh is still there."

"What about the investigation?" Emory held her head with one hand, the other still holding the cell.

"No idea, but that matter's not going to drop. Now before you go getting all worried about Myra Brandt, Ray Thompson is taking care of her stock while everything gets sorted out on that end."

"He is? Where's Myra?"

"Probably in the sheriff's office, if not a jail cell. Everyone seems to think they can get it settled locally."

Despite herself, Emory laughed through her tears. That was, indeed, exactly what they would think.

"I don't know what needs doing for work today."

"Em, check out of the hotel and go home for a few days. Get ready for Mr. Werner's visit. You've been through a lot in a very short time."

And so she had.

LAYING THE PAST TO REST

THE MILES STRIPPED AWAY AS SHE CUT THROUGH RABBIT Ears Pass and looped down into the wide valley of her home territory. No matter how events unfurled, it remained home, for then and ever more. And she had returned. Reluctantly, perhaps, and far sooner than she ever expected. She'd work with her father to get the best story assembled and straight, what details to provide, and which details to keep to themselves. With her father, and perhaps even Monty helping, they would all to explain matters as best she could to Hugo's father.

No doubt a few tears would be shed, she'd show Mr. Werner his son's grave, and if he decided to cuss them all out and curse their name from here to hell and back, they'd just have to take it. In fact, in a way, they even deserved it. They'd saved a way of life for a while, at the cost of his son.

They could never forget that he'd lost his son.

While the Lost Daughter had won the battle, the outcome of the modern range war had yet to be decided. Maybe range wars were never decided—not truly. They just continued on under the surface, erupting in plain sight only now and again. Maybe they just passed down from generation to generation to the point that only the circumstances changed, while their history lengthened and twisted. Like old hanging rope.

Like horse thieves.

And Hugo's father deserved the truth, but that narrative would require careful weaving into a palatable story.

It seemed a tall order indeed.

PASSING beneath the skull still suspended from the crossbar, she took heed of the apparition, having slighted it in the past with nothing short of disastrous consequences. She offered a two-fingered salute—fingers raised from the steering wheel in a self-conscious gesture that felt the nearest thing to futile. The pickup rumbled down the ranch road, and the ranch headquarters came into view. First item of order was Monty's bunkhouse that he had tried to burn down. She slowed as she approached—yes. Charred wood stood out stark and black in the back corner. She hoped that Linda Paulson had been over to investigate—and had given him a well-deserved earful in response. She turned the corner still irritated at the damage done, when she noticed an unfamiliar pickup truck pulled up in front of the house.

Texas plates.

Shit, did she get the date wrong?

She parked her truck, fought a wild urge to pull a U-turn and drive back the way she came.

But damn it, she was no coward.

She hopped out and grabbed her bag. With a deep

breath and a critical eye, she headed toward the front door. The door opened before she reached it.

"Here she is now," Monty called out, like nothing in the world could possibly be wrong.

She furrowed her eyebrows in nasty-looking response. If he noticed, he gave no indication at all.

Instead, he held the door open for her—he still wore his work clothes and his trademark single spur, and appeared like he'd been wrestling with something. "Hugo's father is already here," he said under his breath, worried around his watery blue eyes.

"David? This is Emory," he called out, his words trailing in on the heels of the warning.

A spare, lean man rose up from her father's chair of all places.

His hazel eyes searched hers.

Dear heavens, he bore a strong resemblance to Hugo.

He took a step toward her, hand outstretched.

"I'm so very, very sorry," she choked, then burst into unexpected tears.

The sheer expressions of utter surprise and bewilderment on her father and Monty's faces couldn't escape her as she rushed into the stranger's arms.

He held her as she sobbed. "Oh, dear girl," he crooned, kissing the top of her head. "He thought the world of you, and I can see why."

Which made her cry even harder.

It took a long moment before she could regain her composure enough to release the man, swipe at her eyes, and wipe her nose with the cuff of her sleeve.

All of which felt, coarse, rude, and completely unforgiveable.

She heard Monty drawl, "If that don't beat all."

If he heard it, Mr. Werner didn't bother to grace his words with a reaction.

"I'm sorry," she stammered, catching her father's expression of guarded horror—guarded horror on her behalf. "I don't know what came over me. No, I do. You look so very much like Hugo. I can see you written all over him."

Mr. Werner, for his part, softened down. "Nothing to be ashamed of," he twanged in kindness. "It's called grief, girl. Nothing to be ashamed of."

Although he didn't sense the shift in the room, she knew at that moment he was the only one who held that particular opinion.

As she regained her composure while her father and Mr. Werner sat back down—her father on the couch and awkward—Monty headed for the door.

"I'm just going to go back to the bunk house to clean up a bit," he explained, bolting.

Emory had the feeling that her tears had done him in, causing his retreat. *Coward. No wonder he'd never been married.*

Her father certainly didn't come across as comfortable seated on the couch. In fact, she doubted that he'd ever sat there before. All shut down and fidgeting, he sure looked like he didn't have a damn thing to say after her display.

Mr. Werner cleared his throat. "I came in early," he offered by way of an explanation.

Emory chuckled, relieved to a degree. "I thought I'd got my dates wrong."

"No," he replied, with one, long drawn-out syllable. "I just thought I'd tell y'all that I'd arrived. I made better timing than expected. I was just telling your family that I hope they didn't mind, but it didn't seem right hanging around in the town when everything that mattered was just a short drive away."

"No, that makes sense. I'll go get your room ready."

"I already did that," her father cut in.

"No," Dave Werner protested. "I took a room in town. There is no need to go to all that bother. What I wanted to do was to see my boy's grave for a visit. And meet you. That's all. I didn't want to put anyone out."

He didn't want to put anyone out. That was Hugo all over again.

Tears threatened and shimmered, but mercifully remained unshed. Her father regarded her from a long side-eyed stare that he normally reserved for horses that considered a buck and a plunge. The one that told her not to even consider it.

"I'll take you there," she offered, anxious to get away from her father and his unyielding stoicism. For his part, he acted entirely willing to get her shot of the house as everyone attempted to regain equilibrium.

"You'll at least stay for dinner, won't you?" It sounded like she begged. Sure enough, her father and Monty heard it; she could tell by their eyes.

Hugo's father didn't notice any of it. "If it wouldn't be any trouble," he replied.

Finally, something concrete for her father to do, and he leapt to action. "I'll call Linda and get started pulling something together. You don't mind if she comes, do you, Em?"

A huge sense of relief washed over her—catching her off guard, again. This was turning into one hell of a visit home. "No. Please ask her to come. I can call her myself, if you want."

"No, I'll just tell her that you're asking for her," her father said, all but bolting for the kitchen.

TOGETHER THEY LEFT THE HOUSE, Hugo's father leaning into the trail that rose to the bluff and the graves. They stopped at mid-point, so he could catch his breath.

His words came out in a wheeze. "He liked Colorado, you know."

Emory offered a half-cocked smile and nodded. "The air's thin."

"Or maybe I'm just getting old," he countered. "It sure is pretty."

"The view from the cemetery is even better," she added, pausing. "This ranch has been in our family since 1888—and perhaps a bit before."

Mr. Werner nodded. "I saw the sign."

She shrugged. "That came from some of the money we got from a historical grant. We kind of settled on the year, but it's likely right, or close enough. Anyhow, I don't know what Hugo told you. Maybe I'm repeating everything you already know."

He cracked a smile. "Hugo just told me that he met a girl with good aim…and a chip on her shoulder."

She did a double take. "He told you *that*?"

He lifted a hand, motion pressing something in the air down and notch. "Whoa, not so fast. He also found you intriguing."

"Huh, I think I like that better. I guess. Not sure how he meant that exactly." *Damn, Hugo.* "Now, up on this rise is the graveyard which is a little different than most graveyards. We never buried our dead in the town cemetery but kept them here with us. They belong here, and they are a reminder for the living. We can never forget who came before, and what their sacrifices meant.

Toward that end, we brand our graves with the Lost Daughter brand."

A pause. "I branded Hugo's myself. I hope you don't take offense at that. It's the strongest mark of respect that we have and own."

The man's watery eyes raked over the land. "Your father said that Hugo was trying to get to you when he was shot."

She nodded, silent for a moment and not trusting herself to speak. She leaned over and pulled up her pant leg, revealing the scarred wound. "I stepped through one of the stairs in one of the old houses. I was stuck, and the intruders were coming for me. They shot him…instead."

Her voice trailed off.

"There aren't words…" she said at length. "I never meant for anything like that to happen."

"Of course not," he replied, reaching out for her shoulder and giving it a gentle squeeze. "Shall we?"

They resumed slowly climbing up the rutted dirt thread-road, curving along with the slope of the land. At the final curve, a few of the grave markers came into view. The vantage point offered a wide-open expanse, ringed at the edges with climbing slopes that led to the higher, Never Summer Mountains.

But Mr. Werner directed his attention solely at the markers, searching for his son.

The newest slab, not yet weathered by the elements and the weather.

Hugo Werner
Died defending the Lost Daughter
Buried with loving gratitude
2022

The Lost Daughter brand was etched into the stone, and rebranded where Emory had seared the mark.

Hugo's father knelt down beside his son, and Emory backed away, and stood overlooking the ranch that had claimed the young man's blood, like so many others before.

She pretended not to notice his father's strangled tears.

ABSOLUTION—CROSS FAMILY STYLE

TWO DAYS AFTER HUGO'S FATHER LEFT, EMORY STOOD IN the ranch's graveyard, the wind blowing the tall grass around. It's not as if anyone could ever accuse them of tending to the headstones and the graves that they marked...until the time came for another interment. Then the gravestones and markers would be rebranded with the Lost Daughter brand. She stared at Hugo's grave, shaking her head ever so slightly in the breeze.

Her father made his way up the trail, and for the briefest of moments, she felt his presence and intrusion. As if he intruded upon a private moment—a private matter.

He must have felt it too, for he stood behind her, and didn't say a damned word for a long, drawn-out moment. Maybe he waited for her to say something, but she didn't.

"I want to talk to you," he eventually said.

She turned toward her father.

"Honey," Lance said, eyes dead serious. "Now, you know that I liked that Texan. I truly did. But I can't help but think that in time, you would have chewed Hugo up and spit him back out. I think deep down, you know it, too."

Her eyes watered as she struggled. His words held a lot of truth that deep down, truth that she didn't want to admit.

"I owe you and Monty an apology," she admitted at length.

She stole a glance at her father from the corner of her eyes, to find him scanning the range beyond.

"Maybe for scaring the crap out of us." He sounded laconic and sad. "Your mama was a mistake that I shouldn't have made but," he put a weathered hand on her shoulder and squeezed, "I got you out of it."

She refused to cry. Still, she rushed her father, throwing her arms around him. "Everything all boiled up. I know better than to go retrieve dead bodies with bullets flying. It's time to settle down and raise a family. Hugo would have been a good choice."

"You didn't love him. You just wanted to love him," her father corrected, words spoken over her head and to the ranch beyond. "You would do well to learn from a few of my mistakes. Life out here is tough. You may know it in your head, but not in your heart. You just don't see it because you were raised to it."

Probably he got that part right.

A LOOK AT: ON THE FRINGES

From Award Winning author Randi Samuelson-Brown, a gritty tale about one woman's stark determination to create her own destiny.

Maude Montgomery, gifted with the second-sight, is trapped in a bad marriage to a confidence man who doesn't inspire too much confidence in her. Yearning for a better existence, she gets more than she bargained for when her husband abandons her in a remote outpost of Nebraska.

Alone for the first time in her life, Maude has a decision to make–return back East to nothingness and mediocrity, or head deeper into the West to find her fortune. She chooses to take her chances in the west, and lands in Cripple Creek where she learns gold is *not* scattered about in the streets.

Armed with little more than an untested belief she can sense gold ore deposits, Maude becomes tangled up in the gold camp's underworld and is instrumental in the makings of a mining swindle. Uncertain where to turn, or who to trust, she's about to learn first-hand that all that glitters might not be gold, and freedom demands a hefty price.

AVAILABLE NOW

ABOUT THE AUTHOR

Randi Samuelson-Brown was born in Denver, Colorado, and grew up in Golden. She writes historical fiction and has always enjoyed uncovering strange and obscure historical facts and details. Randi's undergraduate degree is in history, and she continued on to postgraduate research at Trinity College, University of Dublin.

Frontier fiction and the shadier aspects of the Wild West have always held a place close to her heart. *The Beaten Territory* was her debut novel (rereleased as *Market Street Madam* in paperback), and *The Bad Old Days of Colorado: Untold Stories of the Wild West* was her first nonfiction novel and a finalist in the 2021 Colorado Book Awards for History.

Made in the USA
Middletown, DE
04 November 2023